BETWEEN HOMES

The City Between: Book Five

W.R. GINGELL

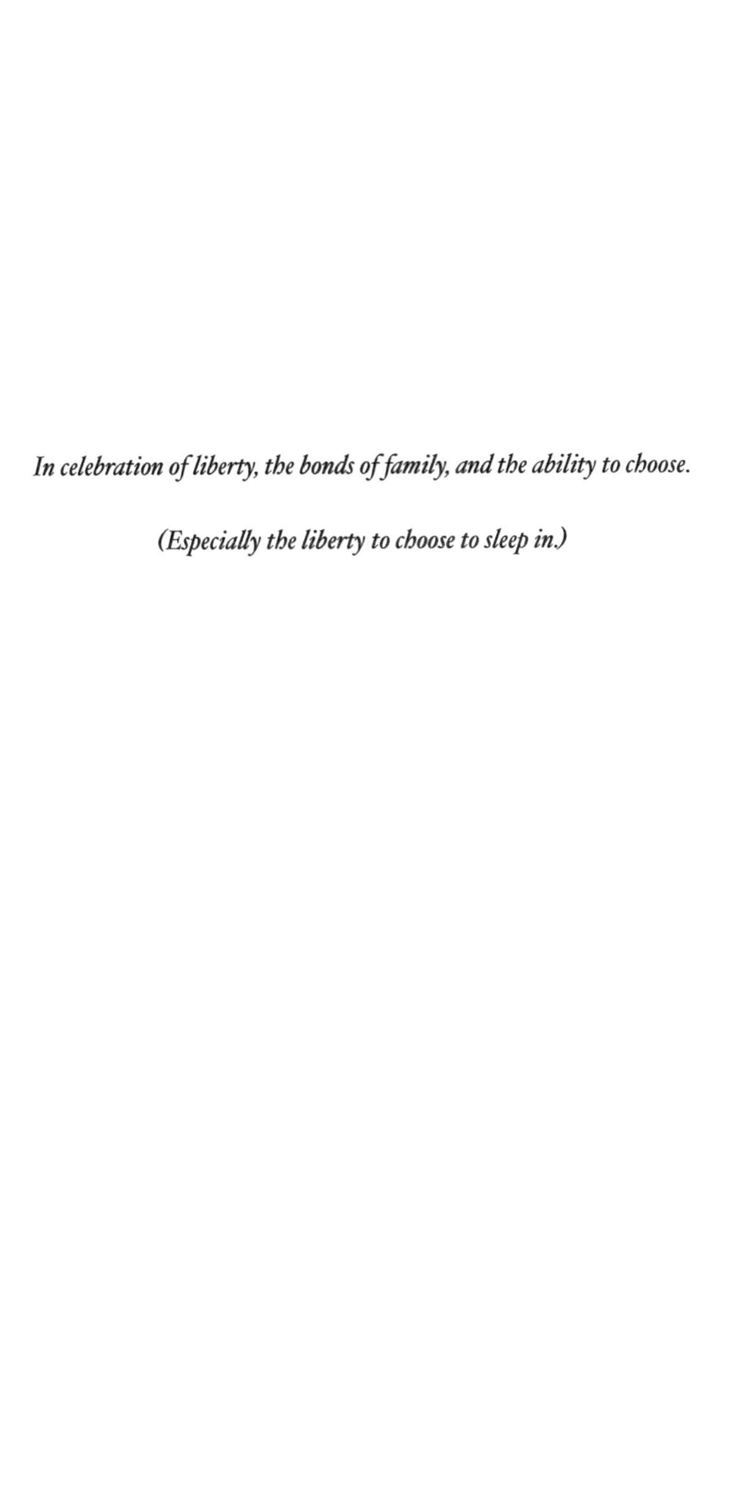

In celebration of liberty, the bonds of family, and the ability to choose.

(Especially the liberty to choose to sleep in.)

CHAPTER ONE

They reckon there are two types of people; that there are two ways of seeing the world. You can see it in a glass-half-full kinda way, or a glass-half-empty kinda way.

That's garbage. There are two ways of seeing the world, all right, but they don't have anything to do with glasses—unless someone out there has managed to make glasses that help you see Between, of course.

Heck, maybe someone has. They haven't shared it with the rest of the world though, so for all intents and purposes, there are only two ways of seeing the world: like a human, and like a Behindkind. Most of us humans see the world in the human way. We see the human world: work, home, city streets, country lanes, seasons that come and go, and a few animals every now and then.

Then there are those who see the world like Behindkind. You probably don't know what Behindkind are, so let me explain how they see the world. They see the human world as though it's the creamy top layer of a trifle. If they want to, they can sink down beneath that layer into the custard—that's Between, the space between the human world and the world Behind, where a walking stick could be a sword, and the nice little old lady next door could actually be a group of gremlins in a floral dress. Between, stuff from the human world sinks down and becomes a bit more, and stuff from Behind pokes up and changes what it looks like, and if you know how to look at it right, you can make it be whichever form you want it to be. Then when they go deeper, Behindkind see the world Behind, a savage place where most things want to kill you for food or fun, and fae learn to kill before they learn to love.

When humans look at the world, they see all they know to see—all they're allowed to see. When Behindkind look at the world, they see layers. And when they look at humans, they see prey—or pets.

But sometimes...sometimes, a human can learn to see the world in the Behindkind way.

Which explains why when I woke up from the same old nightmare, screaming and fighting, I punched a werewolf in the nose. Because I don't exactly see the world like a normal human.

The werewolf fell onto its currently human backside, clutching its nose while blood seeped through its fingers, and made a muffled complaint of "Ow! *Pet!*"

I dropped back down onto my bed in relief, bouncing a bit. Somehow or other, I'd managed to get up into a fighting stance before I was properly awake, which meant that the fighting training I'd had over the last half year or so was beginning to take.

Not that *that* was much good: the fae who'd taught me how to fight had also kicked me out of my own house. It wasn't likely I was going to get to learn much more now.

"Sorry," I said, to Daniel. Without his help, I would have been turned into a werewolf myself a little while ago; he definitely didn't deserve to be punched in the nose. "You shouldn't stand next to my bed when I'm having nightmares."

I mean, technically speaking, it wasn't so much *nightmares* as The Nightmare, but either way, it wasn't safe to be standing nearby when I woke up. These days, I had a habit of being ready to fight before I was aware enough to do it safely.

"You were sweating," Daniel said.

"It's gross that you know that."

"I'm a werewolf. I'm not going to go around with a peg on my nose for you. I came up to see what the go was, and you started yelling. I thought something had got into the house."

"Nah," I said. "Next time, don't worry about it if you hear me yelling. And stop smelling me."

He rolled his eyes at me and got up. "I'm making breakfast for Morgana," he said. "Come up when you're ready. I'll keep you some toast."

"I'm ready now," I said. If someone else was doing the cooking, I was definitely ready.

"Yeah," he said. "I noticed. How come you sleep in your clothes?"

"So I'm ready to punch werewolves in the nose during the night," I told him, and threw the box of tissues at him.

"You can punch me in your pyjamas, you know," Daniel said, dabbing at his nose with a bundle of tissues as I got off the bed.

"I don't have pyjamas," I said. I was pretty sure I hadn't ever had pyjamas. You don't know what's gunna happen in the middle of the night, and there are some times you need to get up and out of the house unexpectedly. Dad never had pyjamas—I was pretty sure Zero didn't have any, either. JinYeong maybe had some. Athelas definitely had them; I wouldn't put it past him to have a silken pair or two about the house—or to be just as deadly in them as he was in his usual clothes.

"That's not normal," Daniel said. "Mind you, I suppose that's what happens when you live with Behindkind."

He wasn't wrong: there's a reason Daniel calls me Pet, and it's not because it's my name.

I am a pet.

Well, I *was* a pet. I used to belong to two fae and a vampire:

Zero, Jin Yeong, and Athelas. All I had to do was cook for them, clean for them, and not be too much of an annoyance. If I did that while they hunted for the murderer they were after, I would have my house back to myself again once they were done in the human world. And this time, I'd actually own the place.

Only there had been a man—probably there had been more than one since they first arrived—they could have saved, and didn't. Someone I might have been able to save, but didn't.

So here I am, staying at a friend's place while I try to figure things out. I'm not quite sure what I am now. Just a human again? Maybe, but now I'm a human who can see the bits of reality that are underneath the human bits, so I'm not quite what I used to be.

I'm not a pet anymore, either.

"Anyway," Daniel said, heading through the door with bloody tissues stuffed beneath his nose, "you don't need to worry about me waking you up again if you're only going to punch me in the nose for it."

"I don't always punch," I said, following a bit more slowly. I felt hard done by. I should have known the nightmare would start up again when I left the house, but somehow it hadn't occurred to me. "Sometimes I just scream at people."

When you live with two deadly fae and a stroppy vampire whose cologne could make a wild pig's eyes water, there's not much that dares to come inside, and that includes nightmares. After being on my own for so many years, I'd too quickly gotten used to the new warmth of movement and tone that came with housemates. I hadn't realised that wasn't all I'd be giving up when I left.

"Yeah, that's much better," Daniel said, his sarcasm echoing back up the stairs at me. Further up, I heard the faint echo of running footsteps, too.

Remember how I said there's layers to the world? Well, there's layers to the house, too: not like Between and Behind, of course, but layers of people. One layer is me and Daniel, just a human and a werewolf, interlopers technically. This isn't our house, but we're allowed to stay because of Morgana. She's the second layer, even though she lives in the top level of the house. Morgana is the first human friend I've ever had—the first really human one. The first real *friend*. Daniel is a lycanthrope, and Detective Tuatu might be human, but he's a cop, which isn't exactly what you think of when you think *friend*.

The third layer is the kids. I don't know where they bunker down, or why they don't want to be seen—Morgana reckons it's 'cos they're scared, but I'm not sure—but all I've ever heard of them is running footsteps. That and muffled, indistinct insults they toss at Daniel over the bannisters. They don't like him much, but they seem fine with me. They don't want to *talk* to me, mind you, but they don't seem to hate me like they do Daniel.

"Oi!" I yelled after him, charging down the stairs as I was reminded of something I'd seen last night, "mind the roller skates on the stairs!"

"Already moved 'em!" he called back, but I'd already caught up by then. To the stairwell above, he yelled, "Stop trying to kill me, you troppo little beggars!"

DANIEL WAS USED TO SCRAPPING WITH HIS PACKMATES, AND THE bruises and scrapes that came with that, and *I* was used to scrapping with the psychos, and all the cuts and aches that came with that, so neither of us thought too much of his nose until we took the breakfast up to Morgana.

When she caught sight of Daniel, Morgana's face went even paler under her makeup. "What happened?"

"Pet punched me," said Daniel, self-consciously putting a hand over his nose to cover it. It wasn't actively bleeding anymore, but since Morgana fainted at the sight of blood, that was probably best.

Morgana's eyes narrowed. "What did you do?"

"Hey!" protested Daniel. "I only tried to wake her up from a nightmare! Why should I get punched in the face?"

"I said I was sorry," I muttered. I pinched a piece of toast, and to Morgana said, "He didn't do anything wrong; I socked him one because I thought he was part of the nightmare."

"You had it again?"

Every night, I thought, but I didn't say that aloud. Instead, I asked, "Again? You heard me last time?"

"The kids did. They said you've been yelling the last couple of nights."

"They said she shouldn't be bringing nightmares into the house, actually," said Daniel, below his breath. The kids might not like him, but at least the feeling was mutual. "I heard them."

"They don't understand about nightmares," Morgana said excusingly, digging into the porridge. "They're just worried about me."

"Nightmares aren't contagious!" I yelled toward the ceiling. When I did hear something of them, it was always from the upper parts of the house. "Anyway, you've already got your own."

"But she doesn't wake me up with hers," interjected Daniel.

I nearly snorted, because if he could smell me sweating, he must be able to smell Morgana sweating, too.

Before I could, Daniel added, "She doesn't belt me one, either."

I was going to say something rude to that, too, but I *had* punched him, so I didn't.

Morgana asked, ignoring him, "Pet, haven't you got any other clothes?"

I grimaced a bit. "What? I don't stink: I've been washing 'em."

Daniel muttered something, but I don't reckon he meant either of us to hear it.

"Yeah," said Morgana, "but you've gotta have more than one set of clothes to wear."

"I'll get something today," I said. Morgana had already offered me some clothes, but I didn't fit her mum's stuff, and there was no way I'd be able to squeeze into Morgana's own clothes. I wasn't much for the black lace, either.

"You don't even have any money," said Daniel beneath his breath.

That was true enough. I had about a hundred in my pocket that was supposed to have been grocery money, but technically it wasn't mine: I'd accidentally stolen it from my old owners. Still, I needed the clothes.

"Got enough," I said. "Oi, Morgana. You reckon the kids'll want spaghetti for lunch? Found some bay leaves and tomato paste up in the cupboards, and there's noodles everywhere."

"I'll ask them," she said. "Sorry they're being like this. I haven't ever had anyone else in the house, you see. They don't like having to share me."

"Put it up on the roof again?"

"Yeah. It's the only place they'll eat if it's not in my kitchen."

"Okay," I said, snagging another piece of toast. "Right, I'm off."

I was opening the front door when Daniel's voice said from behind me, "I'm coming with you. As far as Campbell street, anyway: I've got a shift today."

"When you say *shift*—"

"I've already heard that one," he muttered, shoving past me.

I followed him, grinning anyway, but when we got close to the supermarket on Campbell street where Daniel worked, the grin vanished. I grabbed Daniel by the arm and dragged him back behind the car we'd just walked past.

"Oi," I said. "Reckon you better not go to work today."

Daniel shook himself free. "What? What did you see?"

"Upper Management, I reckon," I said. In the quick, cold glance I'd had of the shop front before I ducked for cover, I'd seen a familiar suited figure with a horrible blankness where its face should have been.

"Typical," muttered Daniel. "Who is it? The Sandman again?"

"Yeah," I said, shuffling backward. "What's the deal, anyway? How come Upper Management keeps following you? They were after you when you were recovering, too. Did you see something you shouldn't have seen?"

"Don't know exactly," Daniel said grimly. "But I don't like it. I reckon they think I know a bit too much about their operation after Erica. If the Sandman catches up with me—"

"Kill you, will it?"

"Nah. It'll take all my memories away, though."

"Oh. Wait, *all* of 'em?"

"Everything since the thing they don't want me to remember. Erica had a bit of a deal with them to keep us better hidden, but I don't know exactly what it was. They weren't really happy about the mess I left in their offices a few months ago, either."

"What are we gunna do about it, then? Sooner or later, they'll manage to follow us home."

"We'll be careful," said Daniel. "Anyway, I've got a plan. Wait and see. C'mon. Let's go get you some clothes, instead."

We got some jeans and t-shirts from the nearest opshop: nothing special, but they were something to wear until I had enough money to buy more. Or got up the courage to go back to the house and get my stuff. After all, just because I'd left the psychos, there was no reason that they should get to keep my stuff.

"I'll have to do something about *that*, too," Daniel said, scowling, when we were nearly back at the house.

I followed his eyes and saw JinYeong with his shoulders propped against the bricks by the front door. I stopped short before the gate, just out of sight, and huffed an annoyed breath.

"How long has he been there, you reckon?"

"Beggared 'f I know," I muttered. Jin Yeong hadn't seen us yet, but it wouldn't be long.

"Great," said Daniel. "As if the kids weren't bad enough, now we've got *two* pest problems. It's probably because you kissed him."

"What? I didn't kiss him!"

"I saw you the other night—you're just lucky Morgana didn't see. If you're going to have a crush on someone, you could at least—"

"I don't have a crush on him! That's flaming weird!"

"Yeah? How come you were kissing him, then?"

"I wasn't kissing the vampire!" I protested. "He kissed me!"

"What for?"

"Give you one guess."

"Beggared if I know, with *that* vampire. The Troika never do stuff for the reason you think they do."

"He wanted to be able to get into the house without asking for permission."

There was a brief silence from Daniel. "What a pain in the neck!" he said, at last. He glared at me when I snorted a laugh. "I don't want him in there!"

"I don't want him in the house either!" I said.

"You were the one kissing—don't you punch me, Pet!"

"For the last time," I said, glaring at him, "I didn't kiss the vampire! He kissed me. It took me by surprise, and I didn't figure it out in time. If you think it's bad for you, what d'you reckon it's like for me? I'm the one that got kissed!"

"Well, at least we know you haven't got fae blood in you!" he said, grinning. "Not enough to matter, anyway. You'd be getting pretty sick by now if you did."

"Of course I don't have fae blood: I'm a human. Hang on, what do you mean, not enough?"

"Well," said Daniel, looking surprised, "if you're half blood, that's enough to get really sick from vampire saliva, and if your mum's the fae, you'd probably die. If your mum's the human and you've got more human than fae, you'll get sick but you probably won't die."

"What about Zero?" I asked, with one eye on Jin Yeong, who had stiffened.

His head cocked, then slowly scanned from side to side, eyes bright, until they fell on me. One eyebrow went up.

"What *about* Zero?"

"He'd die from it, right?"

"Yeah, definitely."

"I thought his mum was human?"

"Yeah, but his fae bloodline is pretty scary. What do you want to know about Zero for, anyway? He threw you out. You're here now."

"*Ya*," said Jin Yeong, strolling toward us. "*Mwohanya?*"

Dark eyes, honey-tinted skin, full lips and an insolent way of walking that made you want to punch him, there wasn't anything from the top of his perfectly brushed hair to the toes of his shiny, pointy shoes that wasn't annoying.

But the most annoying thing? He never speaks in English. Just Korean.

Good thing for me that I like to be annoying, too, or I would never have learned as much Korean as I have. *Or* how to use my supposedly impossible skills with Between to understand the things Jin Yeong chooses to make understandable.

"We're trying to decide if we want to talk to you or not," I said. "What do you want?"

Jin Yeong sniffed slightly, then made a disgusted face at the plastic bag. "*Igae mwohya?*"

"Clothes," I said, ignoring his scrunched face.

"Why," said Jin Yeong, suddenly and startlingly understandable with an edge of Between to his Korean, "do you have dead peoples' clothes?"

"They're second hand clothes, not dead peoples' clothes."

"They are dead peoples' clothes."

I looked accusingly at Daniel. "Did you let me buy dead peoples' clothes?"

"They're not wearing them anymore!" he protested, pushing past Jin Yeong and jogging up the stairs. Over his shoulder, he said, "And they washed 'em first: what more do you want?"

"Clothes that weren't on a dead person!" I told him, following him up the stairs and into the house. To Jin Yeong, who was still behind me, I said, "What are you here for, anyway?"

He shrugged, sauntering past me, and threw himself elegantly onto one of the couches. He didn't say much, but I saw his eyes roaming around the room, and when I made myself a cup of coffee he looked meltingly at me until I brought him one too. I left my bag of dead peoples' clothes on the seat beside Jin Yeong with the rest of my stuff, and took a cup up to Morgana, too.

On my way out, I levelled my finger at Daniel and Jin Yeong in turn and said, "Don't fight."

By the time I got back downstairs Daniel had vanished into his room and Jin Yeong was strolling in through the back door like he'd been out to see what there was to see in the backyard, so they mustn't have fought. It was either that or Jin Yeong had killed Daniel and stashed his body somewhere, but I was pretty sure I would have heard the murder.

I knew there wasn't much out in the backyard because I'd already looked, but I didn't like to think that Jin Yeong had been snooping, so I said sharply, "Don't go poking your sniffer around the place."

The slightest edge of tooth showed. "I have already poked it into the back yard," he said, sauntering across the room. "I will poke it into the second floor now."

"The heck you will!" I said indignantly. "Get away from the stairs!"

Jin Yeong, mockingly, put one foot on the first step.

"You try and get up there, and I'm gunna choke you with your tie," I told him.

Jin Yeong looked back at me, all liquid eyes and slightly bared teeth, then turned swiftly from the stairs on the front pad of his foot, knees subtly bending to put him in a crouch.

Ah heck. That was his hunting look.

Only instead of death in his eyes there was—what?

A low chuckle confirmed it—Jin Yeong was laughing. He wanted to play?

"Try it, *Petteu*," he said, and sprang.

By the time Daniel came out to tell us sourly to stop breaking the living room apart, Jin Yeong's tie was halfway off, a good portion of my hair had come out of its braid, and both of us were staggering slightly.

If you think that I shouldn't have had much chance against a vampire, you're right. But a little bit of vampire venom does wonders in the human body—I mean, so long as I don't bite back —and I was still hopped up and extra fast from the last lot. There was also a *lot* of stuff around the house.

Remember how I said there was a way of seeing things, of pulling another version of things through from that deeper else-where we call Behind? Well, that's something I can do: grab a rusted poker that's a sword in the Behind world, drag it through via Between and use its Behind form in the human world. I don't know exactly how it works, but I've got the feeling it makes a sort of pocket of Between around the thing I drag out, a bit like how Jin Yeong manages to translate his Korean into English for Behindkind.

So when I fight, I can have any number of weapons. I mean, I'm still not that well trained at how to use 'em, but boy am I ever good at grabbing them. And despite how untrained I am, I'm apparently wild enough to worry even a psycho vampire, because he'd done a lot of dancing back and forth to get out of my way.

He was still panting now, hair messy and eyes dark with laughter.

I said, "Oh, what a shame! Your tie's kicked the bucket!"

He stripped it from around his neck and threw it on the couch. "I have another."

"Yeah? You come back wearing it and try to get upstairs again, and I'll wreck that one, too."

Usually Jin Yeong hates being messy—hates his clothes being anything other than perfectly pressed and arranged—but he surprised me by grinning at me, eyes glittering and dark.

"Try it, *Petteu*," he said again, and settled back on the couch to smirk at Daniel, who only snorted softly and went away again.

I DIDN'T ACTUALLY HAVE TO MAKE LUNCH FOR ANYONE, BUT I did it anyway. Maybe it was force of habit. The downstairs kitchen was nice and big, even if there had been dust all over everything the first day I got here, and it was kinda nice to be able to spread out.

Well, it would have been nice to spread out in if Jin Yeong hadn't still been lurking around the place. Or if he hadn't followed me into the kitchen for what seemed to be the sole purpose of watching me make spaghetti bolognese. I dunno, maybe the psychos had gone back to their default of Zero cooking food. From the smell of it when they first came to live in my house, he was pretty good at charring anything that could be charred, and a fair bit that couldn't. Maybe Jin Yeong was just hungry.

And that reminded me that he hadn't answered my question much earlier. "Seriously, why are you here?" I asked him. I wasn't sure if he hadn't answered before because he didn't want to, or if he just hadn't heard me.

Jin Yeong shrugged. "If you die now, it was a waste of time to save you," he said. "Also, you should practise. You still tire quickly."

"Rude," I said, but I wasn't really annoyed. "If you're here 'cos of your missing shoelaces, they're threaded into the bathroom mat—you know, the brown, loopy one."

"Ah, so they were there! You should not meddle with my things, *Petteu*."

"Can't meddle with 'em now," I pointed out.

"Why does the coffee taste so bad?"

"What coffee?" I demanded indignantly. I hadn't given him coffee since the first cup earlier. "If you don't like it, you can flamin'—"

"*Hyeong*'s coffee," he said. "It tastes bad. Why?"

"Oh. I dunno. Maybe he's got the water too hot or something. Tell him to put the milk in first so he doesn't scald the coffee. Hang on—how come Zero's making the coffee? I thought Athelas was meant to do that bit."

"That coffee is even worse," said JinYeong gloomily. "I think he does it purposefully."

"He probably does," I said. "You're not here because of the coffee."

"I want *Petteu* coffee."

"All right, I'll make you coffee. But I still think that's not why you're here."

I put the kettle on while the bolognese simmered away, and maybe that made JinYeong's shrivelled little vampire heart happy, because he smiled at me without any trace of smugness and settled back against the kitchen cupboards. He was in the way there, too, but not enough to complain about.

"I wish to meet your friend," he said, still easily understandable.

It was kinda weird. For the last couple of days, he'd been making a distinct effort to make sure I could understand him—ever since I left the house, really. If it had been anyone else but Morgana he was talking about, maybe that thought might have left me more inclined to be nice about my answer.

As it was, I said sharply, "You're not going to meet her. Stay away from her."

JinYeong's brows went up, and he pouted slightly. "Your friend will like me."

"I don't care if she will," I told him, plunging the coffee. I'd already seen Morgana's reaction to JinYeong's appearance—it was pretty much on par with the reaction of every other woman I'd seen. "You stay downstairs."

This time, just one brow went up. "*Wae?* Jealous?"

I couldn't help the snort of laughter. "Nope," I said. "Just not gunna let a vampire in to visit my friend who doesn't like blood."

JinYeong muttered to himself, then said aloud, "Why are you cooking? Who are you cooking for?"

"Me and Morgana—probably the kids, too."

He frowned. "Children?"

"They run around wild upstairs," I said, passing him his coffee and pouring my own.

"I did not see them."

"They don't like people seeing them," I said, but I felt a tinge of unease. I'd never seen the kids, and neither had Daniel. Maybe I was just suspicious from my time with the three psychos, but it seemed to me that living in the same house with them for nearly a week, I should definitely have seen them at least once. More than the flutter of cloth and the echo of feet, that is.

"I do not smell children," JinYeong said. He thought about that for a moment, and I saw one of his shoulders shrug up and down, as if he had been debating something within himself. "But this house smells of corruption. There are dead rodents decaying in the rooms upstairs. Maybe their scent is lost in it."

"First I've got dead person clothes, and now the house smells bad? You blokes are a laugh a minute."

"What does the dog smell?"

"Sweat, apparently."

"*Mwoh?*"

"Never mind. Shove over, I need to get to the bowls."

He leaned away slightly, *just* enough for me to get to the bowls, and I got out three. It wasn't like the kids would be down to eat with us anyway, so they could wait until we'd eaten first.

"Are you feeding the dog?"

"Daniel likes spaghetti."

Jin Yeong threw me an accusatory look. "I am hungry, too."

"Fine," I said, taking out another bowl. "But you'd better be gone by the time I get back down from taking Morgana hers."

"*Kurae*," said Jin Yeong, back to his usual, unwilling-to-be-understood self. Maybe he was sulking.

I ignored him and took Morgana's lunch up to her, stopping only to drop off a bowl to Daniel. Morgana was in one of her bouncy moods when I got upstairs. I didn't know why, until she said, grinning, "I saw your partner arrive! Although—hang on, you said you're not really a cop, so who is he?"

"Trouble," I said, passing her a bowl. "I dunno, a friend? He's caught up in all this, too."

Morgana frowned. "Wait, then is he one of the three that kicked you out of your house?"

"Oh. Only sort of—it wasn't really Jin Yeong. He came over here with me to make sure I was okay."

Was that really what he'd done? I hadn't actually thought until now that it might have been a genuinely nice action on Jin Yeong's part—the fact that he'd kissed me to make sure he could get into the house at will hadn't made it the first thought to spring naturally to mind.

Maybe, I thought now, sitting down thoughtfully at the foot of Morgana's bed, maybe he was just being like Zero—high handed and pushy in the way he tried to take care of people.

"You sure?" asked Morgana. "Because you're frowning, and if he's going to make problems, I can get Daniel to tell him he can't visit."

"No, no!" I said hastily, swirling spaghetti. If I wanted

Jin Yeong to stop coming to the house, getting Daniel to do something about it definitely wasn't the best way. "I was just...thinking that I'll have to make some boundaries or something."

Morgana's face lit up straight away. "Then he *did* kiss you last week!"

"What?"

"I saw him step up into the portico while you were still there, and I reckon he looked—"

"Yeah, yeah," I said. "He was just trying to annoy me."

Morgana blinked a bit. "You reckon? Oh. Don't you like being kissed?"

"I dunno. It doesn't happen that much." Mind you, it had happened a bit more recently. Only as a vehicle for vampire spit, though, so I didn't think that counted as real kissing. More like mouth-to-mouth in some kind of weird, Between, back-to-front way. "It's like I said—he's just trying to annoy me."

"You probably better make those boundaries clear pretty quick, then," said Morgana. "I know I don't get out much, but I watch a lot of tv, and—"

"What's tv got to do with it?" I asked, bewildered. "I'm just gunna tell him to mind his own business—or at least to ask before he does stuff."

"You want him to ask before he kisses you?"

It was my turn to blink a bit. "You're really weird, you know that?" I said to her, poking my fork at her. "I'm not talking about kissing."

"Oh. What are you talking about, then?"

"Stuff in general. Even if it's stuff that is meant to be helpful or kind. People have been doing stuff for me to keep me safe and look after me, but—"

"You don't like people looking after you?" hazarded Morgana, through a mouthful of spaghetti.

"Nah, that's not it." I wasn't sure exactly what it was, if it came to that. Was it the ruthlessness of the care that had bothered me?

Zero's determination to care for me in the way he thought best, with no consideration for what I thought, or who else got hurt? "It was just...wrong. I should get a choice in who takes care of me. Or how they do it. Or at least I should be able to tell them when to stop."

"You're talking about your housemates, right?"

"Yeah, I suppose."

"Forget those blokes," she said. "They kicked you out because you wouldn't toe the line. There's meant to be some negotiation in relationships, even if it's only between housemates. Me and the kids, we've got our own system—I don't rat on them to mum and dad when they do stuff to upset the neighbours, and they help me out with little things here and there. They know they can't pinch my stuff, and I know I can't yell at them."

"Negotiation," I said thoughtfully. "I'll think about that."

I mean, it wasn't likely I'd get the chance to negotiate with the three psychos, but it might be a good idea to think about it, in any case. If the impossible happened, it might be nice to be prepared for once.

CHAPTER TWO

IT WAS A GOOD THING THAT JINYEONG WASN'T STILL downstairs when I returned, or I might have punched him one for causing me trouble with Morgana. Since he wasn't, and I couldn't, I took a stack of bowls and spoons up to the roof with the last of the spaghetti and left it there for the kids.

"Lunch is up!" I yelled as I went back down the stairs to wash the dishes, but I don't know if they heard me. If it wasn't for the regular accidents around Daniel and the occasional echo upstairs, I'd still be inclined to think that Morgana imagined everything to do with the kids.

That, and the empty plates I'd already brought down from the roof once or twice now. I hadn't seen her parents yet, either, though, and it wasn't like they were fake. Maybe it was some weird, human version of Between about Morgana—gathering weird, oddball people who didn't like to interact with other people, and confining them in a house to sort themselves out around each other.

It was times like this that I was glad there was so little of actual Between around odd corners of Morgana's house. There was just enough of it so that I could make a weapon out of most of what was in the living room, but beyond that, nothing. Much safer for humans who couldn't readily escape from danger, like Morgana. Not like my old house, where every inch had a flicker of the flexible material that edged both the human world and the fae world. Where there was a sword that looked like an umbrella in the hall stand and a way into deep Behind through the linen cupboard.

Which was why when I had run the washing up water and started washing up, it was startling to look absently at the wall straight ahead and see one cracked tile right at eye level.

"What the heck?" I said, in shock.

It was my one little cracked tile. It was one of the tiles above the sink—in my old house. My actual house. The house I had left just a week ago.

Not Morgana's house.

"How did you get here?" I asked it, tapping it with my fingernail. It wasn't just that it was cracked in a very familiar way, it also very obviously didn't match: the tiles in the kitchen in the lower level of Morgana's house were pink, and the one from my old house was *yellow*.

I saw a flicker of movement reflected in that cracked little tile and looked over my shoulder instinctively, but there was nothing there. I shivered a bit and backed away from the sink.

Flamin' fantastic. As if I needed another element of creepy in my life.

"What's biting you?" asked Daniel, from the doorway.

I jumped, then glared at him. I couldn't feel much of Between in this house—didn't know if that was because it wasn't here, or because I was less sensitive when I wasn't around the psychos— but it made it a *lot* harder to know when someone was trying to sneak up on me. I didn't like that.

"See?" said Daniel, ignoring my glare. "That's exactly how you go about not punching someone. Remember how to do that next time I wake you up from a nightmare."

"What's up?"

"Bringing out my bowl," he said, waving it at me. "Hey, did your vampire move the downstairs mirror? Morgana said it isn't quite at the right angle anymore."

"Dunno," I said. "Maybe?"

"Come and help me move it, then," Daniel said. "You can stand in the doorway and tell me when you see Morgana so I know it's in the right spot."

"Reckon that's safe?" I asked doubtfully. "Now that there's people like us coming around?"

"Maybe not, but if I don't do it she'll want to know why," said Daniel. "And we're already lying to her. C'mon, Pet."

The wind picked up as soon as we stepped out of the front door, sending crunchy leaves scuttling along the footpath and under the gate, into the street. I stopped in the doorway, putting up the hood of my hoodie, and caught sight of the gate post.

It didn't look exactly different, it just looked...more. Like there was an extra layer to it, or a bit more reality to it. As if there might even be some flickering edge of Between or Behind to it.

What had the vampire done *now*?

"Oi," I said, trotting down the stairs. "Is there something weird about the gate?"

Daniel turned away from the mirror and frowned at the gate instead. "What sort of weird?"

"Dunno. It feels kinda familiar, is all. If Jin Yeong has put something nasty on it, I'm gunna—"

"It was left so I could find my way here," said someone, her voice the same soft rasp of an autumn leaf against the pavement.

I turned my head, and there was a woman there outside the gate: small and dainty and somehow kinda tumultuous. She had hair so black it was almost blue, and eyes so blue they were almost black. The way she looked at me, with her brows straight and her eyes piercing, made me think she could see straight through me.

Heck, maybe she could. She didn't look like Behindkind, though, and that was the important thing.

Daniel, striding toward us, scowled at her. "You don't smell like you should smell."

Or maybe not.

A sharp, diamond glitter sparkled in her eyes. "You don't look like you should look."

I shivered in the freshness of the breeze, and elbowed Daniel. "Oi. You shouldn't say stuff like that to women. It's flamin' rude. You got up me for asking about Morgana's makeup just a little while ago!"

"I wish to hire you," said the woman. "Mr. Preston sent me."

I didn't know what game she was playing, but I wasn't for hire, and the bloke she said had sent her was very dead. It was one of the bigger reasons I'd been kicked out of my house—refusing to let more humans die because Zero, Athelas, and JinYeong let them die instead of trying to help them.

Bluntly, I said, "Mr. Preston's dead."

"I know," she said.

Well, that was something.

"Do we have to talk in all this wind?" complained Daniel. He was still looking pretty suspicious, and I didn't much blame him.

"My apologies," the woman said, but she didn't make a move to come inside or suggest we go sit in a coffee shop somewhere out of the cold breeze.

I mean, at least the wind dropped, but it wasn't like she'd done that.

Hang on, *was* it?

Living the life I live, you start being suspicious about the *weirdest* stuff.

"Was that you?" I demanded. "The wind?"

"It's early, but not out of season," she said, as if excusing herself. "Usually I wear something milder, but I felt like something more playful today."

Great. A woman who wore breezes had come to hire me.

Hang on.

Hang on. Maybe this was exactly what I'd wanted: a chance to redeem myself. A chance to fix what had happened to Mr. Preston. Well, maybe I couldn't exactly *fix* it, but I could try to find out who had killed the bloke.

It was funny, though. Meeting a woman who wore breezes for fun was a lot more unsettling when I only had a lycanthrope by my side instead of two fae and a stroppy vampire. And speaking of the lycanthrope—

Daniel was shaking his head at me emphatically; he'd probably been doing it for a while now. *Don't do it*, he mouthed at me.

What the heck was wrong with him?

Okay, so he probably wasn't thinking anything that hadn't already occurred to me when it came to talking with a woman who was almost certainly not human.

"What do you mean, you want to hire me?" I asked. That was the most important thing right now. "What do you want me to do?"

I might as well find out what she wanted: I didn't have to do it if it was something I couldn't do, after all. I still had an inkling— or maybe a hope—that it had something to do with Mr. Preston.

Daniel sighed. I'm pretty used to the people around me sighing at stuff I do, but I shot him a reflexive glare anyway. He made a face at me and folded his arms with a sort of *Well, here we go again* look.

Rude. It wasn't like he was the poster boy for reasonable decisions, after all.

The woman didn't answer for a few moments, and when she did, it was to say, "My name is North."

"So long as your last name isn't Wind," I said, grinning in an uncomfortable sort of way.

She didn't grin back, just lifted one eyebrow a bit and waited. "What, it *is*?"

Daniel swore under his breath. "You're *her*?" he said. "You're the North Wind these days?"

"The latest incarnation," she agreed.

That was too big to think about sensibly, but luckily for me, a small thing that had puzzled me for a couple of weeks seemed to click into place. "You sent Mr. Preston to us in the first place, didn't you?" I asked. "To Lord Sero, I mean."

"I sent him to you and the Troika," she said. "I'd heard a few things about you all: I thought they might be able to keep him safe for long enough to win my case."

There wasn't much to know about me, but I wasn't surprised she knew about my psychos. It did explain how Mr. Preston knew a bit more than I'd expected him to know about the world Behind —and the psychos.

"And now you're coming to me."

"Yes. I hoped you'd recognise Mr. Preston's name."

"Why come to me?"

"I have a problem of my own. And I would very much like to know who killed Mr. Preston."

"No, I mean why *me*? Why not go directly to them?"

"Exactly," said Daniel. "Lord Sero's the one with power—Pet is human."

"I don't need power for this," North said. "And what I do need, Lord Sero threw away. So I came to you."

"You need me?" I said, disbelieving that I'd understood her correctly. "That's rubbish."

North shrugged, dark blue eyes velvety. "You're human."

"Tell me something I don't know. What's that got to do with it?"

"I need help with a human problem."

"You're the one Mr. Preston was trying to defend in court?"

"Yes."

"I don't know anything about law."

"This is Behind law."

"Yeah well, congratulations, because I know even less about that."

"I don't need your help with that bit," she said. "I can get another lawyer. I need your help with the human part of my problem."

"Is the human part of your problem still alive?"

North's pearly teeth showed faintly in a grimace that was as small as it was fierce, and the wind snaked into my hoodie and across my neck, sharp as a knife. "*Yes*," she said. "And she will *stay that way*."

"All right, all right, don't get your knickers in a twist!" I protested, but I was relieved. She hadn't called the human *it*, and she hadn't said the human was the problem. I wasn't anxious to tell the personified North Wind that I wasn't going to get rid of a human for her, even if I wasn't. I was glad I wouldn't have to do it.

"All right, then," I said. "Come on in. I'll put the jug on and we can have a nice cuppa."

It sounds cheesy to say that North swept into the house, given who she was, but she did kinda sweep into the house. Dust cart-wheeled and flurried as she passed through the short passageway and into the sitting room, and a soft breeze teased the ancient tassels that hung from the curtain sashes.

Daniel went into the kitchen to boil the jug, which was a nice change of pace for me, and left me to sit down facing North and look as professional as I could.

"All right," I said, pulling my hood back down. "What do you need from me?"

"What do you need from us?" corrected Daniel, from the doorway. To North, he said, "We're pack. You mess with Pet and you'll have a lot more to worry about."

"I don't need you, little dog," said North pleasantly. "Mind your own business. I need The Pet."

Daniel looked a bit yellow in the eyes, but all he asked was, "Tea or coffee?"

"Tea. Earl grey," said North, and turned back to me. "Two months ago, a young human girl, Sarah Palmer, went missing from Glenorchy while she was shopping for new shoes with her mother."

I frowned. I'd heard about that. "Turned back up, didn't she?"

North's pearly teeth showed in a happy smile. "Yes."

"Same day," I said slowly, remembering something else I'd seen in the papers a couple of months ago, "The *exact* same day, a bloke turned up dead in the public loo. The place fell down on him—they said it was an accident."

"It wasn't an accident," said North. "And he wasn't human."

"What, it was a freak breeze?"

She didn't answer that. Instead, she said, "He took the little girl. That is why he is now dead."

"Is that also why you need a lawyer?"

"Yes."

"Did you do it? Kill the bloke, I mean."

"Does it matter to you?"

"Yeah."

"He tried to kidnap a little human girl."

"Yeah," I said, "but it still matters."

North puffed out an impatient little huff of air that came close to bowling me over. "You're a human: you're meant to care about *humans*. Why else would I come to you?"

"Because I also need to know who I'm working for, and what they're capable of," I said. "It's a rule. Sorta. I'm not objecting to you doing it...exactly. I just wanna know if you *did*."

"I could have done it," she said. "I would have done it. But I didn't: he was dead when I got there, and the little girl was crouching beside the ruins. I was arrested almost immediately—"

"A setup," I said, nodding. Someone had done much the same thing to my cop friend Detective Tuatu not so long ago. "Is the kid okay?"

"That's the problem," said North. "I got her back home safely, but now they're trying to take her away from her parents."

"Who is trying to take her away from her parents?"

"Upper Management."

I bit back the hiss of air that tried to escape, and heard a similar sound from Daniel as he brought in the tea and coffee.

I caught his eye as he passed me a mug of coffee, but he only said, "Don't look at me. I'll just tell you we should stay away from Upper Management and you'll ignore me anyway."

"Okay," I said, turning back to North. "But this brings me right back to being confused. How do you think I can help when you're up against Upper Management?"

"I'm not asking you to keep her safe," said North, her chin mulish. "I can do that. And I don't need someone to look after my case—I can take care of that, too. What I need you to do is make Upper Management break their contract with the little girl's parents."

"Oh, right. Easy peasy, then."

"Exactly!" she said, a sparkling smile spreading over her face. "I've heard about you: you think differently to us. If anyone can find a way to break the contract, it's you."

I sighed. "What's in the contract?"

"It's a standard chattel contract," said North, the smile vanishing.

"It's a *what*?"

"Sometimes parents discover that someone is watching them," said Daniel. He was looking pretty grim himself, and I wondered if it was because he had once been human or because some Behindkind actually didn't like Behindkind actions much, themselves.

"I didn't think humans who discovered about Behind lived very long," I said. It wasn't that I'd been *told* that exactly: I'd just gotten the impression. "Behindkind make deals with them?"

"If they want the human enough—or if the human is causing

enough trouble," said North. "It's an investment for Behind, you see: if they've got their eye on a human, they like to make sure they get them as quickly as possible. They wait until they've got leverage, then they swoop down and offer a contract in exchange for whatever they want."

I was pretty sure I already knew where this was going. "And they wanted the *kid?*"

"Yes. They're offered safety from Behindkind at large only by signing a contract that gives the entire family chattel status for a certain period, thus obliging Behindkind to keep them safe as precious goods. The same contract obliges the humans to give up their child if they talk about anything involving Behind."

"They talked about it?" I wasn't sure whether to be appalled or impressed.

"They broke the contract?" asked Daniel at the same time. He was definitely appalled.

"No," said North, her elegant jaw very tight. "There was an extra clause in their contract that they didn't or couldn't see: when the daughter turns twelve, the chattel ownership of the child alone becomes permanent, regardless of whether the parents speak up or not."

"How—how old is she?" I asked, my voice husky.

"Eleven," said North. "Her twelfth birthday is at the end of the month."

"And you want—you want us to find a way to break the contract by the end of the month?"

"I brought you a copy," she said, producing a gossamer piece of paper from nowhere that I could see. "Study it: find a way to break it. I'll send my troll assistant around to get your answer the day after tomorrow."

I took it in a bit of a stupor, but managed to protest, "It's gunna take me longer than a night and a day to find an answer!"

"That's all right," she said. "I'll send her every day after that. Just make sure you solve it within a week: if I'm found guilty and put away somewhere Behind, I won't be able to protect her anymore."

"A *week*—! North, I can't—"

"I'll be busy," she said, surging to her feet as if she had been still so long that she could no longer bear to sit. A hurricane of wind tore a circle around the living room as she stood, then furled into her skirt. "And they'll probably try to kill me so I can't babysit you, too. Make sure you're finished by the end of the week."

"North!" I protested, as she swept toward the door. "I don't think I can do it in a week!"

She stopped there by the door, movement somehow in every line of her though she stood still. "You have to," she said. "There's no one else."

Then she was gone.

"Well, that's just *fantastic*," said Daniel. "First the Sandman, now the *actual North Wind*."

"I don't think she's the actual North Wind," I said. "That's the point of being an incarna—"

"I need to find a way to secure the house," he said, without listening to me. "If you're going to be bringing trolls home—"

"To be fair, I'm not *bringing* them home."

"—and the Sandman's out to get one of us—"

"To be fair, probably you."

"Then we need to look at keeping the house safe. I'm not having weirdos coming around here and endangering Morgana."

"Oh," I said, more soberly. "Yeah."

"Don't worry," he said. "I've got an idea. Just—maybe just stop encouraging Behindkind to visit the house, okay?"

"Encouraging?" I said indignantly. "Since when do I have to encourage Behindkind to stick their snotty noses into my life?"

"Fair enough," he said. "All right, we'd best look at this contract. Might as well figure out what we're up against."

"Ah heck," I said.

"Just realised, did you?" Daniel said grimly. "We're gunna do *great* as private investigators."

"Yeah," I said gloomily. Because as much as this job sounded like it was going to be impossible, there was more bad news. I hadn't asked North what the pay was.

I RELUCTANTLY WORE THE DEAD-PERSON JEANS THE NEXT morning. They were a good fit, at least—and I couldn't smell what Daniel and Jin Yeong evidently could, so I wriggled my shoulders a bit to get rid of the twitchy feeling, and went down to see what there was to eat for breakfast.

On the way downstairs I saw something smashed on the stairs —pottery that had held a plant, by the looks of the mingled dirt and pottery shards, and the tiny bit of greenery in feathery pieces —and a kinda knee-shaped hole in the wall further down.

"Kids try to kill you again?" I asked Daniel as I passed him in the kitchen.

"You need to wash those jeans another couple of times," he said crankily, limping past me with a breakfast tray for Morgana. "You smell like you're close to falling apart."

"Should fit right in, then," I said, remembering what Jin Yeong had said about the house yesterday. Maybe I should be poking around the place for dead rats or something; maybe even dead Behindkind. Hopefully not.

I called up the stairs after him, "Does Morgana know you've been making holes in her parents' walls?"

Ignoring that, he said over his shoulder, "I've called in sick for the week. That'll keep the Sandman off our backs from that direction, but we're gunna have to be more careful while we're out poking our noses into Upper Management."

"What are you talking about, *we?*" I followed him up the stairs with a fresh cup of coffee. Daniel was good at putting the percolator on, too. All things considered, he was a pretty good housemate—probably from all those years of looking after the pack.

"You can't muck around with Upper Management by yourself," Daniel said. "That's how you end up dead."

"Better than both of us ending up dead," I pointed out.

"Who's dying?" asked Morgana, her eyes bright and alive within the dark rims of her makeup.

"Hopefully no one," I said. "We've got a job."

"One with the police?"

"Not really," I said. I'd told her I was a consultant, which was better than the lie I *had* been telling her—and if you squinted the right way, it wasn't actually a lie. I'd helped out my detective friend Tuatu more than once, even if I didn't get paid for it, and the Troika were officially consultants. If I had still been with them, it wouldn't even have been slightly a lie.

If I'd still been with them, there wouldn't be any need to lie.

"You okay?" asked Morgana.

"Yeah, 'course. Nah, it's not a police job; we're trying to figure out a problem for a lady who's being framed."

"What does she want you to do?"

"Find a way to break a contract." I'd had a look at that contract with Daniel last night—it was about as easy to understand as human contracts were, which was to say, complicated as it comes. "Someone's trying to take advantage of a little girl."

"Is that legal?"

"Yes," I said. That was the one thing I was absolutely certain about. This contract was a Behind contract—which meant that sneakiness was not only legal, but expected. It was part of the idea of a Behindkind contract; if you were smart enough to break it, you could do so with no legal ramifications.

"How are you going to do it, though?"

"Don't know," said Daniel, gloomily. "We're going to have to get some sort of leverage."

"I'm gunna go see Detective Tuatu," I said. "Maybe he can tell me a bit more about North and this girl she's trying to protect. Oi, Daniel."

He looked suspicious. "What?"

"You've still got friends in Upper Management, yeah? We need to know why they're going after this family."

Morgana, her eyes bright in all their dark, eye-lined glory, said eagerly, "Is that the gang you used to be in? Upper Management? That's a weird name."

"Who said I'm in a gang?"

"No one," she said. "It's just…I dunno, obvious."

"I'm not *in* a gang: I *run* the gang," he said, unconsciously arrogant. "And they're not friends, Pet! They're trying to—they're trying to send me a message that I should stay away and stay quiet."

"I knew it!" said Morgana. "That's why you were across the road in the hidden hospital, right?"

Daniel sighed. "You're not supposed to know about this stuff."

"Maybe we can use that as our in, then," I said.

He looked interested. "What, use me as bait? How?"

"Dunno. Haven't figured that part of it out, yet. I just reckon we need more information—we don't even know why they want the little girl. If we know that, maybe we'll have something we can work with."

"That'll be some job when we don't even know where to find them."

"I'm thinking, I'm thinking! Oi, what about we split up this morning? I'll go see Detective Tuatu, and you have a bit of a poke about to see if you can get an idea where Upper Management is these days, or what they're up to."

"What about me?"

We both looked at Morgana and said as one, "You stay out of it."

"No fair!" she said, but she didn't seem surprised. "All right, just think of me as home base. Call me if you need anything. I can do internet searches and stuff."

Detective Tuatu wasn't at his desk when I went to find him, so I left a message and wandered up to Maccas for a burger. It was a good place to wait. I hadn't been there long when I looked up to see the detective walking toward me with a frown on his face.

I grinned; it was good to see him again. "What are you doing here?"

"Pet, I've been messaging you for days! Why didn't you answer me?"

"What?" I grabbed for my phone, but the screen stayed as black and reflective as it had been for the last few days since I'd left my house.

Hang on.

Hang on.

Jin Yeong had been sitting next to me the day after I left, glaring at Daniel, then up at the ceiling at the faint scratching noises from the second floor. I'd gotten up to get coffee for everyone—force of habit, by now—and when I'd gone up the stairs to take some to Morgana, I'd left my phone down there.

Suspiciously now, I looked at it more closely.

"Flamin' bloodsucker!" I said explosively, slapping my burger back down into its wrapper. "He's done something weird to my phone!"

"I thought you were dead!" Tuatu said, dropping down on the red-topped stool beside me.

"Oh," I said, taken aback. His face was that combination of anger and frustration that I was pretty familiar with. I'd seen it often enough on Dad's face, a long time ago—and a harder-to-recognise form of it on Zero's face, too, if it came to that. I felt like I should apologise, but that didn't seem quite right, either.

"Look, if you're gunna be mad at someone, go fight with the vampire! He's probably the one to blame!"

"I'm not *mad*," Tuatu said, very carefully. "I am *concerned*."

"Yeah, well—" I began defensively, but there was nothing else to say to that, either. "Thanks, I s'pose. What did you want me for?"

Tuatu's brows went up, as if he wasn't sure whether or not I was messing with him. "I was concerned," he said again. "That one—Zero—kicked me out, and then I heard you shouting, then *nothing*. I've been trying to get back to the house for the last couple of days, but I don't seem to be able to get close to it. When I couldn't do that, I kept trying to call and message you. Did the vampire really mess with your phone?"

"Probably not," I said reluctantly. Truth be told, it was my natural reaction to blame JinYeong when something went wrong —and for the most part, it was a pretty spot-on reflex. But JinYeong was the only one of the psychos who'd followed me out of the house, and even if he'd done it to make Zero angry, as I suspected, I didn't really see him messing with my phone to keep me out of the loop with Detective Tuatu. It was more something that Zero might have done while he was trying to make sure I didn't get killed or something.

Only Zero didn't really care about me—or did he? I was still confused about that. He'd looked after me while I kept within the terms of the contract, and in a lot of ways I'd never felt so safe. But that *looking after* had been ruthless and careless of anyone other than me, and even if it had genuinely been because he wanted to look after me, I couldn't let myself be looked after like that. And I still remembered that Zero was the one who had really kicked me out; even Athelas would have let me stay. That wasn't genuine care: just an icy determination to impose his own will on everyone else.

Yes, Zero was a much more likely suspect than JinYeong.

"Then who did it?"

"Dunno," I said. "Zero could have done something to make sure I couldn't contact you because he's mad."

"That makes sense," he said. "He was pretty clear about me not seeing you."

"But here you are."

"I wanted to make sure you weren't dead somewhere."

"How'd you find me, anyway? Didn't say where I was gunna be in my note."

"I didn't: I came in for something to eat."

"Oh well, it's good timing, anyway," I said. "There's something I wanna talk to you about."

"Is it something for those three?" he asked, his jaw squaring. "Because if it is, I'm not doing it. You shouldn't be helping them with stuff—you shouldn't be there, being treated like a pet."

"It's not for them," I said. "I left that night. Got kicked out, I suppose, or left, or something. I'm still not sure which one it was."

Tuatu's flat islander nose flattened a bit more as his nostrils flared. "They kicked you out? Have you got somewhere to stay?"

"Yeah, yeah, I'm fine. I'm staying with a friend."

His eyes flicked over my face briefly. "You've got a friend? Is it that werewolf?"

"Lycanthrope. Nah, I've got a human friend."

"Good. You need human friends."

"I've already got you," I said. "How many more do I need?"

"You need human friends who aren't cops."

"That's no good to me," I said, grinning, even though I'd thought the same thing myself. "Oi. Buy you a burger if you do some checking up for me?"

The detective grinned back. "Are you trying to bribe a police officer?"

"If it's working, yeah. There's this lady I'm trying to help. Well. A kid, actually."

"What trouble is this kid in?"

"Behindkind are trying to take her away from her parents. I need to know about the parents as well as about the kid—anything you can dig up about 'em. I need to know why they need the parents, or the kid, or both. The kid's name is Sarah Palmer."

Tuatu frowned. "I thought you said this wasn't anything to do with those three?"

"It's not."

"Then why are you trying to make deals with Behindkind?"

"'Cos they're messing with humans," I said. "And these humans don't know what they're up against. Anyway, I'm trying to break a deal, not make one."

"You don't know what you're up against—heck, neither do I! I'm still chasing off otherworldly things with a tiny tree on a pebble because I got into all of this without meaning to. Can't someone else help the girl?"

I thought back to North, with her living breeze and her determined chin, and said, "There is no one else. Just me. You don't have to help if you don't want—I reckon it's going to get pretty dangerous."

"I'm helping if you are," said Tuatu, straightening his shoulders. "It's just—it's not fair on you. You should be able to rest now. Get some normal into your life."

"Don't think I've ever been normal," I said. "Not much use starting now. Here; have half a burger and we'll sort out some stuff."

CHAPTER THREE

"THIS IS YOUR BIG IDEA FOR SOLVING THE PROBLEM?" I demanded of Daniel. "*This* is it? You're the one who told me not to tell Morgana anything!"

And if it sounds like I'm over-reacting, let me tell you what I saw when I looked around the room after I got back from my meeting with Detective Tuatu:

"Werewolves! You thought it was a good idea to *fill the entire lower half of the house* with werewolves?"

"We're *lycanthropes*, sweetheart," said one of them from the group around the telly.

"Don't call me sweetheart!"

"Don't call us werewolves!"

"Okay, fair enough. But how the heck is this flying below the radar?"

"It's not," said Daniel. "It's the opposite of flying below the radar. But c'mon, Pet—what Sandman is gunna have a go at a whole household of lycanthropes? This way we keep Morgana safe, and if things go bad in our investigations, we've got backup."

"Don't remember you doing too well against it when we had to fight it last time," I told him, looking around at the room full of mostly human-shaped lycanthropes. None of the ones in their wolf shape had been very picky about where they changed into their wolf forms, so it was already smelling a bit musty around the place. They were also *very* noisy. Even the older ones who were a bit more sedate than the young twenty-somethings took up a lot of space in their sprawling, yawning way.

"That's because I hadn't fought one before," Daniel said indignantly. "Anyway, you were running, too!"

"I don't have two-inch teeth and a killer smile, either," I pointed out. "And you could have told me this was going to happen before I walked in and nearly had a heart attack."

"You gave me a heart attack first," he said. "Inviting the North Wind into the house—not to mention the night you arrived! I thought you were going to tell Morgana about everything."

"Nah," I said. "But she had to know I wasn't a cop. That's fair."

"She took it all right, didn't she?"

"Reckon she was starting to guess." It wasn't like I was the most obvious candidate for being a cop, after all. I'd just had my eighteenth birthday a week ago, and I was still pretty skinny and young looking—the dark hair that went everywhere didn't do much to take away from that idea, and maybe my grey eyes were still a bit too big and hopeful. "And I think she liked that I told her the truth."

"Yeah," said Daniel, looking a bit uneasy.

I wondered if he was thinking about the fact that he could never be completely honest with her—or if he could actually be wondering what she would say if he told her years later, when things got so complicated or dangerous that he had to tell her or lose her friendship. He seemed to have gotten attached very quickly.

"You're not thinking of *telling* her?" I demanded.

"No!" he said, too quickly. "No. Just, she's our friend, and I don't like lying to her."

"Me either," I said. "But I like her being alive, and if she gets to know too much about us, how likely d'you think it'll be for her to stay that way?"

"I know," Daniel said gloomily.

To take his mind off it, I said, "Oi. How come they're all blokes?"

"The girls are off having a retreat," he said. "I think they said they were going to Alice Springs, but they all have their phones off, so I can't contact them."

"Don't you lot connect in your minds or something?"

He gave me a sceptical look. "We're not mind-readers."

"What about the alpha thing, then?" I protested. I'd been spit-close to turning into a lycanthrope myself, and I still remembered that compulsion to obey the alpha, even if another pull had been stronger in the end.

"That's more of a feeling. And yeah, if I projected a feeling strongly enough, they'd probably come running, but there's enough of us here, and the girls need their time away."

Yeah, if they had to put up with lycanthrope musk all the time, they probably did. Just great. As if the pong of Jin Yeong's cologne wasn't enough, I'd have to put up with the stink of lycanthropes as well. Another thought struck me, and I groaned.

"Ah heck."

"What now?" protested Daniel.

He looked a bit hurt.

"What am I gunna *feed* them all?"

Daniel grinned. "That's all right," he said. "They'll feed themselves. I mean, they'll eat stuff if you cook it for them, but most of them like to hunt for themselves."

"All right," I said. "Then it's chilli and cornbread tonight, and I'll make dinner for 'em every second night, but they have to do the shopping."

"You're on!" said the closest lycanthrope. They'd all been listening and pretending not to. "We like meat. Lots of meat."

. . .

THEY ALL SCARFED THEIR FOOD IN FRONT OF THE TELLY, WHICH wasn't surprising. I took Morgana hers, and was on my way back down with the empty bowl when there was a flutter in the balustrades above—white or pale yellow. Maybe even more of a feeling than an actual thing.

"You kids playing around up there?" I called. "Come down for dinner. I made you something."

Distinctly, I heard a voice say, "She made us *food*."

"Tastes good, too," I said to them casually, but I was startled. Up until now, I hadn't seen so much as a flicker of the kids and I had been almost starting to think that Daniel was eating the food I left out.

Someone muttered, "I'm not *hungry*," like it was a personal insult to be offered food.

Huh. So there was a Jin Yeong-type kid up there somewhere?

"Didn't make it for you!" I called up to that one. "It's for the others."

A chorus of giggles bounced down the stairwell, and just as I was starting to think they'd come down, the front door banged loudly against the wall downstairs.

I heard snarling. A *lot* of snarling.

"Ah heck," I said, and pelted back down the stairs, two at a time.

I shouldn't have been surprised at what I found when I got back downstairs: Jin Yeong, prowling through a gauntlet of werewolves in various states of morph, his teeth showing in a dangerous smirk, eyes black and bloody.

"How did *he* get in?" demanded Cameron, bristling by Daniel's left shoulder. At least, I think it was Cameron. It could have been Dylan. "Who's the moron that invited him in?"

"Sorry," I said. "That was me. I didn't do it on purpose, though."

Cameron—or maybe Dylan—directed a smile at Jin Yeong that was nearly as sharp as Jin Yeong's own, and asked over his shoulder, "Want us to chuck him out?"

"*Haebwa*," purred Jin Yeong at him. "*Petteu, mwoh hae? Yeonsub haja!*"

"What practice?" I demanded. "If you've come in here to chuck swords at me and chase me around the furniture like Zero, I got news for you!"

He grinned at me. "*Shilloh?*"

"No need to chuck him out," I said to the lycanthropes, sighing. "He'd just come back in, anyway."

So that everyone could understand him this time, Jin Yeong said, "I have come to practise, but first I need food."

"She's our cook now," said Daniel. "She doesn't have to make diddly squat for you."

"Also I need coffee," Jin Yeong said, ignoring him. He smiled brightly at me. "Please give me coffee, *Petteu*."

That was a new one: I'd never heard him say *please* before. Mind you, it was in Korean and there is no real *please* in Korean, but it was about as close as I'd probably ever hear from him.

"There's chilli for dinner, too," I told him. I should probably be encouraging good habits or something.

Jin Yeong said graciously, "*Ne*," as if he were doing *me* a favour by eating the chilli, and sat down elegantly at the kitchen table instead of with the rabble in front of the telly.

I got him his chilli and cornbread, and filled one of the random mugs in the cupboard with coffee, then got on with the washing up. The little cracked tile that shouldn't have been there was still there, and this time it had company: a mix of tiles in the four rows around it were yellow instead of pink, and they all had the same pattern as the cracked one.

The heck?

I shot a look over at Jin Yeong, but he was engrossed in his dinner. More slowly, I washed the utensils, gazing at those tiles, and I thought I saw movement within them.

I went on to the cups, and heard someone ask, "What's amiss?"

It was just Athelas' voice. It shouldn't have hurt my heart to hear it, but I felt my chin crinkle briefly. It had been barely a week since I'd seen him—since I'd seen Zero. It was ridiculous to feel the kind of homesickness that was eating holes in my lungs.

"The house is...misbehaving," said Zero's voice, somewhat perplexed.

I could see the reflection of him in the little cracked tile now, faintly, just as if I was in my house washing up while Zero leaned against the kitchen bench behind me like he used to do. That hurt, too.

Soapy water swished around my wrists, and through the doorway the constant squabble of noise that was Daniel's pack-mates faded into the distance, replaced by the sound of Zero's voice. The reflection of him grew until it filled all the tiles that shouldn't have been there.

"The house must have had more of a connection to the pet than I suspected," he said. "Did you know it?"

"I suspected so," said Athelas. I couldn't see him, but his gentle, creamy voice was easy to hear behind Zero's. "If you'll recall, my lord, I did my best to keep her here."

"It."

"She's not here to hear you."

"It."

"Your father isn't here to hear you, either."

"I'm constantly surprised at exactly how much father gets to hear," said Zero.

His face was about as communicative as usual—which is to say, as blank as a piece of paper and about the same colour—but there was an edge of vinegar to his voice. I wondered if that was for Athelas' benefit, or for the benefit of whoever it was he suspected of listening.

"For instance, I'm still curious about how the waystation over the road came to the attention of my father. Upper Management had a good outfit there, never raided, but as soon as we showed up and found out what was going on, Family-led Order Force teams appeared."

"They do seem to have been well informed," said Athelas, and there was no discomfort to his voice. "But I'm of the opinion that the origin of all evils can't be traced to your father."

"They might not all originate there, but a good amount of them certainly seem to pass through. What are we to do with the house?"

"Tame it, one presumes," Athelas said. "If the pet were here—"

"If the pet were here we wouldn't be having the issues," Zero said shortly. "We'll have to make do by ourselves."

"Yes," said Athelas, and I thought a faint sigh lingered in the air. "We seem to be doing a great deal of *making do* these days."

"We've done more when we were on the road before; a pet is not indispensable to us."

"She may well yet be indispensable to the house, however," said Athelas. "Do you have any idea as to why, my lord?"

"Nothing concrete," said Zero heavily. "I suspect it has something to do with the death of her—with the death of *its* parents."

"As do I—yet it occurs to me, my lord, that it is very unlike our murderer not to know that there was a third person in the house. It has also occurred to me that the now very obvious connection our Pet has with this house could have preceded the incident, not been a result of it."

I was so caught up in what I was seeing that I didn't notice the slender hand that reached into the water to pull the plug until the wail of the water draining cut right through the voices and silenced them completely. I didn't expect the hand; I didn't expect the gurgle of water spiralling down the sink to be so loud. I mean, who ever heard a kitchen sinkhole *wailing*? Bathtub drain, sure. Kitchen sink?

It startled me enough to make me look down at Jin Yeong's hand, which was now pinching the plug between two fingers, and when I looked up again, there wasn't even a flicker of movement to the mismatching tiles to show that I hadn't imagined it all.

"What the heck?" I complained.

"You are finished," said Jin Yeong, dropping the plug and wiping his sudsy hand with my hoodie, "so why are you standing there?"

"Just thinking," I said. I would have liked to have hit him, but it probably wasn't a good idea to let him know what I'd just seen if he hadn't seen it for himself. Or had he seen it? I glanced up at him, but he was only looking at me with one brow up in a questioning sort of way.

"Better take the kids some food," I added. I needed some time to think about what I'd just heard.

"I will help."

"You'll stay down here," I told him. Jin Yeong offering to help with *anything* was suspicious—Jin Yeong offering to help with something above stairs was even more suspicious. "Talk to Daniel or something. Watch the telly—get some more coffee."

I left him muttering by himself, and took the remainder of the chilli and cornbread up to the roof. I could hear the kids stomping around and calling out to each other down the other end of the house as I went up, just as if I could suddenly hear them properly now that I'd spoken to them properly for the first time.

It gave me an idea, so when I'd left the food up on the roof I came back inside and yelled out, "Food's up!" Then I made sure I stomped down the stairs heavily enough for them to hear me, and hid out in my room for a while. It was far too early to go back downstairs, now that Jin Yeong was here as well, and I wanted to check on something.

Actually, I wanted to check on more than one thing. I wanted to know what Zero and Athelas meant when they said I was connected to my house, and that my house was connected to the murder of my parents. Good thing I knew someone who was likely to know a bit more about it than I did: I'd have to ask Detective Tuatu a few more questions next time I spoke to him. And, for now, make sure I didn't text him anything that I didn't want Zero knowing about.

I also wanted to know why Jin Yeong was hanging around the house again, because it sure as heck wasn't because he wanted to make sure I kept doing my fight training regularly.

But for now, the only thing I could follow up on was the kids.

I waited for a good ten minutes after I heard them dashing along the corridor upstairs and out onto the roof, before I slipped back out of my room, barefoot, and crept back up the stairs. There was little of Between about the place, but I'd had practise lately in finding all the scraps of it in ordinary life, not to mention the tussle with Jin Yeong yesterday, and I used the tiny filaments of it in the stairs to soften my footsteps.

Quiet, I told them. *There's no one here.*

And there really was no sound to give away my walking. It wasn't that I was afraid of them, exactly. Daniel was inclined to call them murderous little beggars, but that was just because they left their skates on the stairs and weren't too careful about where they left electrical cords when it came to water. And if it came to that, we never saw them actually *doing* it: it was another of the reasons I'd almost thought they were imaginary. Still, I could understand why Daniel didn't like stuff being dropped on his head from two floors above for a joke. Maybe I'd just been a pet for too long: I could understand the impulse to mess with the higher powers, and Daniel *did* take up a fair bit of Morgana's time these days.

But even if I wasn't exactly afraid of them, I'd been afraid to find out what they actually *were*: I was so used to stuff I thought was human not being human these days. I was also just a bit afraid they'd catch me spying on them.

So I stepped quietly, my feet cushioned in silken strands of Between, and opened the door that led to the rooftop by the tiniest, gold-edged crack.

When my eyes adjusted to the gold of the evening sunshine, I saw children. Children—nothing more, nothing less. It shouldn't have made my heart give such a pump of relief, because Morgana had called them children, after all. I settled down where I was to watch them for a bit. They looked happy, not vicious. One of them, with chilli mince all over his chin and two cheeks bulging with cornbread, menaced another with his spoon when the other boy tried to make a play for his bowl, but that was pretty normal. I'd have done the same thing if Jin Yeong tried to go for my chilli.

And *thinking* of Jin Yeong, it seemed like I could still smell him. That was annoying. I wrinkled my nose, wondering how the smell of him had gotten all over my clothes, then remembered that I'd been sharing the kitchen with him and his cologne for the last hour or so. His cologne tonight was strong enough to have followed someone into an alley and mugged them, then pinched their car for good measure. I scowled, rubbing my nose, and went back to looking at the sunlight-drenched children.

The golden hour, it's called, this time of evening. The last, molten sunlight glanced off chubby cheeks and sparkling eyes, and wafted through thin fabric here and there, the perfect picture of cherubs, doused in chilli mince and cornbread crumbs.

At least I knew they weren't Behindkind or something from Between: that had been the thing I was most worried about. I was as well aware as Daniel was that the kids weren't normal. It just wasn't normal for a gang of kids to be living in an old house without any sign of adult supervision, and the kids themselves didn't exactly act like normal kids, either. It was nice to see them with my own eyes; to be sure they had voices and faces and bodies.

Their distinct lack of normality was a different kind, but at least it looked like it was the human kind—maybe the runaway kind. They were wary enough around me and Daniel to make me think they could be afraid of anyone obviously more grown up than they were, and I hadn't ever heard them interacting with Morgana's parents, either.

I might have stayed a bit longer if I hadn't heard growling from downstairs. That wasn't unusual, but I didn't particularly want to go back down and find shreds of Jin Yeong's suitcoat strewn through the living room with strips of lycanthrope amongst them.

I sighed, and eased my way back into the house.

Maybe it was because I'd been out in the bright, golden sunshine just a few moments before, but the passageway seemed darker than it had on my way up. It was always pretty cold up here on the top level—old houses are like that, all sneaky chills around the ankles and ears—but now it was cold *and* creepy. I raised my hand to tap on Morgana's door in passing, just in case she wanted anything, but then I saw, with a small buzz of shock, that the door opposite hers was cracked open.

I'd never seen it open before.

That door led to her parents' quarters. They didn't like to be bothered, Morgana had explained. They didn't care if it was noisy in the house, but they didn't want to talk to people. Her father did something with stocks and the economy and her mum was a romance writer. Which kinda explained how the three of them were able to live in this huge old three-storey heritage house that was meant to take boarders, without fussing too much about whether or not they *had* boarders. And it also explained all the *very expensive* technology that was lying carelessly around Morgana's large suite, half of it forgotten and at least a third of it unused.

I must have stood still with a stupid expression on my face for a good minute. When I started forward again, my eyes had adjusted to the point that I could make out a face hovering in the gap, a good foot higher than my own.

It gave me another buzzy sort of a shock, that face. Pale and narrow, with elegant, mournful eyes and elegant, mournful hair done in a Gibson girl style, it was a shadow play of cream and charcoal.

I cleared my throat and said a gruff, "Hi. I'm Pet."

A silky shiver of darkness below the paleness of the face and long neck made me realise that the head wasn't floating: it was merely attached to a long, graceful body clad in a black silk wrapper.

"Don't feed the children too much," said Morgana's mother, in a whisper that was just like the movement of silk against silk.

"Right," I said. "You want something? There's chilli mince."

But she had already closed the door, without either acknowledging my question or saying goodbye. I stood where I was for a moment longer, until I was jarred out of my reverie by the sound of Daniel's voice in Morgana's room, then shrugged and went back downstairs.

To my surprise, JinYeong was sitting at one end of the red couch, one leg crossed over the other and a very obvious space between him and the lycanthrope nearest. He had a put-upon look on his face, while the lycanthrope had an irritated one—probably on account of JinYeong's cologne.

I plopped down on the couch between them, and JinYeong sighed, "Ah. You smell like dead person."

"I washed the jeans!" I said indignantly. "Turn your sniffer off if you're not happy."

"You know," said JinYeong, looking at me beneath his lashes, "that it cannot be turned off. Then you are saying so just to irritate me."

I grinned at him. "Ya reckon?"

"Do not irritate me, *Petteu*. I shall bite."

"Yeah? Well, that'll just make me faster, won't it? I mean, I can wreck another one of your ties if you *want*."

He looked at me with narrowed eyes, then stood up and said, "*Chamkan nawabwa, Petteu. Cheom iyaegihaja.*"

"Come out to talk about what?" I asked, but he was already stalking toward the front door. "Fantastic," I grumbled.

I got outside to find him leaning against the wall by the door, just where he was out of sight of Morgana's mirror. He was so perfectly positioned, in fact, that I said, "What? Been scouting out the place, have you?"

He grinned, because he could see that I was just in the right place to avoid Morgana's mirror, too. "*Wae? Kisseu hallae?*"

"Try kissing me again and I'll wreck more than your tie," I said, glaring at him. "Oi. You were over yesterday; if you had something to talk about, how come you didn't mention it then? How come I've gotta come outside with you?"

"That is the point," he said, the edges of the words glowing with filaments of Between. "I wish to talk when I wish to talk. I will live in your friend's house."

I stared at him. "What?"

"There is no *coffee*," Jin Yeong said. "And *hyeong* burns the food every night: I smell of charcoal. I will live here with you."

Jin Yeong living in Morgana's house was not the sort of thing I was thinking about when I told her I was going to have to make boundaries.

"*Heck* no," I said.

His eyes narrowed at me, but instead of objecting, he said, "You are having dreams again, I think."

"I'm used to it," I told him. It was true, but maybe not as currently true as it had been while I lived with my three psychos. "It's the same one I've had since mum and dad died."

"Shall I frighten it away?"

"What?" I said, my grin a bit twisted, "Finally admit you've got a scary face, do you?"

"Ah!" muttered Jin Yeong, as if to himself, but still understandable, "why is it that the old man is always correct? He said you would be dreaming."

"If you're talking about Athelas, I'm gunna tell him you're calling him old behind his back," I said.

"Why can't I live here? I will be helpful."

"I don't want you to," I said. It wasn't that—not exactly. It was more of a nebulous feeling that had something to do with what I'd talked to Morgana about: the feeling that I didn't want to walk into being looked after again without knowing what it was going to cost me and the people around me. "Anyway, if you're helping me, I'll bet you're helping yourself, too."

Jin Yeong surprised me by grinning. "Perhaps it suits me, too," he said. "Why should it not help both of us, *Petteu?*"

"No," I said. "The house is already full of lycanthropes. I'm not chucking a vampire into the mix as well. I told Morgana I'd look after the house and make sure it's kept tidy."

"I will restrain myself from killing the dogs."

"Well, that sounds like a fantastic living arrangement," I said. "But it's still no. I'll make you some kimchi this week."

"Ah," said Jin Yeong, his eyes momentarily fluttering shut. He seemed to fight with himself for a few moments before he said, "I do not require kimchi. I will live here."

"Yeah? Got that supermarket kimchi, have ya?"

He made a very small noise that was close to a growl.

"Oi," I said, to distract him. "I need your help."

"What trouble are you making now?"

"Gotta find where Upper Management are keeping themselves these days," I said. "And what they're up to."

Jin Yeong's lips curved. "If you wish for my help—"

"Nope," I said. "No bargains. You help if you want, and don't if you don't want. I'm gunna do it with or without you. I'm *asking* for your help; I'm not gunna do a Behindkind swap sort of thing."

"That—" JinYeong stopped; said accusingly, "*Ya, Petteu!* You cannot do that!"

"Can too. All you have to do is say yes or no. No bargains."

"That is a human way of doing business," he said disapprovingly. "Then if I betray you? You have no protection."

"Yep. That's me: human. I'm doing things my own way now. Are you in or not?"

"I am out. I refuse."

"Okay then," I said. "See ya."

I left him on the doorstep and went back in, but I was pretty sure I could still sense the fuzzy ball of distemper that was JinYeong on the front step for a good ten minutes after I went back in.

CHAPTER FOUR

I was expecting a knock at the door the next morning, but not the person who did the knocking. North had said she was going to send her assistant, but I didn't expect that assistant to be waist high and apple-cheeked, with bright, button-like eyes.

She also had a serious dandruff problem. It flaked the shoulders of her fluffy cardigan, and when she bashfully scratched her head with the pen in her left hand, a few more flakes drifted down.

"Hello," she said. "My lady North sent me. I'm here for your answer."

"Oh," I said. "Well, I haven't found a way yet, if that's what you mean. I'll know more tomorrow, hopefully."

"All right," the girl said, and carefully wrote my exact words down on the little clipboard she held, in huge, blocky letters. "I'll be going, then."

"You can come in for a cuppa if you want," I said. "Just boiled the jug."

"No, thank you," she said politely. "Oh! My lady also asks whether you trust the human detective with the pendant."

"With my life," I said. Flaming heck! How had she gotten a

bead on Detective Tuatu? "A couple of times now, actually. She doesn't have to worry about him. You sure you don't want a cuppa? It's no worries."

She smiled at me with much less reserve. "My name is Hyacinth," she said, as if it was a thank you. Maybe it was.

"Pet," I said.

Hyacinth turned her head to the side as if she was thinking about that. I wasn't sure if it was because she was offended I'd given her my title rather than my name, but it wasn't like I had a proper name to be called these days, anyway. Maybe one day if I got away from dead people and Behindkind and stuff—maybe I could go back to being called by a human name then.

"I'll come back tomorrow," said the troll girl. She didn't *look* offended, which was nice.

I went back inside to the slowly stirring house and put on two pots of coffee for the lycanthropes that were just starting to stagger out of bedrooms and picking themselves up from a drooling mess on the living-room carpet.

The house looked a bit different today, as if a filter had been laid over it to silver it into an old fashioned photo—or as if things weren't quite exactly where they were meant to be. I was still trying to figure out whether it was the colour or the place-ment of things that wasn't quite right when I walked into the kitchen.

Over by the stove, Daniel froze, mid-yawn. He abruptly shut his mouth and asked, "How did you do that?"

"Do what?" I asked, looking askance at him. "Oi! Your eggs are gunna burn!"

"They're not mine, they're yours and Morgana's," he said, hastily scooping them out. "Didn't you—you just walked through the wall, I swear!"

"Reckon you haven't woken up yet," I told him. "There's a doorway there."

I pointed at it without looking, then glanced over my shoulder and found my aim was off by a of couple feet and corrected it. "See? Came through there."

"Okay," he said, but he didn't sound exactly convinced. "There's bacon, too."

"Thanks!" I said, pinching some of the bacon out of the pan before it could get to the plate. I slipped one of the eggs onto a piece of toast. "How come you cook so well?"

"Because when the new ones turn I have to make sure I can feed them without finishing off the job of killing off the human part of them before the change is complete," he said. "It's safer if they don't hunt right away, but the meat also needs to be just raw enough to appeal to the wolf part. But if I don't cook it enough—"

"Food poisoning," I said, nodding. I licked up the few drops of runny egg that had spilled onto my fingers. "How come you were looking after the newbies?"

"I still do," he said. "That's what an alpha's meant to do: look after the ones that can't look after themselves. That, or—"

I looked up at him, aware of a change to his voice. His face didn't look too different, but there was a shade of sorrow to it.

"You have to kill the ones that are savage, as well?"

"Yes. If they're a significant danger to humans and there's no hope, it's my responsibility to kill them. Most of the packs don't do it unless there's danger to the pack as well, these days, but originally there was the expectation that we'd live safely by the humans."

"But that's what you were already doing when Erica was still—"

"Yes," he said briefly. "Are you going out today?"

"Changing the subject, huh? Yeah; I'm gunna go see Detective Tuatu. Reckon he might have some info for me by now."

"That North's assistant at the door before?"

"Yeah. What's the go with North, anyway? Being the latest incarnation of the north wind, I mean. How does that work?"

"I thought we were trying to investigate the little girl—Sarah Palmer—and Upper Management," said Daniel. "Why do you want to know about North?"

"Because she's protecting this girl for a reason, and I reckon it'll end up being important. Personal stuff is always important."

"All right. I've got a bit of an idea about how to get some intel on Upper Management, so I'll—Pet, if you want some, come upstairs and eat it! Stop pinching it out of the frying pan!"

"Nah," I said through a mouthful of bacon, and shoved in a piece of toast for good measure. Thickly, I added, "I'm off. Call me if ya need me, but be careful what you say—reckon they've done something to my phone."

I left him with a frying pan in one hand and a cup of coffee in the other, muttering sourly about *why would stuff ever be easy? Where's the fun in that?* and took myself off to the police station again.

Detective Tuatu was at his desk, looking a bit more frazzled than usual.

"G'day!" I said cheerfully, and he jumped. I raised my brows at him. "You're a bit jumpy this morning, aren't you?"

"I get that way when I haven't had enough sleep," he said pointedly.

"What? I didn't keep you awake."

"Someone came to visit me last night," he said.

Oh. That explained the twitchiness: visiting Behindkind are never a good thing. Still, he was alive, so the dryad I gave him must still be doing a good job of looking after him.

"Who was it?"

"Someone with more arms than they should have had."

"Ohhh. Yeah, those ones are pretty flamin' creepy."

"Who are they?"

"Dunno. Fae, maybe. If I had Zero's library, I could look 'em up. Oi—"

"Nope," he said, straight away.

"I haven't even asked you yet!" I protested.

"I'm not pinching one of the Troika's books for you. I already have more contact with that world than I really want."

"Fine. Maybe Jin Yeong will pinch it."

"Maybe," said Detective Tuatu, but he sounded pretty unconvinced. "Pet, why am I being visited by four-armed fae?"

"How come *I'm* to blame? If you've been doing stuff you shouldn't have been doing, don't blame it on me!"

"I did something Athelas asked me to do," he corrected me. "And straight afterwards, there were four-armed blokes at my windows."

"You did *what?*"

"Athelas asked me to find some information for him—said it would go some way toward the debt I owed him."

I closed my eyes briefly. I'd known that would come back to haunt him some day, but I'd been hoping I'd misjudged Athelas.

"I don't know why he wanted the info, but I didn't seem to be able to *not* do what he asked me to do. Any idea about why that is?"

"Yeah," I said grimly. "An idea that says next time you're with Behindkind, don't say stuff like *I'm happy to pay whatever you think it costs* in exchange for your safety. They're pretty flamin' serious about collecting on things they think they're owed. They love balance—especially when the balance is in their direction."

"So you're not working together at all?" He closed his eyes briefly, then opened them again. "I just thought you were coming to a more healthy living arrangement and doing your own thing."

"We're definitely not working together on anything. What did he ask you to check on?"

There was a moment of silence before the detective said, "I can't say."

"What, you're not talking to me now?" I said indignantly.

"No, I mean it won't come out. I can show you what I showed

him, though. I made a copy for myself: I'll bring it around tomorrow. Make sure you tell me where to bring it."

I grinned at him without acknowledging the attempt to find out where I was living these days. Instead, I said, "You've gotten braver lately."

"Nope. I just don't like not being able to say things with my own mouth. What about the terrifying little woman with black hair?"

"Heck," I said. No wonder he looked frazzled. I knew she'd gotten a bead on Detective Tuatu, but I hadn't expected that she'd actually go to *see* him."

"Pet, who is that woman?"

I couldn't help grinning. "North? Dunno if I can exactly say it. Definitely can't *prove* it."

"She said she was *the North Wind*! Why did you send the *North Wind* to my house?"

"I didn't send her. How come she came to see you?"

"She said she was concerned about me looking into her case."

"Why *were* you looking into her?" I hadn't asked him to do it, even if I'd been thinking along the same lines.

"Because every time I tried to explore a facet of the Palmers' lives, there was a connection with her as well."

"Hah!" I said. "I knew it! What's her human name?"

"Selma North. I dug up everything on her—including her present legal troubles, I might add. Pet, you do know that she's on trial for murder, don't you? I don't even know how she's walking around free—her bail was *massive*."

"Came by to tell you to get your mitts off, huh?"

Detective Tuatu, looking very ashy for an islander man, closed his eyes briefly and opened them again. "I *wish* that's what she came to do," he said fervently. "No, she wants my help, Pet! What did you tell her about me?"

"Just that I trusted you."

"Thanks a lot."

"Oi." I grinned at him. "Reckon it would have been better if I told her you weren't to be trusted?"

I think he actually went paler. "Good point. She would have been a *lot* less happy with me digging into her. Is she a murderer?"

"Don't reckon she killed the bloke they say she killed."

"That makes me feel *much* better." He thought about that for a while, then said unexpectedly, "Oh well, I suppose it does. The dryad went mad trying to keep her out, then let her in. It was a bit of a shock."

"What did you find out about the family, anyway?"

"From our side, not much until recently: there was a report filed when Sarah disappeared as a baby, but she was found again so quickly it never became an alert. Then there was a spate of attempted abductions in the last few months that led to a uniformed patrol past their house every half hour starting a few weeks ago. It's weird—the Palmers aren't into anything danger-ous, and they don't have biker or mob connections: I couldn't even find a parking ticket on them, for pete's sake!"

"You said you kept finding traces of North while you were digging into the Palmers."

"Ridiculously many for someone who isn't connected to them by blood."

"What sort of traces?"

"The first traces of her are in Claremont. It's also where Sarah Palmer was born, and where the Palmers still live. They've been offered very good money for their house several times and turned it down every time, but that's another story. Until she was arrested, your friend North was also the librarian at the school Sarah attends."

"So they live in the same town and go to the same school. Not a huge deal, yeah?"

"Not alone, no. Interesting, but not suspicious. But then a friend of mine who works at a certain law firm tells me that North's will is made out to Sarah Palmer."

"Is your friend allowed to do that?" I asked suspiciously.

"Legally, no," said Detective Tuatu. "If she told me straight out. And if she were a lawyer. She's actually corporate counsel, so she can get away with a lot of things that lawyers can't. And *more* than that—"

"There's more?"

"In the last three months, North has been there just in time to prevent the abduction of Sarah Palmer five times. That's not including the time where she was accused of murdering the bloke who kidnapped the girl."

"She's really invested in this kid," I said. It looked like I would have to ask North a few questions myself. There had to be something important in why North was so invested—something that would help when it came to breaking the contract Upper Management had with the Palmers. "All right. You got an address for her? I'd better go and see her."

"Is that safe?"

"Dunno. Oi, that reminds me."

"Of what?" asked Tuatu. He looked wary, and I really didn't blame him.

"Don't dig too much into North's case—keep to her connection with the Palmers. If you come across anything about that Mr. Preston, leave it alone for now."

"Why?"

"Or keep away from water for a while if you *gotta* look into it."

"Pet, if I'm going to have Behindkind coming up through my toilet, I'm going to—"

"Yeah? You're gunna what?"

"Pee somewhere else," he said. "Literally."

I grinned at him. "See, I knew you were getting braver. Just stay away from the case and you should be fine."

"*Should be*, that's nice," he muttered.

"Oi," I said. "There's one more thing."

Detective Tuatu sighed. "What is it?"

"Take it easy, it's not about North or the Palmers. You said you'd been keeping an eye on my house since my parents' murders."

"Off and on."

"So how come you didn't know I was in there? At first, I mean? And there's something else, too: how come the power was still on? I could still take showers and use the jug. I mean, I wasn't dumb enough to use the lights, but they were still on, too."

"I wanted to know the answer to that as well," the detective said. "They didn't tell me at the agency that someone was paying to have the water and power kept on, but they must have known. I'll look into it, if you like."

"Oh," I said. I'd been hoping I was wrong, and that it wasn't weird. "I thought that was just so that they could keep showing the house to people."

"Not for years like that," said the detective decisively. "Not for a house that had seen a double murder. And as for how we missed you in there—we didn't see lights or movement, no one coming through the front door. And the house itself is easy to walk past if you're not looking for it. I presume someone was responsible for that."

"Well, yeah, I usually used the door at the back," I admitted. I didn't know what he meant by *easy to walk past*. I'd never had the kind of trouble I'd once had with the house across the road. It had been spelled to make people look past weirdness. "Oi. You reckon you could get the file on my parents' case for me?"

"Pet—"

"S'pose it's illegal?"

"Very," he said dryly. "But anything hardcopy we've got is already over at your house: the Troika took it all with them as soon as they turned up. If you want to look at what there is, you'll have to ask Zero for it."

"Flamin' heck!" I said, disgruntled. "Talk about bad timing! They've still got my money, too."

"They took your money?" Detective Tuatu stood up. "Come on. We're getting it back."

Startled, I said, "What, this is something you're all gung ho about? They didn't *take* it, I just didn't get the chance to grab it before I left: it's hidden all over the house."

"Still—"

He didn't look convinced but lucky for me—or maybe him—my phone rang.

"Sorry, gotta take this," I said, scribbling down the address of Sarah's house from the notepad beside Tuatu's mousepad. "You can bring me copies of whatever you've got from Athelas as well as anything left of my parents' case tomorrow. I'll make you lunch."

I left while I was still talking, and answered the phone as soon as I was out of earshot of the detective's desk. It was Daniel.

"Hey, Pet," he said. "I've got some good news for you."

"Yeah?"

Carefully, he said, "You remember you wanted me to find out what some old friends of mine were up to these days?"

"You found out?" I said, almost astounded enough to say something without thinking it through first.

"Not exactly," he said. "Got a good chance of finding out where they are at the moment, though, if we play our cards right."

"What—I mean, how did you do that?"

"Still doing it," he said, a bit tersely. "That friend of mine who was looking for me—"

"Did you let—"

"Gave 'em a quick look at me. So if you wanna wait where I got the clothes last time, you might be able to follow 'em back somewhere useful after I lose 'em."

"Gotcha," I said. "Gimme fifteen minutes to get there."

. . .

I'M STARTING TO LEARN THAT THERE ARE CERTAIN PLACES THAT are more likely than others to have bits of Between clinging to them. Places like the building restoration at the corner of Davy Street and Salamanca Place, for instance, where there's an old building being restored—that's prime real estate for Between. It's old, it's in flux; constantly changing between old and new, with pieces of the old that will never be new, and bits of new plastered over the old. The exact sort of spot where things never look exactly like they are.

That was useful to me, because that was where Daniel had told me to meet him. We'd fought off a Sandman and dropped in for some clothes afterward, so that he didn't have to run around Hobart in the nick. There are a lot of things that locals don't see when it comes to Between and Behind, but a naked teenager isn't one of those things.

I jogged most of the way there with the churning feeling in my stomach that I had done a Very Bad Thing. I hadn't meant Daniel to set himself up as bait when I asked him to find out what he could about what Upper Management were up to these days.

But then, I thought as I jigged up and down behind cover of one of the flaps of hessian that were printed with *Do not enter* in bright yellow, wasn't it because I had known he could do something like that, that I had asked him to do it? I already knew it was a dangerous job, and I'd encouraged him to do it in that knowledge.

While I was still uneasily thinking about that, I felt a flurry of breeze, or maybe a flurry of Between, and Daniel said from behind me, "That was close!"

I turned, cold with relief, and said, "What the heck were you doing?"

He grinned at me. "Don't get all indignant with me, Pet! I know the kind of stunts you got up to with the Troika! I saw a chance, so I took it. Keep an eye out to Davy Street side: they're still scanning it to see if they can catch me again."

"Reckon they'll go back to base when they can't find you?"

"It's a good chance," he said. "And if they don't go to home base, I'll bet they go somewhere useful, anyway. There! There they are!"

"Get back!" I hissed. It wouldn't be much good Daniel escaping once just to be seen again.

"Do that thing where you're harder to notice," he said.

"What thing?" I demanded, bewildered. I'd had a bit of success with softening my footsteps with whatever scraps of Between were lying around to quiet the noise, but it was a far cry from making myself hard to be seen.

"You know, when you put up your hood and just kinda fade into the background."

"Dunno what you're talking about," I said, but I put my hoodie up anyway. Through the patchy cover of the *Do not enter* fabric, the Sandman and someone a bit too lumpy to be human scanned the street up and down, then spoke together as if trying to decide what to do next.

"Yep, that's it," said Daniel, giving me the thumbs up. "That's the thing."

I would have asked him what he meant by that, but the Sandman and his lumpy friend started back along Davy Street in the direction of the main shopping district at that exact moment, and I knew my cue. I hung back by about a block but no more, to account for the swell in the ground that came with Hobart's hilly streets, my hood up and my hands in my pockets. It was noon, and the streets were just busy enough to be a decent camouflage, but I stayed at my one-block distance anyway.

Daniel wasn't the only one who had reason to be worried about the Sandman: it knew my face, though I wasn't sure about whether or not it knew who I really was. There was no way I wanted it catching sight of me.

I followed the Sandman all the way up the hill and back down into the shopping district. Just before we got to the opposing shop fronts delineating the Cat and Fiddle Arcade from Centre-point, the lumpy bloke took a hike toward the cinema and left the Sandman to wend his silent, creepy way into one of the stores that had only recently opened after the fire that destroyed the whole block they were on.

It was one of those expensive clothing stores with a French or Italian name, a lot more high-class than I was used to shopping at, and with more shelf space than clothing, which made me nervous.

I didn't dare to hang around outside because there was nowhere to hide in the arcade that was on one side of the shop, and out the front there was only a hipster coffee place where I would have been boxed in with nowhere to run if the Sandman saw me hiding behind one of the plants.

Lucky for me, there was a huge clothing rack in the middle of the store, which meant I could nip in through the arcade while the Sandman was at the counter with one of the girls and keep well out of sight but in hearing.

I don't know what was said before I got in there, but when I prowled along my side of the rack, I heard the Sandman say in its muffled voice, "You're lacking the size I require."

Well, it sure as heck wasn't talking about the clothing: the Sandman was dressed, as I'd always seen it, in a grey, slimline suit of the sort that JinYeong would have worn if he wasn't usually inclined to go for something more dramatic in the way of colour. This shop was far more flamboyant about its suits: they were flowered, polka-dotted, and striped. If I'd had a spare six hundred hanging around, I probably would have bought one of them just to see if JinYeong would wear it.

I didn't, and the Sandman mustn't have either. The girl passed it a card that looked suspiciously like one of those cards you take into the changing rooms with you, and it walked out the front of the store with the card and not so much as a hundred dollar tie to take with it.

I sauntered along toward the front of the store, pretending to check out a gorgeous blue-lined, suede jacket as I watched the Sandman continue down the street toward the shoe-store and vanish inside. I left my position and headed down just in time to see it through the shoe-decorated window, descending the walled staircase into the employees-only area. I sauntered onward and crossed the road at the corner, heading for the pizza place on the other corner. From there, I could keep an eye on both entrances to the shoe shop, which also opened out into a sister store for kids' shoes around the corner from the main entrance. I wanted to be able to see if the sandman came out that way.

I would have liked to have sat in the pizza place at their counter that looked out on the street, but no matter what Daniel said about me being unnoticeable, I figured that would be stretching it a bit. Instead, I sat on the green-painted wrought-iron bench, one arm hanging over the back of the seat to rest my chin on as I watched through the palings of the likewise green-painted wrought-iron safety fence.

By my phone, I waited for at least an hour. Someone must have sat down next to me at some stage, because I smelled the distinct scent of someone who definitely hadn't had a bath in far too long. I huddled down into my hoodie a bit more, feeling tendrils of Between from the bench curling around me. Maybe it made me harder to see against the bench, or maybe it just made people uneasy enough not to sit down there, because the scent wandered away after a bit, and no one tried to sit down there again.

Still, it spooked me, and after another half hour passed I left my spot and wandered back toward the clothing store. Maybe I could ask a few sneaky questions without tipping off anyone— pretend to be interested in buying some of their frighteningly overpriced clothing. Maybe I could afford a sock or something.

I mean, probably not, but it was worth a try.

There was no one behind the counter when I went back in, and I sauntered around the place for a few minutes, trying to look like I was an interested potential customer, but although I heard the sound of voices, I didn't see a single sales girl.

"What the heck?" I complained, beneath my breath. It was going to be a lot harder to look disinterested and casual if I had to seek out a salesgirl instead of having one come to me. I could have *sworn* I'd seen about four girls wandering around when I was here earlier. I followed the vague babble of conversation that bubbled up from somewhere over the top of one of the racks that was sequestered away in a private little corner. At the same time, I sensed just a *pinch* of Between from the same direction.

Not enough for something to be coming through from Behind. Not enough for it to be a regular patch of it. Just enough so that it could have been a bit lingering from having walked out of Between and into the human world recently.

That wasn't all that was lingering, either. The scent of a familiar cologne tickled my nostrils.

Ah heck. That's where the sales girls had gone.

I headed around the racks of clothing, dodging through a flurry of two-hundred-dollar shirts and fifty dollar socks, and sure enough, there the sales girls were: grouped around a smug, suited figure.

"Did you need to take *all* of them?" I protested.

"I took nothing," said Jin Yeong, even more irritatingly smug. "They came to me of their own volition. I am irresistible."

"Says you," I muttered.

Jin Yeong said something soft and caressing in Korean to the shop girls, who scattered, then sauntered over to me.

I glared at him. "Oi—were you following me?"

"Of course," he said, shrugging. "Why else would I be here?"

"Dunno, looks like your style in here. Figured you could be shopping."

Jin Yeong sent a faintly approving look around the shop and said graciously, "The style is good."

"If you say so," I said.

"Not for you," he said. Again, his eyes roamed the store, and stopped on the blue-lined suede jacket I'd used for cover earlier. "Except that. We will buy that."

He started across the shopfloor before I was prepared, and I had to break into a trot to catch up with him.

"Hang on, we'll what? I'm not buying anything!"

"The Sandman said something to that woman at the counter," Jin Yeong said, swiftly flicking through the hanging jackets. "This one is your size. This one, too. You should not be sniffing at a Sandman."

"Wasn't sniffing at it, I was following it," I told him. I took a quick look at the price tag on the brown, tooled leather pants he'd grabbed as well as the jacket, and felt myself go pale. "Put them *back*!" I whispered. "They're two hundred and fifty bucks each! If you scratch 'em, we're dead!"

"You wished for my help," said Jin Yeong, turning decisively. "I shall help."

"This is not helping!" I hissed after him as he carried away the clothes back into the store.

Jin Yeong stopped briefly at a rack of soft t-shirts. "If you are going to sniff at a Sandman—"

"I'm not sniffing at anything!"

"—you need more teeth," he finished. He moved on to a display of deep yellow, cowl-necked shirts that were silky soft in texture and came with a price tag that was bigger than the amount of material that had gone into their making. "Ah. This, too. *Caja!*"

"*Please* stop picking up clothes I can't afford to breathe on!" I wailed softly, but it was too late.

Jin Yeong was already sauntering toward the checkout desk. I caught up with him just in time to hear him address the counter girl in Korean that was untouched by Between and mostly beyond my understanding.

He caught my eyes and tilted his head toward the sales girl.

"Oh, right," I said, suddenly understanding. What a relief! He was just using the stuff to give us a reason to go to the desk. "You don't have the size I need," I told the girl.

"Oh!" she said, surprise in her voice. "But they look the right size! Are you an odd number size? We only go by the standard sizing here."

Again, I met JinYeong's eyes. What had the Sandman's exact words been? "You're lacking the size I require," I said, this time sure that I'd gotten it right.

"I can—I can look out the back for you if you know what size you want," said the girl. She looked more confused than surprised, now.

"*Ah, dwaesseo!*" JinYeong said impatiently, and directed a rapid spate of Korean at her that I couldn't follow.

The girl smiled dreamily and said, "Thank you, sir!" and began to fold and pack the clothes into delicate paper, then a bag.

"Hang on!" I protested. "You can't just take the stuff!"

"*Mothae?*"

"No! It's stealing!"

JinYeong sighed, then reached into his inner pocket and held up a plastic card. Painstakingly understandable, he said, "Then I will *pay*. As if I were a peasant."

"You are a flamin' peasant," I said. "As far as Behindkind go, you're pretty much lowest of the low."

"Not as low as you, *Petteu*," he said, smiling maliciously at me. He passed the counter girl his card, and she took it with a starry sort of look.

"I'll pay you back," I told him, ignoring the insult. I didn't like owing him stuff. It might not be as dangerous as owing stuff to Athelas, but I was pretty sure it was still dangerous. "Make sure you keep a record of what I owe you. When I get paid, I'll give you the money back."

His eyes narrowed on me suddenly. "You, get paid? For what?"

"Got a client," I said.

"Who is your client?"

It wasn't until I realised how dark and liquid his eyes had become that I realised what he was trying to do.

"How many times do I have to tell you that your mojo doesn't work on me?"

JinYeong made an impatient hissing sound and muttered something that might have been, "Ah, I forgot!"

"Can I get you anything else today?" asked the counter girl, passing the bag to him. Her eyes were just a little bit clouded due to his proximity (or maybe just the strength of his cologne), so I said, "Thanks. That's all we needed," and towed JinYeong away by one of the front flaps of his suitcoat.

"Stop vamping people!" I hissed at him on the way out. "What if they're watching out for interference? They'll catch us before we know they're onto us!"

"*Shilloh*," he said, tapping his teeth together very lightly. "That one is a human. *Caja*. We will drink coffee here."

"What?" I said blankly, surprised enough that I didn't let go of his jacket and was towed along into the hipster coffee shop. "Why are we having coffee?"

"What, will you stop your investigation here?" He sat down at the table opposite me, and called out an order in swiftly flowing Korean that I couldn't understand.

Maybe he'd been here before—but more likely the bloke behind the counter was just as susceptible as the girls in the store to JinYeong's vampiric charm—because I saw the bloke start on our order straight away.

"No," I said, hoping JinYeong hadn't ordered me something weird with soy. "But it didn't work, so I need to think about what to do next. Maybe go up to the other place to see what they say."

"They will not say anything there," said JinYeong. "Because we have failed here. Here, are humans. There, I think are fae."

"Flamin' fantastic," I said gloomily. "So we gotta make sure we get it right here."

The barista brought over a tray, momentarily cutting into the conversation, and left us with coffee and a few sugar-dusted friands that looked too pretty to eat.

I picked up one anyway, and said after the barista had gone, "If it's not about the exact words the sandman used, what is it about?"

Jin Yeong's eyes flicked back toward the store. "*Akka, mwoh haesseo?*"

"The sandman wasn't doing anything. It just stood there and said they didn't have its size. I don't think it even had something to take to the counter. Oi."

"Mm," he said, as if he knew what I was going to say. Then, surprising me by being quite right about that, he added, "We will check the CCTV next."

"Yeah," I agreed. "Remember how I told you to stop vamping people?"

Jin Yeong smiled dreamily. "I will charm the human."

CHAPTER FIVE

"Yeah, thanks," I said, trying not to roll my eyes. "Just get us into their security room and try not to talk the assistant into going out for a bite."

"I think you snickered at me," he said, with a touch of sulkiness.

"If you've only just noticed that, you're gunna have to work harder on your investigative instincts," I told him.

"You should appreciate me, *Petteu*," said Jin Yeong, fastidiously splitting a friand to avoid powdered sugar on his suit.

"How come you can't just vamp the information out of her, anyway?" I asked him idly. "Without us having to go for the cameras, I mean? Usually you ask 'em stuff and they tell you. You losing your touch or something?"

Jin Yeong leaned across the table, his eyes slit and glittering. "I have lost nothing, *Petteu*. Shall I demonstrate?"

"Your mojo doesn't *work* on—"

"I do not need to use my talents to make people do what I wish them to do," he told me. "Shall I charm you?"

"Only if you want me to puke on your shoes," I said. "Can you stop dipping your cuffs in the cake? I'm trying to eat here."

He sat back with a snarl, muttering in Korean. He didn't limn it with Between to make it possible for me to understand, and if I'd had the energy, I would have tried to understand it just to annoy him. Since I didn't, I just sat back and ate cake.

At length, he stopped sulking and said with painstaking plainness, "If they are clever, they know they can be found. So they will program—"

"They'll do *what?*"

"Input directions in their minds," said Jin Yeong. "If a Behind-kind attempts to withdraw information—"

Withdraw? What the heck?

"Do not scowl at me," he said, folding his arms. "I am *helping*. If there is an unauthorised withdrawal—"

Okay, maybe it was something in the translation.

Jin Yeong stopped again.

"What? I wasn't glaring this time!"

"You made a face at me."

"Aren't you a bit touchy today?"

"My feelings are hurt."

"Oh. Why? And if you say it's because I glared at you, I'm gunna feed your tie through the coffee machine."

"I am helping *without payment*," he said. "I am not supposed to do that. And you will only make faces at me."

"Oh," I said again. "Okay, sorry then, I s'pose."

Jin Yeong turned his head to the side and said slowly, as if he wasn't quite sure whether or not to be waiting for the other shoe to drop, "*Cheongmal?*"

"Yeah. Sorry. Here, you can have the last cake."

"I paid for the cakes," he said, but he took the last one anyway. "Drink coffee, *Petteu*. We will go back."

"Okay," I said, grabbing my coffee in one hand and the bag of clothes in the other. "But we're bringing this stuff along with us so we can return it."

I stayed behind Jin Yeong with the clothes and my coffee cup, and was surprised to see him flash a very official-looking ID along with his too-rapidly-spoken Korean. It reminded me that he and the other two psychos were officially adjuncts of the police force here, and impressed me just slightly—if Jin Yeong was trying to avoid leaving traces of himself behind, this was a good way to do it. If I had correctly understood a few of the words I'd been able to make out, he was telling the counter girl that we needed footage from their CCTV to help catch a shoplifter. He must have vamped her just enough to make sure she didn't find it weird that her customers from before were back as police to look at the camera feeds, because her eyes were still pretty bright when she took us out the back into a small, elegant office.

"You can use the computer here," she said, double-clicking an icon on the desktop that spawned a split-screen of four sections, and a control panel on the right. "I'll be out in the shop if you need me."

To my relief, she also shooed away the other three girls who were trying to crowd into the room with Jin Yeong. It would have been a bit hard to talk freely with them in the office, even if they were at least partially starry-eyed from vampire proximity.

"This one," I said, opening the camera feed that pointed directly at the customers and the register from behind the counter. "Looks like we just have to enter the time and select a section of the record."

We settled back to watch, me in the chair and Jin Yeong hovering to look over my shoulder, as the video went through its frames. I was watching closely, but I was still taken by surprise when Jin Yeong said, pointing, "*Chogi.*"

"What? Really?"

I'd forgotten that Behindkind often look different in modern image capture: I'd been able to pick the Sandman out of a photo when other humans couldn't see it at all, but I hadn't expected it to look completely different in motion capture.

I could still see the grey suit—that was the one thing that

never seemed to change, no matter what else did. And with the Sandman, when you could see its real body, a *lot* else seemed to change. Its face, for example. And its hands and body, and—

Let's just say that you don't want to meet it out on the streets.

Its face looked like an ordinary face in the video. Not a fuzzy sort of mess that just suggested a face directly into your mind, and not the mothy face with the fluffy antennae I knew was the real face beneath it, but an actual, human face. It was ovular and tidy, with a high hair line and an air of quiet self-possession. Ordinary and kind of nice. If I didn't know what was underneath, I would have thought he was just another bloke.

"How come it can do that? It looked like itself when I took a photo of it."

Jin Yeong shrugged and said something about more sides and movement, without an edge of Between to the words.

"You mean it's got more dimensions to play with, like time? So it can layer the idea of itself onto the security feed or something?"

"*Maja*," he said.

"Your translator turned off, or what?" I demanded. I could understand most of what he said, but maybe I'd gotten used to him being more understandable lately, because I resented having to go to the effort of understanding his Korean without the edge of Between.

"*Choshimhae, Petteu*," he said, glancing significantly toward the door.

"Oh, right," I said. Fair enough: there was no use triggering anything in the assistants' heads, if they'd been programmed in any way by Upper Management.

I turned my attention back to the computer, and watched the Sandman approach the register. From this perspective, I could see it picking up a package of two handkerchiefs that it placed on the counter, and its lips moved briefly.

"So it's the handkerchiefs *and* the words?" I mused aloud. It didn't do anything else before she handed it the card, so it must have been that.

The Sandman left, and my attention wandered to the right side of the screen, where numbers ticked over, second by second.

"Flamin' heck!" I said. "Just as well we came today!"

Jin Yeong frowned at the computer. "*Wae?*"

"It's one of those cameras that rewrites," I said, pointing at the display to the right of the multiple camera screens. "Look, there's only twenty-three hours left before it writes over the files. Wouldn't think that's much good for a shop, but what do I know?"

"For shops, not much good," agreed Jin Yeong. "For Behind-kind, it is convenient."

"Good point. Right," I said, clicking out of the screens. "It's probably asking a bit much to try getting a card today."

"I can do it," said Jin Yeong. "But it is unwise."

"Yeah, figured. I'll get Daniel to do it tomorrow, or maybe wait until we're ready to go in. On our way out, make sure you tell 'em we didn't need to make copies of the files, all right? Don't want 'em getting spooked."

"*Jal haesseo, Petteu,*" he said in a congratulatory sort of way. "*Kurolgae.*"

"You don't need to sound surprised about it," I told him, following him back outside. "I'm running my own investigation these days—if I'm not careful, I'll end up like Mr. Preston."

Jin Yeong narrowed his eyes at me again. "*Petteu—*"

"Forget it," I said hastily. "I'm not investigating Mr. Preston and I'm not telling you what I really am investigating."

"*Wae?*"

"Don't want it getting back to Zero," I explained. I already suspected he'd done something to my phone; I wouldn't be surprised if Jin Yeong was still reporting back to him.

Jin Yeong grumbled something in Korean that might have been *Rude!* then added, "*Caja!*" and led the way out. He spoke briefly to the girl at the counter, but it wasn't until we were walking up the street toward North Hobart that I realised not only had I started up the street toward my old house, but that I also still had the bag of clothes dangling from one hand.

"Flamin' fantastic," I said gloomily, dodging across the road before the lights could turn. Now I was stuck with a few hundred dollars' worth of clothes that I couldn't—didn't want to—afford.

If I'd hoped that Jin Yeong would have to hustle across the road after me in a way that was unbefitting him, I was doomed to disappointment: he stared down the drivers of the cars that tried to start forward when the light turned, and they each stopped as if entranced until he'd finished crossing the road.

That was enough to put him in a pleased mood all the way home, his steps light and jaunty and his mouth smug. I felt the itch to destroy that smugness but restrained myself. He'd actually helped me—helped me without asking for anything in return, and without any reason. Well, without any reason that I *knew*.

I asked suspiciously, "Zero tell you to do this?" but I didn't need his derisive sniff of laughter to tell me that Zero had given no such order.

"*Ani*," he said, still sauntering. "*Nae maumiya*."

So he'd done it because *he* wanted to.

"Okay," I said, and continued along beside him silently all the way home without trying to irritate him out of his good mood. It wasn't exactly payment, but it was a kind of acknowledgement: I don't think I'd really expected him to help, even though I'd asked.

A good half of the lycanthropes were home when we got back. A good half of *those* growled or glared at Jin Yeong as he followed me into the house, but he only showed the tip of an incisor in a very small snarl, so he must have still been in a good mood.

By the time we'd had a cuppa and I'd put on a pot of coffee to percolate for the lycanthropes, half of them were still either growling or glaring, but at least it was a different half this time.

Jin Yeong looked at them beneath his lashes and sent a derisive laugh in their direction, which they took a lot worse than I'd taken the one directed at me earlier, and said, "Practise, *Petteu*. You wriggled away yesterday. Today there will be no wriggling."

"Says you," I told him loftily. Daniel must be upstairs, so it wouldn't hurt to exercise for a while before I saw him. "I can tell you, if you're gunna be trying to pin me to the wall with a couch again, I'm gunna be doing some flamin' wriggling!"

"I do not need to use the couch," said Jin Yeong, lofty in his turn.

"Lost your temper last time, did you?" I asked, grinning at him. I knew he had. The couch had come just after I ruined his tie, and I'd had to move *very* quickly to avoid being pinned between the couch and the wall.

Jin Yeong turned away and stalked out the back door, but it was too late: I'd seen the sudden grin that he tried to close his lips over.

"I knew it!" I said, chortling as I followed him out. "Better watch out for your tie this time!"

JIN YEONG IN NORMAL LIFE WAS IRRITATINGLY BEAUTIFUL, thoroughly exasperating in his carefully groomed elegance. In the fight, he was lean and deadly in a swift-moving streak of raw energy that was somehow more elegant than his coiffed and perfumed self.

I don't even know why I noticed. Maybe it was because it wasn't so terrifying fighting Jin Yeong as it was fighting Zero. I felt like I had a chance to breathe, to watch, to appreciate—to learn. Maybe it was just because Jin Yeong's hair couldn't help but be disarrayed, his tie loosened, and I found that less irritating than Jin Yeong all dolled up, so I could appreciate his beauty instead of being annoyed by it.

I mean, it actually seemed like there was a good chance I

could mitigate Jin Yeong's annoyance to me on a personal level if I could just destroy his tie or mess up his hair every now and then.

We had stopped to rest, me crouched below a tree and him leaning against it like some kind of knightly hero. I leaned on the two handlebars I'd grabbed after he swatted away the original stick I had, my eyes narrowed at him consideringly.

Jin Yeong, still panting a little, said, "*Wae?*"

"Nothing," I said innocently, pulling my weight back from the two handlebars. They might look like handlebars from the windows of the house, but I could see their curved, sharp-edged other form, and that form was far too quick to slice into the earth. "Just I'll have to make sure I get your tie next time."

"You," he said, pointing at me with a stick that wasn't a stick, "are a frightening little whirlwind. Why do you always take up two weapons? Will you really try to cut off my tie?"

I shrugged, trying not to grin my pride. "Dunno. It just happens: I keep finding two of stuff when I'm reaching for weapons."

"Then why do you not remember what I showed you?"

"Dunno, been busy trying not to die," I said, with a touch of sarcasm. He *had* shown me how to hold them, a couple of months ago, but training was always such a scramble that it was hard to remember. "Thought I was keeping up."

Jin Yeong made the same, small *tsk* of annoyance he had made when he first saw me take up two blades. "*No.* This one, lower—that one, above, like so."

He demonstrated, and I rose with far less ease to copy him. The stance felt comfortable but still kinda perilous. Like I could cut off someone's head, but also maybe my own.

Suspiciously, I asked, "Are you just trying to get me to cut my own head off?"

"Not like that," he said, casting down his own weapon and stepping toward me. He observed me from directly in front, then twitched my upper blade into a better position by adjusting my right wrist. "Lower, like so. I *showed* you."

That put his tie in a very tempting position proximate to both blades—blades that were now near enough to being scissored. I blinked at the tie, then gazed up at Jin Yeong, who was very close and utterly still, watching me intently.

He probably knew what I was thinking.

"Your hair's messy," I said to that intent face. It wasn't what I'd meant to say, but that's what happens when you open your mouth a bit too much.

Jin Yeong stiffened, then stepped back. "If my hair is messy, it is your fault!" he said accusingly. "I am going home. My tie is still alive."

"There's always next time!" I called after him. I must have hurt his feelings—we'd only been practising for about half an hour so he couldn't be tired already.

I reckon he must have meant to walk home—to just step through the thinning patch of reality that leached the feeling of Between, avoiding humanity and human traffic.

I had a moment of panic. How many mirrors did Morgana have pointed at the back yard, and exactly how much could she see? But since it didn't seem very likely that Morgana, who liked to know what everyone else was doing, had very many mirrors on her own back yard, and since I didn't remember seeing any that focused in that direction, I squashed back the panic.

Still, I'd have to tell Jin Yeong to stop pushing through Between when he was near Morgana's house, anyway. Fighting was okay if it looked like we were only practising with sticks, but disappearing into thin air because he wanted to take the familiar route home was far less explainable.

That's what I *thought* Jin Yeong was doing, anyway, but when I'd finished tidying up the mess we'd made of the back yard and started to head for the house again, I stopped short.

At the back door, just stepping through the frame of the door, was Jin Yeong again.

Why was he coming back? And how was his back to me, as though he'd walked through me to get to the back door that he was currently entering?

I turned a considering look at the outline of the house, and it seemed to me that I could see something else layered over it as if someone had put Christmas decorations for a two story house on a three story house instead. The roof was lower, the shape different. Familiar.

"Oi!" I said. "That's my house!"

Jin Yeong's head tilted a fraction, and I shut my mouth. He couldn't hear me, right? Despite his apparent presence here, he was definitely entering my old house through the back door, and he shouldn't be able to hear me. I mean, I shouldn't be able to see him, either, but here we were.

It must have been a coincidence, that faint tilt of what had looked like acknowledgement: he continued on back inside, and I dashed to follow him. As I ran up the few steps to Morgana's back door, the world smudged around me and I saw the doorway of my old house as I passed through it on Jin Yeong's heels.

That doorway layered over Morgana's, the soft green of my old house's hallway paint fluttering against the bold striped wallpaper of Morgana's hallway. I saw the faint traces of a door where the bathroom was, the linen cupboard opposite, and the stairs that led to the upper floor just beyond that, even though the room around me was a huge living room filled with lycanthropes and old, dusty furniture. I softened my footsteps and put my hood up almost by instinct, which earned me a few weird looks from the nearest lycanthropes before they turned back to the tv, ignoring me.

For a moment or two I considered trying to walk up those stairs that rose faintly to my right and vanished into the more solid ceiling here at Morgana's house, but Jin Yeong was still walking, so I followed him into the living room instead. He threw himself onto his side of our usual couch and sent a look of dark dislike across at Athelas, who was also sitting in his usual chair and sedately sipping a cup of tea.

"Ah," said Athelas, his voice just a thread of sound in the tapestry of the air. "I see the Pet has kicked you out yet again."

JinYeong snarled at him, but said only, "There is no coffee, I suppose."

"Who would make it?" gently asked Athelas.

I left them to their fight, since in Morgana's house I was still in the part of the living room that was filled with a lot of lycanthropes and led toward the stairs, and threaded my way slightly dizzily toward the almost matching doors that led to the kitchen in either house.

I took a moment to make sure I knew which one was the one I was supposed to be walking through, but I still managed to get it wrong. If I'd gotten it wrong in my old place it would have been fine: the framed doorway between living room and the combined kitchen-dining area was about the width of three doors. As it was I had the unpleasant experience of walking through the wall of Morgana's place with my eyes wide open. Somehow I usually close my eyes when I'm walking through stuff to get Between.

"I knew it!" said Daniel, his voice triumphant and far too loud, just as I caught sight of Zero, sitting at the dining table in my old house, books spread out before him.

I jumped, the sudden loudness of Daniel's voice vibrating against the faint framework of my old house that lingered in the air and shivering it nearly to nothing.

"What?" I said in annoyance, and my own voice was too loud, too. When had Daniel come down to the kitchen?

Faintly, *very* faintly, I heard Athelas say, "Did you take care of the other thing?"

It vibrated against the world around me like the tap of a spider's leg against the web. I would very much have liked to know what they were talking about, but Daniel's voice, unwelcome and disruptive, said, "You walked through the wall! Again!"

"Yeah," I said, trying to speak a bit more softly. I didn't know exactly what was happening, but it had started with the little cracked tile. It was as though my house, as stubborn and unwilling to give into unreasonable Behindkind demands as I, was trying to find me again. "Hang on. Shut up for a bit."

"If you want me to give you some of the toasties I made for afternoon tea, you're going about it the wrong way," Daniel said.

"I'm trying to hear something."

He snorted and said, "Good luck, around here," but I pushed his voice to the back of my mind with all the other lycanthrope noise, and concentrated on seeing Zero.

When I could see him again clearly, I heard Athelas' voice again. Zero was listening, too: I could see his eyes resting on the kitchen wall instead of his books, even if he wasn't looking toward the other two.

I turned my eyes curiously toward Jin Yeong and Athelas, and it seemed like their voices became just a little easier to hear once more.

"I really advise you to be more careful," said Athelas, and sipped his tea. Despite his words, his tone was tranquil. "I have the feeling that you're more deeply enmeshed than you would like to admit."

"I am enmeshed in nothing," Jin Yeong said coldly. "I am doing as I'm told and having fun. When I am not having fun, I will do something else."

"I see. You're playing with your food, then. Perhaps you're aware that my lord is not happy about it?"

I grinned. Whatever *other thing* they had Jin Yeong doing, he must have found someone interesting to play with. Zero didn't let him bring humans home unless they were there to do a job, but I'd seen Jin Yeong at work, luring women from the other side of the room to where he was—for, I was assuming, the pure fun of it, since he could have simply taken one of them by the hand and drawn them into the street for a quick snack.

"It's not my concern if *hyeong* isn't happy," said Jin Yeong. "And when it pleases me to walk away, I shall walk away, regardless of his happiness."

"Do you really think you can?"

Jin Yeong threw him an offended look. "Certainly I can."

"I look forward to it, in that case," said Athelas, and he was definitely smiling into his tea.

Weird. It sounded like more than just playing with his food. Had Jin Yeong fallen in love? With a human? That would be... interesting. I mean, it would probably be a bit of a pain in the neck as well, but it would be interesting.

Hang on—was he *allowed* to be in love? Zero seemed to take a dim point of view on any kind of love, and I definitely couldn't see him letting Jin Yeong date a human.

"Pet, can you stop scowling at the blokes on the stairs?" Daniel said, under his breath. "They didn't mean to knock the antennae off the roof—they were just looking for whatever dead animal's making the stench up there and started playing. They've put it back, and Morgana says it's fine."

I blinked a bit, and found that I was looking at two very guilty-faced lycanthropes on the stairs. They each made a slight grimace instead of a grin, and looked significantly more relaxed when I tentatively grinned back at them.

"Sorry," I said. "The house went a bit weird for a while."

"Yeah," said Daniel. "I noticed: you walking through the wall kinda gave it away. It's been like that for a day or so, yeah?"

"Yeah."

"Is it something we should be worried about?"

"Nope," I said. "Reckon it's something *they* should be worried about, though."

"The Troika?"

"Yeah."

"Good."

He was still in a good mood about that when we went upstairs to eat with Morgana, and I didn't blame him. Things were still a bit too raw with me to be exactly happy about stuff like this, but I was conscious of a feeling of lightness. I might have felt a bit lighter if I could figure out if my lightness was because I could keep an eye on the psychos for business purposes, or because I still had a connection with them on a personal level.

Don't get fond of psychos. It's a bad idea.

We found a sleepy Morgana waiting for us when we got upstairs, but she brightened when we walked in, and shuffled herself forward, away from her pillows.

"You came back *ages* ago!" she said. "What were you doing? I wanted to know what was going on—Daniel came back with *wounds*."

I looked accusingly at him. "You said you just gave them a look at you!"

"I had to let 'em get close enough to make it worthwhile!" he said uncomfortably, tugging down the sleeve of his t-shirt. There was something there, dark and a bit sticky beneath a patch of something medical. I hadn't noticed it when I met him at the restoration site, so at least it couldn't have been too bad. Still...

"Did you make Morgana faint?" I demanded.

"Out like a light!" said Morgana cheerfully.

Well, that explained the bags under her eyes, at least. I glared at Daniel.

"I didn't know it was there!" he protested. "Anyway, you're one to talk: what were you doing in the back yard with the—with Jin Yeong?"

"I wanted to know that, too," Morgana said, turning traitor and grinning at me. "I'm going to have to get the kids to move the mirrors a bit."

"Don't," I said. "You'll just see me being trounced in training by Jin Yeong. It's already embarrassing enough that I can't beat

Mr. Shiny Shoes without people being able to take a gander at it as well."

"Hand to hand stuff?" asked Morgana. She sounded envious. "I always wanted to be Lucy Liu and beat up people while looking glamorous."

"Sorta," I agreed. "But it's not glamorous. I'm still just trying to avoid grass burn."

"Did you find out anything useful today?" she asked. "You said you were going to meet with your detective friend."

"That's what I wanted to know," said Daniel, passing around the toasted sandwiches, "but someone went straight into the back yard without coming to see me and trained for half an hour instead."

"Sorry," I said, grinning. "But you were up here making Morgana faint, and I didn't want to walk up the stairs. Oi, Detective Tuatu found out some stuff, so belt up while I tell you now."

"What, he found a connection between the Palmers and North? Or between her and Upper Management?"

"They're all connected," I said, "but we don't know exactly where the connections are yet. Everywhere Sarah Palmer goes, North goes. Wherever North goes, Upper Management is there. And both of them are trying to keep tabs on the Palmers. It's gunna be hard to find a way to break the contract if we don't know why it was made."

"You better not be leading up to us invading Upper Management now that we know where they are," Daniel said. "Because I'm not going to do it."

"Not exactly."

"You *did* find it again, didn't you? I wasn't just chased around Salamanca by those wallies for nothing, was I?"

"No, we found it," I assured him. "Or at least, we think so."

"Hang on, *we*? Jin Yeong was with you then, too?"

"You're not the only one who's important enough to be

followed," I told him. "He was following me while I was following Upper Management."

"Flaming fantastic," he muttered.

"Oi, that's *my* thing."

"Is this going to turn into a Troika job now?"

"Nope," I said, and hoped it was true. "Only Jin Yeong's helping me."

"Yeah? What's it costing us?"

"It's a favour."

Daniel gazed at me with an open mouth for a very long time.

"You broke him," Morgana said. She looked like she was considering shoving a piece of her toastie into his open mouth.

"Pet, those three don't do *anything* without a cost. *None* of them do!"

I shrugged. "This time, it's a favour. No cost."

"If you say so," he said unconvinced. "But I'm not poking my nose back into Upper Management's business if things are going to get complicated."

"You don't have to do it," I said, surprised. "I can go by myself if I need to go. It's not like we've gotta attack or anything."

"That's not what I—"

"What if you're looking at it wrong?" interrupted Morgana. "What if you don't have to actually go there yet? You're trying to get leverage, yeah?"

"Yeah. Well, kinda, I suppose."

"What if the biggest connection is between your client and this private company? What if the Palmers are just leverage to these guys?"

I exchanged a look with Daniel. He said slowly, "It's possible, Pet. Every time Sarah's in danger, North's *there*. If they're trying to control her through them, it's a likely pattern to produce."

"So if we're trying to get leverage on Upper Management, we need to know why North is so invested with the family, and what they mean to her," I agreed. "We'll probably also need to know why Upper Management wants to keep North under control, but we shouldn't need to get too close to Upper Management just yet for *that*."

"I knew she wasn't telling us everything," muttered Daniel. "It's just like—"

I cleared my throat.

"—just like a lawyer," he finished lamely. "We'd better go see her again, I reckon."

"Maybe have a bit of a squiz around Mr. Preston's office and house if we can, too," I added. "Oi, Morgana, reckon you can find his home and work addresses?"

"Pay me in coffee: I'll find you everything," she said, grinning. "You got a first name for him?"

"Nope. He didn't tell me. But he's a lawyer too, and he works here in Hobart. If you combine his name with *Selma North* and *murder trial*, I think you'll find it easy enough. I'd call and ask Detective Tuatu, but I reckon my phone's tapped."

It was also why I couldn't do an internet search without worrying that Zero was going to see what I was up to.

Morgana's black-rimmed eyes widened impressively. "You're being tapped already? What did you investigate with those bosses of yours before this?"

"Stuff," I said. "Anyway, it's probably them doing the bugging, so…"

"Are you *sure* the Korean bloke should be hanging around here, then?" she asked. "I mean—"

"That's what *I* said," Daniel said, obviously pleased to find himself agreed with.

"*You* try and stop him hanging around!" I said indignantly. "Anyway, I told you—he's helping me. He might be reporting some stuff back to the others as well, but I think he's trying to annoy Zero at the moment, so it won't be much. I just won't take him anywhere really important."

"It's too late for him not to know about the new location of Upper Management," Daniel said pointedly.

"Well, if you'd given me some *notice* that you were gunna try to get yourself killed, I would have had a chance to make sure I wasn't being followed!" I retorted. "All right, so we'll leave Upper Management for a little bit later and focus on asking North a few questions, and having a bit of a sticky-beak around Mr. Preston's office and house."

"He's barely been dead two weeks," Daniel said gloomily. "Do you reckon there'll be anything left? The police have been there, but whoever killed him would have been there first to clean up anything interesting."

"Dunno," I said. "But we'd better take a look, anyway. He's connected to North, so it was probably Upper Management who killed him."

Daniel huffed. "I suppose that means we're going out again this arvo."

"Not you," I said. "It's not like I'm gunna run into any trouble over at Mr. Preston's office: they're just lawyers, and if Upper Management killed him, it's not likely they're still interested in his work space."

"It also means there probably won't be anything to find," muttered Daniel.

"Yeah, maybe," I said stubbornly. "But Behi—those people always think they know more than anyone else, and they're not too good at thinking like—like normal people. They're bound to have missed something."

"I keep feeling like *I'm* missing part of the conversation," said Morgana, uncomfortably perspicacious.

"There's still stuff we're not supposed to talk about," I told her. "Even though I'm not a cop. Oh! And that reminds me! You said a while ago that you'd had a cop here before I came along, didn't you?"

She nodded. "He was checking out the place across the street before Daniel arrived and everything got messy."

Daniel muttered in the background, but I ignored him. "How long ago was that? Was he taking pictures?"

"Just a month or two ago, not long."

"He take photos?"

"Yeah," she said. "He started by trying to run a camera feed through the window, but there must have been something wrong with it, because he was always complaining about stuff not turning out right. After a while, he just started taking lots of photos."

I exchanged a look with Daniel. He probably already knew what I'd just found out today: Behindkind in general could mask themselves much better on something as relatively low-tech as surveillance video than they could in photographs. Even if normal humans couldn't recognise them in photographs, other Behindkind *could.* I was pretty sure now that even Behindkind couldn't recognise other hidden Behindkind when it came to moving records.

"Why did he stop coming?" I'd been meaning to ask her since I'd heard about the bloke, but what with everything else that had happened lately, I'd only just remembered. "I would have thought he'd find it really useful here."

"I don't know," Morgana said, and she sounded a little bit sad. "He just didn't turn up again one day. There's still a flannie somewhere around the room that was his."

"'Zat all he left?" I asked eagerly. It sounded like this cop had known *something* of Behindkind. That being so, he was likely dead by now. If he had left anything useful behind, now, that would be something.

To my disappointment, Morgana nodded. "Yeah, just a flannie. It's why I wasn't worried or anything—he took everything else with him. He must have forgotten it, that's all. It should be somewhere over in that corner if I've still got it."

"All right," I said, my mind very full of questions and potential timelines. It wasn't that long ago that a body had been thrown at me and Detective Tuatu while we were in a cop's house. Maybe a month or two. I very much wanted to know if the two things were connected. "I'll head out as soon as you've found those addresses, then."

Morgana looked very slightly disappointed. "Wasn't it useful information?"

"Don't know," I said frankly. "I think so, but I haven't got enough other info to be sure. Once I know who to ask a few more questions, it should be easier. You got those addresses?"

"What am I supposed to do while you're out?" interrupted Daniel. I didn't know whether he was trying to stop me from talking too much, or just annoyed.

"Sniff out that flannie," I said, grinning. I couldn't help it, even though he scowled at me. "Tell Hyacinth we're still working on it when she comes around, if I'm not back by then. Oh yeah, and put something up on the roof for the kids to eat this evening."

Daniel grumbled, but I knew he'd do that, too. For a big, bad lycanthrope, it looked like he was pretty much putty when it came to Morgana: if she wanted the kids looked after, he would look after them.

I scarfed down another toastie, while Morgana finished her internet search for North and Mr. Preston, and very nearly gave away the whole thing by texting me the one she found instead of writing it down. When I got over that heart attack, I took the piece of paper from her, trying not to laugh at her crestfallen expression, and tucked it away in my pocket.

"I'll bring back coffee," I said.

CHAPTER SIX

I WENT TO MR. PRESTON'S OFFICE FIRST. MORGANA HADN'T been able to find North's address for me, so it was a good, logical first step. Even if I didn't find anything else there, I was sure to be able to at least find her address. I couldn't help feeling annoyed with North: she'd asked me to do a job that needed doing quickly, and hadn't bothered to tell me all the details. If I'd known she was connected with both Sarah and Upper Management, I would have asked a lot more questions—questions which, I was pretty sure, would be helpful in working out how to break the contract Sarah's parents were labouring under.

"Flamin' Behindkind," I muttered to myself as I double-checked the address Morgana had written down against the number on the side of the building. I was down in Salamanca again, and after wandering through heritage sandstone buildings, past an itinerant blacksmith and the awful Marilyn Monroe-inspired cat and dog statues in bronze, I had found myself by an unmarked door.

The number was right, and it was the right lane, but there was no sign of—well, a *sign*. Shouldn't any lawyer worth his salt be advertising? Or, I wondered, remembering a few things that Mr.

Preston had told me, had he worked purely for the benefit of Behindkind courts when their law intersected with human law? I knew he'd been paid very richly for taking on North's case, at least.

The door was open, so I went in. The inside was just as atmospherically heritage-styled as the outside, with wooden floors that echoed footsteps and long carpets that made them boom instead of echo. There was a bad smell in the air, too; or maybe not so much in the air as it was in the walls and carpet. I was pretty sure that was because of the staircase on my left: the grain of the wood in the stairs ran with the possibility that they could lead somewhere else other than an upstairs office, so it was likely that there was something gross and deadly up there.

I left them for last. Just in case there was something up there I didn't want to meet with until I'd checked down here and could run for it without feeling like I'd missed something important. I saw the receptionist's desk up ahead through a door at the end of the hall and headed toward that instead. As I did, it seemed like the smell grew worse, which was worrisome.

If it was something upstairs, with all the Between leaking down, it was likely to be something weird but not necessarily something I needed to worry about. If it was down here, it was more likely to be something human and weird that I definitely needed to worry about.

The floorboards creaked underneath my feet, setting the hairs up on the back of my neck as I came around the edge of the doorway, and I stopped with a jerk. There was a dead receptionist behind the desk. She reclined in her office chair with her head tilted back and her eyes open to gaze sightlessly at the ceiling, and I swayed a bit in the doorway, the floorboards moving beneath my feet.

It would have been nice to be able to say it looked like the woman had just fallen asleep. Would have been nice to see that instead of what I actually saw: a bloated and discoloured caricature of a human woman whose eyes had popped nearly all the way out due to decomposition. Something brown and gooey leaked from pretty much every hole on her face; nostrils, eyes, mouth. With the last warm, summery week we'd had, that must have been where the smell was coming from. It coated my nostrils like a paste of spam that had been left out too long in the sun and dredged up an urgent desire to puke from right at the bottom of my stomach.

I forced that urge back down and said aloud, a bit thickly, "Oh, right. It's dead body smell. Why didn't I know that?"

Maybe because all the bodies I'd come across were fresh? And the ones that weren't were in a kind of frozen stasis, which must have really put a lid on the smell.

When my stomach was under control again, I made myself step forward once, and then again. After that it seemed like I could keep walking around the desk, even though I didn't really want to. The computer was behind the desk, too, and once the police got here, I wouldn't get another chance to look at it.

I skirted around the poor woman as best I could, hitching up my hoodie to cover my nose, but it didn't do any good. The smell seeped through, right to the skin.

I didn't know how long she'd been dead, but I reckoned she must have been killed a few days after Mr. Preston was. She must have come back to clean her desk out after the police were done: the drawers on the right hand side of the desk were each slightly open, and there was a box on the desk with a few pens in it. A water cooler stood against the wall beside her, just a normal office one that bubbled when you got a drink. On the floor near her chair was a paper cup that had once been soggy and now was stiff in the form it had taken when it fell to the ground. Around it, and around the base of the receptionist's chair, there was a stain of water in the carpet.

I remembered Mr Preston's wild eyes as he told me of crea-tures crawling up through the drain and coming through the sink, and shivered. She must have thought she was safe here—what human would think something could come after them from the *water cooler* of all places? Who could have wanted to kill a receptionist who was just coming back for her things? It was just so *senseless*.

I cleared my throat carefully, just in case my lunch tried to crawl back up my throat again, and tried to breathe through my mouth as I leaned around the dead woman to get at the computer. It didn't help. It might have even made it worse, because now instead of just smelling it, it was like I was drinking it.

I gagged into my hoodie, but my lunch was pretty much aware of where it was meant to be by now, so I just hunched my shoulders and got on with my search, trying not to look at the poor receptionist. There wasn't much on the computer apart from basic client files, unless they were hidden by the Behind equivalent of a firewall or something. I didn't think so, though: Behind-kind are usually too much in love with themselves to realise the use of blending human tech with their skills.

Maybe I should be thankful for that.

Still, I managed to get the address they had for North—even if it wasn't her real one, it was somewhere to start—before I wiped away any fingerprints I might have left and hurried away from the poor dead receptionist to have a quick stickybeak around the rest of the lower floor.

There wasn't much to be seen; dribbles of Between ran down the walls everywhere like water trails or mould, but they weren't doing much except *being*. I wondered if the present, quiet Between was just because it was an older building, and that made me curious. Was it possible that Between could just exist in a kind of benign way? Just being there, without it having to be an opening for death and dismemberment, because the place was old and new at the same time.

Yeah, probably not.

The presence of a dead body along with the trickles of

Between was a pretty obvious veto of that idea. Still, it didn't look like the dribbles along the wall had been responsible for her death: they were there but they were still quiet, like they'd been there for a long time without trying to reach out further into the human world. If I'd had to guess, with my very small experience of Behindkind and Mr. Preston, I would have put my money on it being something to do with the empty water cooler and the deep liquid stain below the receptionist's chair.

I wished, for a brief, homesick moment that I could see Zero and Athelas' reaction to the scene and pick their brains, but shoved the thought away energetically. I had Daniel. I had JinYeong. I could ask either of them. I didn't need Zero. Didn't need Athelas.

I took a few pictures before I went back down the hall, mindful of the fact that my photos might be something Zero had hacked into as well as my calls. I didn't want the psychos showing up here while I was still in the process of checking out the whole place, so I made sure I covered up the business cards and anything with Mr. Preston's law firm's name on them.

I mean, there was no reason for Zero to be turning up, anyway: now that I was out of the house, he didn't have to try to keep me safe. He might want to keep me out of Behindkind business, though, and there was no use taking risks, after all. I was still very much confused between the Zero-who-seemed-to-care-about-me and the Zero-who-let-humans-die. There might be some intersection between the two, but if he was willing to let a human die because he didn't want to get involved with humans, how long would it be before he realised he didn't really care enough to keep me alive? It was much better not to trust him; much better to learn to trust only myself again.

Which meant that if one of those Zeros *did* turn up, whichever one of them it was would be more trouble than he was worth. If he wanted to keep me safe, he'd probably kick me out and then do nothing about the receptionist, and that wasn't fair.

She'd been here at least a week, which meant no one had missed her. If no one else was gunna even report her death, I was going make sure it got done.

I paused with my finger hovering over Detective Tuatu's name in my address book, and slowly put my phone back in my pocket. I still had to check around upstairs. Once the cops came, I wouldn't be able to poke my nose into things, and while that brought with it certain advantages—being able to ask Detective Tuatu for the cause of death, for instance—it also meant I wouldn't be able to see what I assumed was the office upstairs.

I didn't much want to go upstairs after the scene downstairs, but I went anyway. I couldn't let myself stop doing stuff just because I wished I had a sturdy, white-haired fae in front of me or a vampire next to me. If I did that, I'd be pretty useless as an investigator.

Anyway, the smell of downstairs was too sickening to stay there.

It followed me as I climbed the stairs, and I had the feeling that it would follow me all the way home, too, but at least the overwhelming sogginess of it crawling down into my lungs lessened as I climbed.

As I drew closer to the top of the stairs, the hollow wooden sound of my footsteps grew more solid, and a pattern traced itself through the wood beneath my feet. The stairwell itself rounded and smoothed out, chocolate shadows flowing along the newly curved walls that blended seamlessly into the curved ceiling. There was light, but I didn't know where it was coming from. I paused to look around and saw pinpricks of light everywhere that looked like glowbugs; tiny, matte luminates in the woody shadows.

Heck. I was definitely walking inside a tree right now. There was no way it was boards beneath my feet anymore. The stairwell opened out again ahead of me, but the entrance was round instead of rectangular or even oval, and I had to duck my head to pass through.

I didn't exactly expect more dead bodies, but I suppose I expected what I'd seen of Upper Management: a chilly, antibacterial kind of atmosphere that was more human than Between, where fae and humans alike could easily move around. Instead, I found a place that wasn't human, or even Between—here was a place that was deep Behind. I felt the difference of it as soon as I entered; the deep silence and profound sense of peril and something not quite...right. Or was it just that the place was so utterly inhuman? I hadn't felt that sense of deep, abiding peril since I'd been lost Behind by myself the first time. Or perhaps the first time I'd laid eyes on the Troika.

The furniture was furniture, but it was also part of the room itself: growing from the floor, growing from the ceiling. More glowing things instead of electric lights, though I was beginning to think that the bugs weren't bugs, but delicately formed, inanimate replicas. There was a desk, a chair, and even a window. A kind of dumbwaiter, too, by the looks.

And, incongruously, a computer.

This must have been where Mr. Preston did his work. I looked around at the room, and although I'd known he hadn't been telling me everything, I knew now that he had barely been telling me anything. He'd said he didn't know anything about his clients, that he just did what he was told, but if he'd worked in here there was no way he didn't know at least a good part of where his clients came from, and how to move around the world Behind.

I went around the room once, being careful to duck below the windowsill as I moved, but there wasn't much to see. The computer wouldn't turn on for me, either, but since I was pretty sure that was because it would only work for Mr. Preston, I didn't try too hard. I didn't want to give away the fact that someone was here, poking their nose around the place. I opened the dumbwaiter door as well, and found that it wasn't exactly a dumbwaiter.

Nope, it was a tiny prison. I stared at the very small Behind-kind in there, and it bared its teeth at me, pressed against the back of its prison. It could have been a fruitbat if it was back in Australia in the human world. Even here, it looked a *lot* like a fruitbat: all huge amber eyes and peaky leatherish ears, fur everywhere. Instead of wings it had four arms, all of them waving at me like a huge, demented spider, and legs that were nearly arms, too.

"Flaming heck!" I said, trying very hard not to be repulsed. It probably didn't care whether or not a human found it appealing. Goodness knew how long it had been imprisoned here. "You'd better get out while you can. *Don't* bite me!"

It just snarled at me and gnashed its little teeth again, burbling in some language I didn't understand. With the thought of Jin Yeong in my mind, I let the feeling of Between seep into me, and distinctly heard a tiny voice saying shrilly, "The information was correct! The information was correct! I will swear to it in the courts!"

I let the feeling of Between flow out with my words when I said again, very clearly, "You'd better get out while you can. Don't bite me."

Its eyes grew wide. "You can't do that!" it said.

I sighed. "Yeah, people keep saying that. You want out, or are you gunna stay there?"

It darted past me on all six limbs, and sprang to the floor. I expected it to go for the window and fade into the Behind world, but it ran for the stairs instead.

"Oi!" I yelped.

To my surprise, it stopped. "What does the human want?"

"You—are you going out into the human world?"

"I do not wish to die," it said, as though that was an answer.

"What—what were you doing in there?"

"I am an intelligence unit," it said. "I receive vibrations. Questions are given, answers are found."

"Oh," I said. Maybe I'd been too quick to let it go. But I couldn't just have kept it in a cage while I forced it to give me answers, after all. "You're not gunna hurt anyone, are you?"

"I do not wish to die," it said again. "Humans do not harm me, and I shall not harm them. I shall find a plump lap."

"You're gunna find a what?" I asked, startled.

"You may call me for precisely one favour," it said. "I will answer. Speak the words *big ears, big ears, answer my call* and I will answer."

"That seems a bit rude," I said, but the thing was already scarpering for it.

Heck. Hopefully I hadn't just let a dangerous ankle-biter out into the human world. And *speaking* of the human world...

Hardly daring to breathe, I stooped and entered the stairwell again, hoping against hope that I would be able to find the path that led back through Between. It had obviously been made safe for a human like Mr. Preston, but now that he was dead, would it still be so?

Luckily for me, either someone had forgotten to turn off any human-assisting bit of magic, or the little vibration-receiving creature had left the way open enough for me to get out. I tumbled down the last few stairs, feeling the familiar movement of floorboards beneath my feet in heart-stuttering relief, and was hit anew by the smell of death and decay.

I phoned Detective Tuatu on my way out the door, as I was wiping my fingerprints off the doorknob on the inside. There was no reason for the poor receptionist to stay where she was any longer: she deserved to be able to be buried. It wasn't like I was saying anything that would be useful to Zero if he overheard it, anyway.

"Oi," I said, when the detective picked up.

"I thought you weren't supposed to be calling me," he said. "Pet, I can't talk now. I'm slightly busy—ow! Can you *please* keep that thing down!"

"Yeah, but I've got a body for you. Don't you want it? Wait, who's there with you?"

The line went dead.

"Mongrel!" I said indignantly. He'd hung up on me.

My phone bingled with a text from him. *Where?* was all it said.

I texted him the address, and the next text was just as short. *Wait there.*

The heck I would. I felt as though I needed to get away from that smell before it followed me into my dreams as well.

Can't, I texted. *Got somewhere I gotta be. Bring a mask, it's ripe in here.*

Then I shut the door behind me, wiping off my prints from the outside as well. It was a shame to get rid of anything that might have been useful, but I'd already messed it up by putting my fingerprints over what had been there and I was wary of leaving traces. I was pretty sure Behindkind wouldn't hesitate to use the human legal system if they wanted to get rid of me. After all, they were using it on North, and I would have thought that was much harder to do.

I mean, I'd rather they didn't find out about me at all, but if they did, I wanted to cover myself from potential repercussions in the human world.

The evening was golden by the time I got to the place Mr. Preston's records said North lived. It was out at Sandy Bay and too far to walk if I wanted to get home before dark, so I used up a couple of the last few gold coins I had left on me and took the bus.

I already knew the place was a unit based on the address, but I hadn't expected it to be quite so posh. Instead of being in a heritage kind of building that I would have expected from Behindkind, North's place was one of the new, modern complexes that had a common garden and a pretty solid gate at the front for the private car park.

"Pretty flamin' swish," I muttered, matching my walking speed to the pearl-wearing grandma ahead of me. I wouldn't even have offered a bet on the likelihood of there being either a security guard or a pin-pad sort of system to get through the door, and I wanted to make sure I got in.

It was a pin-pad system, but I followed smoothly after Grandma Pearl with my hood up and my footsteps quiet, and I don't think she even noticed me. I took the elevator right up to the top floor, raising my eyebrows at the sheer spaciousness and richness of it, and came out onto a floor that was even swankier than the first floor had been. It was more like an expensive hotel than a block of units, and up here I could understand why North had picked this place instead of something more connected with Between. From here, through the long windows at the end of the hall, was a clear, airy view of the sea and sky and clouds: exactly what you'd expect the incarnation of the North Wind to want to see.

I knocked on the door of her unit, and it just sort of fell inward with a dull thud onto the carpet.

"Ah heck," I said.

The place was a mess. I don't just mean a human mess, even though it was that. If you looked at it with normal human eyes, the pot-plants were smashed, spilling dirt all over the place, and pretty much everything in the house that could be smashed, *had* been smashed. Holes gaped in the walls, with plaster in crumbs and jagged pieces inside and outside of them, and one of the ceiling fans had been torn from the ceiling and now dangled brokenly about half a metre from the carpet.

If you looked at it with the help of the copious amounts of Between that hung over the place like mist, there were weird bodies on the floor with dirt for blood and hessian for skin, black blood splattered everywhere, and something soggy and furry and very dead hung from two of the blades of the ceiling fan, dripping on the carpet.

"Ah heck," I said again. Whatever had happened here, it didn't look like I was going to get the chance to speak with North today. I just hoped she wasn't dead.

I mean, could you even kill the North Wind incarnate? I suppose that's the point of an incarnation, but how do you kill the bit that makes them the North Wind?

I hunched my shoulders a bit against the crawling feeling that had started up again, and took a slow walk around the main room. I didn't know whether North's attackers had been looking for North herself, or something around the place, but I wanted to make sure I saw everything there was to see before I went home to Morgana and Daniel and gave them the bad news.

The living room was pretty empty if you didn't count the dead bodies, and there didn't seem to be a lot around that was personal, just the broken potted plants and a few dishes. There was a cup of water sitting on the kitchen bench, with a bit of water sloshed around it, like North had been getting a glass of water when her door was smashed in. Hadn't she seen them coming? That was weird: beside the door was a digital screen that showed a split view of the outside of the unit block, and a slightly cracked view of North's ceiling, which would once have been a view of the outside of her door. Splinters of Between also protruded from all over the door, as if they'd been smashed in as much as the door had—a Behindkind sort of first warning system, I was pretty sure.

Chilled, I hurried around the kitchen, then went for the bedroom. It was as much of a mess in there: everything that could be torn apart had been torn apart, and in the remains of the mattress an iron box had tumbled across the sheets, coming to rest between wall and mattress and surrounded by padding. Scattered over the mattress and the floor were photos; a good fifty or so of them, torn and dirty from being trod on, some of them with dirt or slime or whatever the searchers had had on their boots or possibly feet.

North's version of a safe? If so, whatever really important things had been in there were gone: I could see the bare inside of it through the broken lid. I had a quick look at the photos that were scattered around, too, but they were all of the same little girl and sometimes a pair of adults. The Palmers, I would have guessed, though I wasn't sure why North had their photos. They didn't look like surveillance photos: they looked like the kind of photos a family friend takes.

They obviously hadn't interested the searchers, however. I couldn't see anything left to sift through.

Hang on, though. Underneath a wad of carelessly tossed photos was a flicker of royal blue. I leaned over to pinch that sliver of blue between my fingers, and came back up with a scrap of silky material. It was a ribbon: you know, the sort you get for running in races or winning the art competition at school. Just a silky blue ribbon with *first place* embossed on it. It didn't look special, but I was pretty sure it must have been if it was locked away in a box of North's stuff. I put it in my pocket to think about later, and went back out into the main room to frown at the glass of water on the bench.

It was just...weird. Not broken, for a start, while everything else was. It was a cut glass cup with lots of facets, and there was no reason for it to be where it was. If North had been taken by surprise, she would have dropped it or thrown it as a weapon, not set it down on the bench, regardless of how careless she was as she did so. If she hadn't been taken by surprise, why was fetching herself a glass of water the last thing she did before being attacked, especially since the sloshed water suggested she had set it down hastily?

I picked up the glass, holding it up to the light of the window, and at first saw only water and refracted light. Then it occurred to me that there was a small golden gleam somewhere in the depths of it that was just a bit more solid than the spangles of gold the sunlight made. It was tiny, that flash of gold: about an eighth of the size of my little finger-nail, with nothing Between to it or the glass. If I hadn't held the glass up, I wouldn't have seen it. Even gazing into it at eye level with lots of light, it could almost have been part of the golden sunset refracting through the water.

I tried to fish it out, feeling carefully for the flake of gold, and my fingers touched something unexpectedly much larger than the gold. Rectangular and smooth, it was as slick as glass. I pulled it out and gazed at the transparent wafer as it dripped onto the bench.

What the heck?

I turned it over between my fingers, trying to work out what it was. The flake of gold seemed to be some kind of a chip, though I wasn't sure about that, and when I dried it off, I could see very faint scoring marks at the other end of it.

What the heck was this thing? Why had North hidden it from her attackers?

I mean, if I kinda squinted at it sideways, those barely-there marks could almost be...

I felt a grin spreading across my face.

It was a USB: a tiny glass USB with the same depth as a couple of glass microscope slides and only two thirds as wide. The faint scoring on it was from someone sliding it in and out of a USB port pretty regularly.

I still didn't know whether it was something that was helpful to North's case, or something else entirely, but I *did* know it was something she hadn't wanted to get into the hands of whoever attacked her. Question was, who had she left it for? She hadn't seemed as though she was willing to have anyone but me helping her on the case, which would suggest she'd left it for me, but she couldn't have known I'd make it here to find it.

Obviously it was my duty as North's hired investigator to appropriate it and see what was on it. I was still grinning as I slipped it into my other pocket: despite the fact that North was goodness-knows-where by now, despite the fact that I didn't even know what I was going to do next.

There wasn't much more around the place, so I just did another quick circuit around the house and decided to make a day of it. It was already getting toward evening, and I was pretty sure

Daniel would start hassling me by text to know where I was if I didn't check in soon.

That reminded me that even if Zero had my phone magically tapped somehow, I could still send a careful text to Daniel to let him and Morgana know everything had gone well, and that I was on my way home. I did that, strolling along with my head bent and my eyes on the phone as I came out of the apartment, and when I nearly walked into someone, my first instinct was to just step aside and keep walking.

A firm hand grabbed me around the neck, but I'd already seen, if not processed, the extra set of arms on the torso.

"Ah heck," I said, for the umpteenth time that day.

I think my feet left the floor. The four-armed Behindkind shunted me effortlessly across the hall, and I caught a brief glimpse of someone tall and open-mouthed at the end of that hall. I would have hoped that whoever the human was, he had more self-preservation than to try and help, but as the four-armed creature hove me through the doorway of the apartment opposite North's, I caught the faint but certain flutter of Between to the figure.

Well. Behindkind. What a surprise.

Still whoever that Behindkind was, he obviously wasn't with this lot: they shut the door behind them, and I could suddenly feel carpet beneath my feet again.

No. Not carpet. Grass.

I was standing on grass.

"You lot bring this stuff with you everywhere you go?" I asked, before I could stop myself.

"I do not bring it," said a very deep voice that didn't belong to my current captor. "However, it springs beneath my feet where I go."

"Oh," I said, catching my breath and my balance. And then, because I didn't know what else to say, I added, "I s'pose that's pretty convenient."

The speaker emerged from the kitchen as I spoke. He was a big bloke—well, if he'd been a bloke, he would have been a big bloke. He was actually fae; sorta golden in a quiet, warm-sand type of way, and he was big even for a fae. He looked nice or something. Maybe he reminded me of someone? I wasn't sure, but his face was pleasant and open and friendly...and utterly without wrinkles.

That made me look again, because people should have wrinkles. Even fae should have wrinkles—just enough to show which part of their face does the most moving. There should be faint lines around their eyes to show that they smile, and maybe one or two at the corners of their mouths. Even if they're inclined to be grumpy beggars, there should at least be a ridge between their brows.

Even Athelas has lines around his eyes, for pete's sake! Even Zero has a nearly constant line between his brows.

This bloke—this fae—he had *nothing*. Just smooth skin.

And suddenly I didn't feel like he was so friendly and warm.

"G'day," I said.

He sat on the couch, dwarfing it, and said, "Talk to me."

There was a huge weight of command with it: command that said I should tell him about my life, my connections, my current situation. No, not a weight: a worm. A worm that burrowed into my ear and chewed through my brain looking for *truth* and *lie* and gnawing, gnawing, *gnawing*.

I talked a *lot*. I talked about waking up from the Nightmare and drinking coffee. I talked about my annoying friend who was very close to being a big brother, and about how much of a pain it was to do the washing up after I'd fed all his friends. I talked about the previous house I'd been in, the one I'd been kicked out of, and skated around the edges of everything by telling an awful lot about things that weren't important.

That helped with the awful, itchy feeling of the worm that was burrowing in my head, and I reckon it must have tired him out, because he said impatiently, at last, "Stop. Where is Lord Sero?"

"Dunno," I said. The worm considered that and grew still for just a moment.

"He didn't kill you, I see."

"I'm a good cook," I said, off the cuff, as the worm wriggled itself deeper.

"I see," he said; and he said it like he really did see. Like it made sense to him. "Yes, it's no use killing a good cook."

"Exactly," I agreed, very cold around the ears. I wanted to put up my hoodie but didn't dare.

"What are you doing here today? Is this interference under the aegis of Lord Sero?"

"North asked me to help with something," I said. "I said I would, but she didn't tell me everything I needed to know, so I came to ask her some questions."

He considered that for far longer than I was comfortable with. Did he not believe me, or was he going to ask questions about what North wanted help with—stuff I wasn't comfortable answering, but would probably be dead if I *didn't* answer them?

Dead, or chewed to pieces by the worm in my brain, the worm that had started burrowing, *burrowing* again.

"She has an assistant," he said.

"Yeah," I said, "but I'm not with Lord Sero anymore."

I knew it was a mistake as soon as I said it. One of the fae standing beside the big fae asked, "Should we take care of it, my lord? If it's unaffiliated—"

"I'm not unaffiliated," I said. "I'm with North now."

That was true, too. I mean, probably not in the way that he meant it, but what mattered was how it looked to me. That's what I told the little worm crawling around in my brain, and it seemed to be happy with that.

"I won't alienate the North Wind," the fae said. "Not at this stage. Flesh bag: did you take anything from her place of residence?"

The truth. Only the truth was safe while the worm burrowed. "Yeah," I said. "Got this."

I held up the ribbon, expecting the worm to bore deeper, looking for the rest of the truth, but it didn't. Oh. Right, I thought after a sick moment. I had told the truth, and that was all that was demanded of me. The worm wouldn't specify *how much* truth I had to tell, just that I had to tell it.

Just like Athelas, I was free to tell just enough truth to quiet the worm. Enough to confuse. Enough to conceal. I wondered, suddenly and coldly, if Athelas had become the way he was in part because there had once been a little worm crawling around in his head, and he had never been able to get rid of it. Maybe that was why he was so torturous with the truth. Maybe he'd forgotten that he could talk in any other way because he'd been watched and controlled and used for such a long time.

Maybe there were worse positions in the Behind world than Pet.

"Useless," said the fae, and the worm crawled out of my ear again even though there was nothing there when I reached up to feel for it, to crush it to bits. "Throw the fleshbag out. You. *Forget.*"

Unlike with Jin Yeong, I had absolutely no desire to let this Behindkind know his mojo didn't work on me. I actually kinda expected it to work, since the worm had gotten in. My surprise must have made my face blank enough to be believable, because the fae didn't even watch as the four-armed man dragged me back out and threw me into the corridor.

I didn't look back, either. I just ran for it.

CHAPTER SEVEN

I ONLY JUST GOT INSIDE THE HOUSE.

I *just barely* got inside the house when someone howled, "Who dragged in the body? I'm not cleaning it up!"

"Rude!" I yelled. I still felt cold and creeped out and wriggly, and it was comforting to yell at something that wasn't scary. "See if I get you lot any more coffee!"

"They wouldn't drink it if you got it now," said Daniel, from the stairs. He leapt the last couple of steps and strode toward the kitchen. "It'd smell like a dead thing."

"Thought you lot liked that sort of thing," I grumbled. "Don't you lot roll in dead things?"

"That's racist," he said, but he was grinning. "Only the young ones do that. When we're older we've got more of a sense of humanity back again, and the human side doesn't like dead things."

As if to prove him right, one of the younger lycanthropes shuffled close and rubbed his cheek against my sleeve, giggling.

"What the heck!" I protested. "Get off!"

Pressure, against the other arm. I looked around and there was another of the teenaged ones, gazing up at me.

"You get lost, too," I told him, but the warmth of lycanthrope on either side had already helped with my cold, creeped out feeling, so I didn't say it with as much of an attitude as I would normally have done.

"You okay?" Daniel asked, in spite of that. "I was starting to get worried. I got your text that you were coming and then you didn't reply."

"Yeah," I said. "I'll give you a rundown once I've had a shower. North's vanished off somewhere and I'm gunna need coffee."

"North's what?" he demanded, stopping short of the kitchen.

I kept going for the stairs, ignoring him. "Tell you after. Gotta shower!"

A flutter of movement was my first notice that someone was watching me from above the bannisters as I climbed the stairs. I looked up curiously, and saw them lining the stairs high above me on both sides: two rows of heads shoved between bannisters, gazing down at me.

Dust flickered through the very last, golden sunshine of the day, lending a distressed photographic sort of look to the whole scene, and I wondered if I looked the same to them from up there.

"Didn't Daniel get you any food?" I asked them.

"We already ate it," said one of them, his voice filtering down through the sunshine just like the dust. It was the bold little boy with golden curls who had threatened one of the others with his spoon the other night. He rested his chubby chin on tiny fists and added, "We want dessert."

"Okay," I said. "But you gotta wait until I have a shower: the others said I smell."

"We don't care about that," whispered a girl, who was just a little bit taller than the boy.

"You might not, but the boys downstairs care," I told them. "I'll bring some cake up after, okay?"

They didn't answer, just watched me in silence as I climbed

the stairs to get to my own room. Still, I didn't feel like they were about to drop anything down on me, which was nice. They must still like me more than they liked Daniel.

I DID *NOT* EXPECT THAT I WOULDN'T BE ABLE TO WASH THE smell out of my hair.

Or my skin, for that matter. I scrubbed until my skin went red, and washed my hair until the water was threatening to run cold, and I could still smell dead receptionist.

I huffed my frustration in a spray of water droplets through the golden sunshine that still streamed through the west-facing window, and then yelped when something shuffled over near the door.

I popped my head around the shower curtain, wondering if I could use the loofah in a deadly enough way to be any use, and saw one of the kids standing next to the door, blinking sleepily in the sunlight. At her feet was a small plastic bucket with cut lemons in it.

"What the heck?" I complained.

"*He* told me to give it to you," she said, looking down at the bucket. Reckon she must have been a bit miffed about it, because she wasn't carrying it: she was sort of shunting it across the floor with one foot, sulkily.

"Who's *he*?" I asked, but as the bucket made a small plastic *tic!* against the bathtub, I smelled the faintest whiff of cologne.

"He says it will help with the smell," she said.

"Right," I said, and reached out to take the little bucket. She stared at me unblinkingly, so I added, "Thanks. Make sure you shut the door on your way out, all right? I'll bring up cake later."

I retreated back behind the shower curtain, hoping she would take the hint and leave me to my shower. She must have, because although I didn't hear the door open and close, the next time I looked around the shower curtain she was gone.

That left me looking down doubtfully at cut lemons, wondering what the heck they were supposed to do about the smell of dead person. Mind you, if anyone would know about dead people, it was Jin Yeong. I shrugged, and grabbed the first lemon half.

It actually worked. I mean, I had to squeeze it over my hair as well as the rest of me, and I still did another round of shampoo and conditioner, but by the time I was done I smelled acidic instead of disgusting, and my skin didn't have the creeping feeling any longer.

Daniel was waiting for me outside the bathroom with a disapproving look and a mug of coffee when I got out of the shower. I accepted the coffee, ignored the disapproval, and said, "Sorry, forgot to bring some home. I got distracted by a dead person."

"The vampire is back," he said, surprising me by ignoring the open lead I'd given him. Apparently he was more annoyed about Jin Yeong's presence than a dead body somewhere.

"I can't help it if he comes around here," I argued. "You're just lucky he gave me a tip about lemons, or I'd still smell like sticky dead person."

"Who's dead? It's not fresh body smell on you."

"The receptionist at Mr. Preston's place," I told him. "She can't have been dead more than a week and a half, but she was... she was falling apart."

"Those are the worst," he said. "I prefer the fresh ones, even if there's blood. It sounds weird, but the bloody ones don't turn my stomach like the weepy ones."

I reckon he meant to be comforting, but how comforting is it when the people you know have a preference for a type of dead body?

"You said something happened to North?"

"Yeah. I got to her place and everything was tossed over like there was a full pitched battle and then someone went through everything with a knife to find what they were looking for. North was gone, and there were fae in the room across the hall."

"What fae?"

"Dunno, some bloke who said something about bringing grass with him wherever he goes. He was sprouting flowers in the unit, too."

"*Shingihae*," purred Jin Yeong's voice, from the top of the stairs.

"You're not allowed up here," I told him. Maybe the lemon juice had burned out my nostrils: I hadn't smelled him before I saw him. "And what the heck do you mean, it's interesting?"

"He means that you saw one of the high fae. They're the ones that spontaneously grow flowers where'er they walk and stuff. Lord Sero's dad is one of 'em, too, so if it's him we're dealing with, we're going to have to be a lot more careful. North must have been involved in something really big if she's got high fae chasing her when she's already due to be seen by the courts. Fae usually step back when the Behindkind courts are involved."

Heck, I thought, a bit worried. Had it actually been Zero's dad I'd met? I said, "Whatever it was they wanted from her, they really did a number on her unit. It had to be the fae across the hall, right?"

"*Kurae*," agreed Jin Yeong. "Certainly."

"Unless they were with her and arrived too late to help," Daniel said. "No one's ever been sure which side North's on: Family, or anti-Family."

"Whoever it was that took her, they went for whatever she had hiding in an iron box as well as whatever she might have had around the place."

"What did you get?"

"This was in the box," I said, showing them the ribbon. I wasn't yet sure if I wanted to show the glass USB while Jin Yeong was here.

Daniel's brows went up. "That was in an iron box?"

"Yeah." I thought about that, and added, "Hang on, that means the people who came after her were definitely fae, right?"

"It means that's who she was hiding that stuff from, at least," he said. "Might have nothing to do with the fae that were there."

JinYeong made a small, unconvinced noise, and said so that we could both understand him, "It was Family. She had information that they didn't wish to become known."

"Hang on," I said, frowning. "*Hang* on. This has to mean that Upper Management are the ones defending North, right?"

"It sorta makes sense," said Daniel. "I mean, it's a good way of controlling her: do as you're told, and we'll make sure you get off the charges, right?"

"Yeah, that's fair enough—especially if they were the ones who got her charged with it. It would also mean that's why she needs someone else to break the contract between them and the Palmers. But if it was Upper Management who were defending her, how come they killed off Mr. Preston? I was pretty sure it was them."

"You can replace lawyers," Daniel said. "Maybe he found out something that was too useful."

I thought about that for a bit. "*If* they're the ones who made it look like she did it, and *if* they're using it as a way for control to get what they want from the Palmer family, then they wouldn't want her getting off the charge too quickly. Or," I added slowly, thinking of the huge fae in the unit opposite North's, "Upper Management weren't the ones who killed Mr. Preston."

"I think you are being distracted," said JinYeong, leaning into the wall. "I thought you had something else in your mind."

I looked at him with suspicion. "What do you know about what I'm investigating?"

One of JinYeong's brows went up again. "You are involved with North. But you would not help in such an issue if there were not a human in need of help. So you are helping some human who is connected with North: perhaps a little girl who is contracted to Behindkind. Am I not correct?"

"You're annoying, is what you are," I retorted, which just made him look smug. To Daniel, I said, "I'm gunna get something to eat. We'll figure out how much to tell Morgana tomorrow."

"All right. I'll let her know you're back. Don't let the boys talk you into making anything for them—they've already had about twenty kilos of pizza. There might even be a couple of pieces left in the fridge."

I grinned and went back downstairs with Jin Yeong following me. I wasn't sure what he was doing here again other than getting the kids to pass me lemons to make sure I didn't stink too much for my housemates. Still, he didn't do anything more annoying than sit down next to me on the couch when I decided to watch tv with Daniel's pack in the living room, so that was refreshing.

Jin Yeong was still there when I came back from putting cake up on the roof for the kids, but it didn't seem worthwhile to complain about it. I went to sleep with my back against him and my legs in the lap of a confused but willing lycanthrope, and when I woke up again the tv was off and I wasn't the only one sprawled around the room.

I shuffled back a bit into the warmth that was Jin Yeong, and wondered why it felt like someone was watching me.

Oh. Someone *was* watching me. It was Zero, sitting in his chair back at my old house with his eyes unnervingly on me.

"What is it?" murmured Jin Yeong. I knew he didn't need to sleep, but he sounded sleepy anyway. "You are wriggling. Go back to sleep."

"It's nothing," I said, a little bit shaken. I could still see Zero there, looking at me, but I didn't think he could really see me. He was in the fae version of rest, sitting perfectly still with his eyes half-slit and unseeing: he was looking at whatever thing was in the same position as me in the house he was in.

I wriggled a bit more until I was shoulder to shoulder with

Jin Yeong instead of leaning against him. The lycanthrope I'd had my feet on growled in his sleep, but didn't wake up, and Jin Yeong flicked a look down at me as if to say *what?*

I shrugged and tried not to look over at Zero again, but it was difficult. His eyes were always piercing in real life, and even half-shut and unseeing they were hard to meet.

Jin Yeong followed my eyes, but he mustn't have been able to see Zero, because his gaze panned over the wall without stopping, then came back to rest on me.

"Go to sleep, you," he said.

Jin Yeong was still there when I woke up the next morning, but he wasn't quite *there* there. He must have left some time during the early morning, because now he was back at my old house, and my old house had come here, bringing him with it.

I groaned at the living room ceiling and tried not to think too deeply about it. Things were already confusing enough. The lycanthrope in whose lap my feet were resting growled in his sleep and seemed to be trying to catch a flea, so I stopped wriggling, and after a while he settled back down to sleep again.

I sat up carefully, watching a not-quite-there coloured shadow of Athelas carry his teacup to his favourite seat and sit down near Zero. Jin Yeong was sitting in his usual place already, looking sulky, and if I had a guess as to why, it would have been because he had no coffee.

By the looks of it, Zero and Athelas had been talking for a little while already, and since they both had their coffee and tea respectively, Jin Yeong must have arrived back home too late to be given the same benefit.

"You're late," Zero said to him shortly.

Jin Yeong shrugged and got up again to pad over to the kitchen and fetch a blood bag. I heard him say, "I am busy," before he came back into sight with it in his mouth.

"Then you'd better have something useful to show for it," Zero said.

"Mm." JinYeong took the bag out of his mouth briefly while he sat down. "There is something."

I stood up in my indignation. Was he about to tell Zero about what I'd been up to? Well, I wasn't gunna put up with that! I shuffled around behind his couch and leaned over it.

"Oi," I breathed in his ear. "You *better not* be about to spill the beans."

JinYeong choked on his blood bag and twitched around, his hand brushing against his ear as if to brush away a spider. I saw his eyes roam the space behind him, narrowed and thoughtful, and the realisation as it dawned in his eyes. As soon as it did, he saw me. I don't know how, but he definitely saw me. Maybe it was just the knowledge of it that triggered his sight.

His eyebrows went up challengingly, and he said over his shoulder to Zero, "The North Wind has been taken."

"I know it," said Zero shortly. "My father has been busy. He must have heard she had something for me."

Heck, I thought, distracted at once. It really had been Zero's dad I'd met.

"Then I suppose we can at least surmise that the information she has is the sort to prove useful," said Athelas. "How delightful. It would seem we have found ourselves a true lead this time."

I glared at Athelas; not that he could see me. Flamin' fae. Always so cold-blooded, even about other Behindkind. Trust him to be more interested in the information than he was in the disappearance of North.

JinYeong grinned a bit and turned back around, biting into his blood bag again.

"I was supposed to meet her a few hours ago," said Zero, rather grimly. "If, in fact, we have found a true lead, it would also seem that we've lost it again. I'm quite certain my father now has in his possession whatever it was North would have given me. He has been disturbed by her outside connections for the last few years at least. Even if she is yet alive, she has no knowledge of what it was she was giving me: she was merely the courier. I've got a suspicion that it wasn't originally intended for me, if it comes to that; I suspect it was meant for Upper Management."

Okay, so whatever it was on the USB, it was something Zero wanted—and possibly something to do with the murder of my parents, his own mother's death, or both.

I didn't realise I'd climbed over the back of the familiar couch until I plopped down onto a seat that wasn't really there. Jin Yeong looked across at me, his eyes very wide for an instant, then dropped his eyelashes to hide his surprise before Zero could catch him at it.

"The pet is keeping herself busy," he said, looking straight at me. His mouth curved mockingly, he added, "You were correct, *hyeong*. She is involved with North, but only in regard to a human. It is nothing."

"Make sure she doesn't get in my way," said Zero briefly. "I don't care if she's busy, so long as she doesn't turn up in my investigations."

I glared at Jin Yeong. What a rat. Funny, though. He still hadn't mentioned anything about Upper Management, or our outing to find it together. Nor had he mentioned our practise bouts, or anything about my presence at North's place yesterday. He only told Zero what Zero already knew.

I stopped frowning and instead narrowed my eyes at Jin Yeong, who looked almost indecently pleased with himself. I stuck my tongue out at him, but he only grew a little more smug.

"The Palmers will be out tonight," Zero said. "There was a necessary meeting with the school, and they'll planning on eating out. While I still have an agreement with North, I'll make sure they're kept safe. Athelas, you look for North: see what you can find out about who took her or if she managed to get away. Jin Yeong—"

"I am busy," said Jin Yeong in a lazy voice that nevertheless left no room for arguments. "Do not involve me in your plans."

"May one ask what you will be busy doing?" enquired Athelas, his voice deceptively pleasant.

"What are you doing?" said another voice, causing my sight of all three to shudder.

"Spying," I said, and came to the realisation that I was perched, not on the couch, but the third step of the stairwell. Goodness knew how I'd gotten there: if I'd walked the way I seemed to remember walking and climbed over the back of something, it was also likely I had walked right through the wall and the stairs to perch where I was.

"The troll lady's at the door," said Daniel, because of course it was him. "I think she wants to speak to you."

That jolted me right out of my desire to segue back into the other house with the psychos. If I'd thought about it earlier, it would have occurred to me that with North gone, there would be no more Hyacinth, either. I was glad to know I'd been wrong, but I was also anxious to ask Hyacinth a few questions about her mistress now that I could do it.

She was less pink and cheerful about the face than when I'd last seen her. There was a slight look of strain to her eyes, too, and this time when I asked her to step in, she came without politely declining first. Hyacinth was obviously worried about her mistress.

It was a good thing that I'd done some research before she came back, or I might have tried to offer her a cuppa again. As it was, I did offer her a cuppa—but of fine gravel, not tea. And yeah, I got it from the back yard, but it was finely graded and Daniel had said it was the fine stuff they liked.

Which is to say that I did research, but my research was mostly asking the lycanthropes about trolls. Apparently everyone knows you don't offer liquids to a troll. Probably the same everyone who knows humans can't do magic, or escape Behind, or use Between.

When Hyacinth was seated at the kitchen bench, rather

nervously tipping gravel into her mouth and crunching softly, I said, "You know North's gone, don't you?"

"Yes. Miss North was not there this morning when I went to see if she had further questions for you."

"Do you know where she is?"

"No."

"Do you know if she's alive, at least?"

There was a very short pause before Hyacinth resumed crunching. "No," she said, in a very small voice.

"The fae in the unit across the hall seemed to think she was still alive," I said, by way of small comfort. At least, the big one had let me go because he didn't want to offend her.

Hyacinth brightened. "That is a little bit cheering. If she got away from the Family, she will find a way to contact me. She is very concerned about Sarah Palmer's case."

"That's what I wanted to ask her about," I said. So Hyacinth, like Zero, was certain it was the Family and not Upper Management who had come after North. "North's connected with that little girl a heck of a lot more closely than she let on. I need to know why if I'm supposed to break her contract. Why does North care about her?"

"I don't know why Sarah was important to Miss North," Hyacinth said. "That was before I came to be with her."

I blinked a bit. I hadn't expected that. Hyacinth had the quiet, polite demeanour I'd come to expect of the long-term servants of Behindkind. Enslaved so long that they'd almost come to trust in and respect their owners.

"Oh, right," I said. "Did you know anything about the kid herself?"

"She escaped from Behind," Hyacinth told me. "Or that's what Miss North said. I didn't know it was possible."

I blew a breath out into my cheeks. "Me either."

I mean, I'd done it, but I was pretty sure I'd had help each time. If this kid had escaped from Behind, there was a good chance she was interesting to Upper Management in the same way that I was to the Troika.

On a whim, I asked Hyacinth, "Who was North supposed to be meeting last night? Did it have anything to do with Sarah Palmer?"

I already knew the answer—one answer, anyway—but I wanted to know if she would tell me at least the part I knew or not.

"I couldn't say," she said guardedly.

I couldn't help grimacing slightly in disappointment, but at least the answer told me more than Athelas' responses usually did, while being not much more openly communicative. It told me that whatever Zero had been about to get from North the other night, it had had something to do with the Palmers. Their protection, probably, but she would have had to purchase it with something pretty big to interest Zero in guarding three humans. That must be what was on the glass USB.

It also told me that Hyacinth wasn't going to answer any other questions about Sarah, whether or not she knew the answers to those questions.

I dug the blue ribbon out of my pocket and waved it at the troll lady instead. "Know what this is?"

"That's Miss North's! How did you get it?"

"Took it from her apartment. What do you mean, it's hers?"

"She won it in a feat of great strength, she said. May I have it?"

"All yours," I said, passing it to her. I had no use for it, and I wasn't even sure it was important. The USB, on the other hand, I was definitely not going to be handing over. I wouldn't even be mentioning it until I knew a bit more about it: not to North or her assistant, not to Zero or the rest of the Troika.

Hyacinth left after she finished her gravel, passing Daniel in the hall as he entered it from the stairway. He watched her go, eyebrows up, and when the door shut behind Hyacinth, he asked,

"Does she know North is gone? Or does she know something we don't know?"

"Everybody knows something that we don't know," I complained. "Even Detective Tuatu."

"What about Detective Tuatu?"

"Nothing. He's just got some info for me. I gotta go see him today because I didn't tell him where I'm living now."

"You want coffee? I made a pot up in Morgana's kitchen. Just came down for more milk."

"Beauty," I said, and ducked into the kitchen to grab the milk. "Any food?"

"Only if you want to make toast," he said through the doorway.

"That'll do," I said cheerfully. "All right, let's go."

On the way up, to get it out there before Morgana could hear, I said, "She escaped from Behind, Hyacinth says. Sarah Palmer, I mean."

Daniel turned his head to stare at me and tripped over a step. Regaining his balance, he said, "That's not possible."

"Yeah, I'm starting to think you guys say stuff like that just because you have no explanation for stuff. I s'pose Behindkind think tv is magic, too."

Daniel coughed away a laugh. "All right, but it's supposed to be impossible. When impossible stuff starts happening Behind, it means trouble."

"What sort of trouble?"

"Change of succession, usually. It's gunna be dicey if the same thing happens again with the King Behind—I wasn't around for the mess last time, but your lot must have been."

"So it's what, a sign that your king is about to die so you can find a new one in time?"

"There's a bit of disagreement about it," Daniel said. "Some people think it's like that. Some of them think it's a catalyst for the old leader to die and a new one to come in."

"That's what I said."

"No, it isn't. I mean, some of 'em think this sort of thing *brings about* the death of the current leader. Like, if he can stop it happening, he can reign for another cycle, however long that lasts. There was a bit of a scandal about it when this king came in. They say he tracked down and murdered all the heirlings *and* the harbinger for good measure, and that kicked everything into a new cycle. I'm told it happens every now and then. It's why the Family is being so careful about Lord Sero now that he turns out to be an heirling for this cycle. The King Behind won't mind one or two heirlings around, but once the harbinger shows up as well, things are gunna get messy pretty quick."

I thought of the old mad bloke, who had been wandering around the neighbourhood for years. If he was afraid of being killed for being a harbinger, it was no wonder he was so lost, and mad, and scared. He probably didn't even know enough about what was happening to know exactly why fae were trying to kill him.

"Oi," I said, lowering my voice as we got closer to Morgana's room, "reckon it's possible that Sarah Palmer's part of all that stuff?"

What if Upper Management weren't after Sarah Palmer because they didn't like loose ends, but because they actually needed her? They hadn't killed her or her family, after all, and from what I'd seen of Behindkind, that was the standard response to loose ends. It had definitely been the Family response.

"That's what I'm worried about," Daniel said, drawing in a breath. "I don't like the way this sort of trouble keeps following us. We get away from it, and up it pops in another spot. It feels like it's being forced on us, and I wasn't ever one of the Behindkind that thinks harbingers are catalysts, either."

"Not to worry," I said. "I've got a plan."

"Yeah? Well, so do the Family, Upper Management, and the Troika, not to mention the King, so it better be a good one."

CHAPTER EIGHT

"I've got a good mind not to give this to you," said Detective Tuatu, when I went to hassle him at work.

"What for?" I demanded. My already nebulous plan was very quickly on dangerous footing. "I gave you a body, didn't I? Just 'cos I didn't give you my new address so you can pretend to bring around info and and poke your nose in there while you're at it—"

"I didn't *want* a body! Why would you even think that's an acceptable exchange?"

"You're a cop, you're meant to like bodies."

"We're not meant to like them; we're meant to investigate them!"

"Well, now you can investigate it. Can't believe your lot didn't find it before me."

Goaded, the detective said, "We can't help it if people go back to crime scenes after they've been processed to clear out their desks. We certainly don't encourage—"

He stopped, and I grinned at him. "Glad to know you're not encouraging murder, anyway."

"I'm not so sure, these days," Detective Tuatu said, and his eyes weren't on me. They were on a red USB that balanced between his fingers, and a deep line had etched itself between his brows.

I narrowed my eyes at him. "There's something you're not telling me, isn't there?"

"There's a lot I don't tell you, thank you very much," he said. "You're not even in the force—I shouldn't be telling you anything!"

"Okay, fair enough," I said, grinning. I nodded at the red USB. "I s'pose the stuff you were looking into for Athelas is in that? C'mon, you said you'd give it to me."

"It's not much," he said, giving up and tossing the USB at me. "But maybe it'll mean more to you than it does to me. I don't see what use it's going to be."

"Thanks," I said. "Still having trouble talking about it?"

He glared at me. "Yes."

"What?" I protested. "You can't blame me for that!"

"I blame you for *all* the things I can't talk about!" he told me. "And let me tell you that the little tree you gave me is selective about who it lets in and out!"

I couldn't help grinning. "What, it wouldn't let you out the other night? Or it wouldn't let a date in?"

"Never mind!" he said grumpily. "And next time bring me a cuppa if you're going to invade my space and grin at me like a scrawny Cheshire cat."

I COULD HAVE GONE TO AN INTERNET LOUNGE TO TAKE A LOOK at what I'd been given, but that seemed about as ideal as checking out the USBs at Morgana's computer or at the library: far too much chance of being overseen by someone who definitely shouldn't be seeing the kind of stuff I was kinda afraid would be on the USB.

Yanno. Someone normal.

So I went home. Not to Morgana's place, mind you: back to my actual home.

You say crazy, I say crafty. I mean, I knew they were out; Athelas was trying to track down whatever had come after North, not to mention North herself, and Zero was already out there as well, probably scouting out wherever it was that the Palmers would be going whenever they left the house.

And yeah, the psychos *might* have put up something magic to stop me getting through, but I doubted it. Behindkind constantly underestimate humans because they think we're stupid and confuddled half the time. They don't take into account that ignorance is our biggest problem, and that we're perfectly capable of dealing with fae and other Behindkind if we have the knowledge to do it. Physically, there's a big difference, but when it comes to the mind, Behindkind are definitely not as clever as they think they are. I think most of them are just used to dealing with humans who don't know about Behind and are interacting without the full set of rules.

Me, I'm operating with a full set of rules and an advantage. They'd still wipe the floor with me if they caught me but I had a really good chance of not being caught, especially since I wasn't planning any fancy footwork to get in. I was going to sneak in the human way—by breaking in.

Besides, I needed more cash before I ran into trouble, and if they caught me at it, I could just show them the money I'd come back for. Reasonable. Normal.

So I sneaked in the way I'd always snuck in. The window at the back on the second floor was still cracked open by about a finger's width: I suppose none of the three thought there was enough of a threat from human housebreakers to bother shutting it properly after I wasn't there to use it anymore. Typical.

The familiar smell of the house hit me like a blow to the chest: a mix of coffee, Between, and Jin Yeong's cologne, with the faintest smudge of lavender from Athelas' tea. Familiar, overwhelming, and nostalgic, even though it had barely been two weeks since I lived here.

I cleared my throat, settled my shoulders, and went for one of my money stashes. It was no use allowing myself to be distracted by feelings. This wasn't my house, and they weren't my psychos anymore. They hadn't ever been.

I emptied out the stash in my bean bag and raided half of the one that was seeded between the pages of the *Lord of the Rings* trilogy, then came back out into the upper living room to sit down at the computer. I started it up and then took a couple of minutes to stuff my boots with cash while it warmed up. It wasn't likely that I was going to be mugged on the way home, but I'd prefer to make sure there wasn't anything for anyone to find if it happened.

It was just going on for twelve, and I knew I shouldn't need to be out of the place too quickly, so I took my time. I knew exactly how long the Troika could stay out while they were engaged on a job, and if they were trying to find North, I figured they had a decent bit of work ahead of them.

I tried the glass USB first, of course. The stuff on it was probably even less my business than the red one, but despite that—or maybe because of it—I didn't even have to think about it. I put it in the right way first time around, which was pretty impressive. It slotted right in, but nothing happened.

"Rude," I said. I pulled it back out and put it in again, and this time an icon flickered on the bottom taskbar for a few seconds before a dialogue box popped up, asking for a password.

Well, *that* was flaming typical. What sort of passwords did fae put on their computer files? I would have bet a pretty hefty amount that Zero didn't even know about passwords, let alone how to enter one—or make one, if it came to that. Fae might be clever and stuff, but when it comes to technology, they're mostly granddads. That's probably the only thing that stops humanity from being wiped off the planet—the fact that fae don't seem to be able to work out computers with any more literacy than your average eighty-year-old.

That's why it was so flamin' annoying to be stopped at this hurdle. I knew a bit about North, and I knew a bit about Zero, but I didn't know enough about either to be guessing at a password for either, let alone a password that they had in common. I didn't even know how they knew each other.

What I needed, I thought darkly, was a hacker. Someone who wasn't close enough to Zero to want to shield him, but probably not a human, either. I had distinct concerns about asking humans to do fae stuff for me. There was too good of a chance that they'd be hurt, especially since the 'good guys' wouldn't prevent it.

"This is your fault, too," I said testily to Zero, even though he wasn't in the house and couldn't hear me.

Fine. I'd find a hacker who wasn't afraid of fae lords or their fathers—or of the North Wind, for that matter—and they could do their technological wizardry on the USB. In the meantime, I'd go on to the one Detective Tuatu had given me.

It didn't ask me for a password when I put it in, but when a window opened on the screen, it didn't have in it the kind of things I'd expected. I'd expected to find documents, or files—and *yeah*, they were documents and files, but they were photos of the documents, not the actual documents.

What the heck? If Detective Tuatu had wanted me to see them, why hadn't he just shown me the paper originals, or copied the files? Unlike the fae, the detective knew very well what he was doing when it came to computers and files. It looked like he'd ferreted out a series of documents, taken photos of them, and put the photos onto the USB.

And I mean, maybe he hadn't wanted to send them to me via my phone when I wasn't sure how badly I'd been hacked, but what use was a photo of the current rental agreement on my old house, or the power bills for the last...was it *ten whole years* he'd gone back? Why? I quickly scrolled through the rest of the images, but it was all the same sort of thing.

"Flaming heck," I said crossly. "What's the use of this garbage!"

I'd been hoping for something more interesting. Something... at least something to do with me that wasn't about bills or rent, or maybe something about Zero. Whatever Athelas was up to when he wasn't around Zero, wasn't just for the fun of it. Or at least, that's what I'd always assumed. I'd always assumed that he was off doing things in ways that Zero wouldn't approve of rather than stuff that had nothing at all to do with the others.

I printed it all out, anyway, two sheets to a page, and hoped I'd have a bit more luck with figuring out what it meant later. Maybe Morgana could have a look at it. That was an idea.

It took a good half hour to print all the documents, and another half hour to rearrange the paper stacks so it didn't look like I'd used any paper. Then I put the chair back exactly where it had been, checking carefully for stray hairs, too. You never knew what Zero and Athelas were going to notice. Jin Yeong wasn't too good at getting a scent of me when he wasn't expecting me to be there, so at least I didn't have to worry about being smelled out. I cleaned my fingerprints from the window on my way out, too. No use taking chances.

A CHILLY BREEZE TICKLED MY EARS, SHARP AND COLD WITH THE early promise of autumn, and I eased up the hood of my hoodie. That meant it was harder to hear, but at least my ears weren't hurting. All I had to do was sit still and do nothing. No movement, no giving my position away if anyone was watching.

Preferably no breathing.

I was outside the Palmers' house—in a tree, to be exact. I'd taken my documents home earlier and had a bit of kip and food before I came out again, prepared for a long night. I'd already done a circuit of the house in the shadows, and I couldn't find a way in from the first floor that wasn't likely to have the cops called on me by the family in the other side of the semi-detached house.

I clung to my tree, fingers sinking into the soft paperbark trunk while the same bark tickled my ears. For a few moments it almost felt as though the breeze that swept through and stirred the curls of paperbark also stirred my hair, which was somehow more paperbark than hair just now. I held onto that feeling as much as the tree, my breathing slow and shallow, and traced my route with my eyes once again. Up and across the tree limb, right into the shadow of the limb and through the wall. I could see the way it looked Between, and I knew I could do it.

I waited until the breeze was moving through the trees, creating shadow and movement and noise, and then I walked across the branch and straight through the wall.

Nice! That was easier than I'd expected. Maybe my accidental walking-through-walls back at Morgana's place had been good for practise or something.

I came out in the kitchen—or at least, that's what I guessed it was. The outside light might have been left on downstairs, but there were no lights on up here. There were tiles under my feet, though, so kitchen seemed likely. I fumbled for my phone and turned on the flashlight. Yep. Kitchen it was. It looked a bit grubby and dusty at the corners, but it was a pretty normal kitchen apart from that.

I wandered around the connected living room, peeking behind pictures and knick-knacks, thankful for the thick curtains that would do a good job of hiding my light from the outside. The top floor looked like being kitchen, laundry, and living room, so downstairs must be the bedrooms. I couldn't decide if that was safer or not—Zero would have been the one who could tell me. Maybe Athelas.

I panned my light over the pictures on the wall as I went

down the stairs, too. They hung along the wall in descending lines, and I felt a chill of discomfort and danger. That was another thing my family hadn't kept around the house—photos.

"We don't keep anything we can't pick up or burn in five minutes." That's what dad had said. I didn't remember having to pick up or burn anything, but dad had been a bit funny like that. As I stepped quietly down the stairs, it seemed to me that a few of the pictures were missing: there were empty spaces on the walls that should have been taken by photos or at least paintings, the wallpaper beneath just a little darker than the surrounding areas.

I stopped in my tracks, and headed back upstairs, leaving the bedrooms for later. I'd seen the photo albums upstairs, under the coffee table. I hadn't thought anything of them at the time—they were at least portable, so they could be picked up in five minutes —but now they were the first, tiny not-quite-right thing. I needed any tiny, not-quite-right thing that might turn out to be a not-so-tiny wrong thing.

I propped my phone against a candle holder on the coffee table to illuminate the albums without shining directly at the curtains to test their thickness, and plopped the two fat albums on top of the table.

I went through the first album page by page for a while, but it looked like just normal family stuff. Surprisingly familiar, but that could have just been the fact that it was hard to see the faces properly with the glare of the flashlight against the glossy paper, and my mind wanted to insert familiar faces in the glaring white.

Or, I thought, frowning, was it because I'd seen the exact same family in photos at North's unit?

Soon I was leafing through it a couple pages at a time, and it wasn't until I began flipping through the second album that I came across the missing pieces there. It wasn't just one or two missing like on the walls, either; here, it was a whole year or two missing. They hadn't just not taken photos that year or two, either—there were empty leaves where they hadn't replaced the pictures, along with a slight yellowing of the album. The photos directly after those ones were subtly different, too; the Palmer parents each had a hand on their daughter in every photo, or both hands. As if they were afraid she would run away—or as if they were afraid she would be taken from them.

I put the albums back where they had been and went looking for the missing photos downstairs in the master bedroom, but I already knew exactly where they were.

Those fifty or so empty spaces had once held the photos that I had found in North's unit.

Why had North taken from the Palmers photos that had absolutely nothing to do with her? I could understand it a bit more if she'd actually shot the pictures as a family friend, but this looked more as though she'd literally lifted them from the family photo albums and taken off with them.

When I was sure the photos weren't still in the house, I finally went to Sarah's room. Something shuffled beneath the soles of my feet as I crossed the threshold, a small, almost musical clutter of sound. I crouched down, directing the light from my phone at my feet, and saw a wide, curved swathe of dark sparkles across the doorway.

Hang on. Were those *iron filings*?

I stared at them, then sat back on my heels, a laugh of disbelief soft in the darkness.

Heck. Whatever else the Palmers had gone through, they were very much aware of fae and their basic conventions, at least.

I tidied up the shards I'd accidentally moved and stepped over the dark line to check the window. Sure enough, there were iron filings there, too. More than that, there were iron filings all around the room, a trail of them following every wall to completely surround everything in the room.

Okay, so the Palmers also knew that Behindkind didn't necessarily use doors and windows, too, which probably meant they knew a bit about Between. Which meant they most likely knew about Behind as well, not just that their daughter had vanished and come back from somewhere Other. Enough to know exactly what Sarah had escaped from?

Who the heck were the Palmers? North had said they were human, but—

Hang on. Had she, though?

She'd said that *Sarah* was human. She hadn't specified that the Palmer parents were human. Was it possible that they were something else? But if they were something else, I couldn't see North fighting to keep Sarah with them when she was fighting so hard to keep her away from Upper Management.

I stored that thought away to chew over later and wandered over to Sarah's dressing table. It was a mess of fake flower, hair things, cute plastic toys, and one hidden lipstick tucked away behind an artful flourish of the fake flowers. Underneath the lipstick was a single photo, but there was nothing contraband about it.

It was a photo of Sarah Palmer, grinning as her parents embraced her on some sort of sports field, her knees grubby and her school uniform running shorts dangling a hem. One fist was up in the air, a clear sign of victory. It must have been a favourite day for her, but maybe it wasn't so favourite for her parents, with the picture hidden away like that.

Had something happened on that day that her parents didn't want to remember?

I would have to add that to the list of questions I needed to ask North next time I was able to get in contact with her.

I took a photo of the lipstick and the photo, just in case, and had just started toward the hall that led to the front door when I heard a car pull up outside. Heck! The Palmers were back already? It was barely nine o'clock.

I could have made a run for it back upstairs and taken the same way out that I'd come in, but I had a suspicion that Zero would have followed them all the way home to be sure they were safe. He probably already knew about their precautions against fae, so it was likely he wouldn't hang around for long after he saw them get safely inside. It was much safer for me to stay in the house for another half hour or so until he left.

I made myself comfortable behind a big potted plant in the hallway, putting up my hood and feeling the shiver of Between seep into me and flatten me until I was more of a shadow than a person. It was a weird feeling. I was still there, still myself, but somehow I was in a different space where there was...more space. Maybe I was sitting in a little patch of Between, while just my shadow came out in the human world.

I didn't know, but whatever it was, the Palmers didn't see me when they came in, and they were pretty cautious. All the lights went on first thing, and if I hadn't had my bit of Between to sit in, I would have been easy prey. Mr. Palmer came in first, looking around swiftly, with Sarah close behind him, one hand curled in a fist full of his woolly jumper. After them both came Mrs. Palmer, glancing toward the rear until she could close the door safely on them.

Oh, they were *jumpy*. I mean, I'd probably be jumpy too, if someone was trying to pinch my kid, but they were knowledgeable about how they moved, and that was interesting. Maybe that was because there was a feeling of familiarity to it.

Mr. Palmer went upstairs briefly, and I saw the flood of light down the stairs as he turned on every light upstairs, too. When he came back down he said, "All clear," quietly to his wife and daughter.

I could understand North's urge to protect them. I could feel it myself. They were trying so hard, and they were obviously so tired.

I just couldn't understand why *North* had that urge. It wasn't something I was used to seeing in Behindkind. I had the feeling that if I could just understand that, I might be within a hairsbreadth of understanding how I could break the Palmer's contract with Upper Management. Right now, I had nothing to grasp that could potentially turn into leverage, and that was a dangerous position when I was dealing with Behindkind.

I waited until they went to bed, and then for another half hour after that, watching shadows that shouldn't be there moving in the hallway. I heard noises, too, that weren't the Palmers moving around to settle down for the night.

That made me look a bit more closely at the wall that separated the Palmers' side of the house from the other side as I crept toward the front door. There was definitely a bit of Between there. I would have liked to know if the Palmers knew that, and if so, *how*. The iron filings curved around the exact section of wall that seemed most contaminated. To me, it looked like most of the action must be taking place in the semi-detached place next door, and since the main entrances were reversed for the two dwellings, that would make this section the spare room in the other house. Would there have been enough noise to worry Sarah's parents without them being able to actually see the slow seep of Between down the wall? It was one thing *knowing* about fae and potentially Behindkind as well—it was entirely another thing to be able to *see* them. I'd always been pretty sure that I wasn't the only one who could see stuff like Between and Behind, even though Zero and Athelas disagreed, but I could only see it being trouble if the Palmers could see it, too.

No wonder they were being harassed by Upper Management, if so! The Palmer kid had escaped Behind, after all, and I found myself wondering once again if the interest in Sarah was less to do with North's connection to the kid and more about the kid herself. Still, that didn't help me with how to break her contract with Upper Management, either.

I puffed out a silent breath, discouraged to find myself with as little useful knowledge going out as I had had going in, and very carefully, very quietly, slid through the front door. After crouching for so long behind a potted plant, that wasn't the easiest, but I didn't dare try to massage some feeling into my legs until after I was out and shaking off filaments of Between from my shoulders.

Earlier, there had been a painful warmth somewhere near my pockets where the USBs were digging into my skin. The sudden absence of that warmth made me pat my pockets in a start of remembrance, fearful that I had somehow lost them as I was crouching and exploring inside the house, but they were still there.

I let out a relieved breath, and trotted toward the front gate, careful to scoot around the soft beam of light that now lay on the lawn from the hallway window. It was well beyond time to be going home. I had learned a lot of things that seemed utterly disconnected and useless, and I wanted to sit down quietly and chunter about them to myself for a while. Preferably with coffee. If I was lucky, there would still be a pot of coffee on the percolator, and we could each percolate for a while: the coffee, and me with my thoughts.

With happy designs on that imaginary pot, I stepped out onto the street, smiling at the dark.

And stopped dead in my tracks.

Across the road opposite me was Zero, a deep cleft between his straight brows. Ghostly in the moonlight with his white hair and far-too-pale skin, those pale blue eyes stared straight at me.

Ah heck.

"Pet, what are you doing here?"

Could I get away if I needed to? Where could I run? He'd catch me along the road in no time, and there's no way I'd beat him if I dodged into the tempting patch of mossy Between that existed in the stormwater drain just a short drop away.

I began, "I'm actually not your pet right now, so—"

"Don't play with me."

I bit my tongue before I could tell him that playing was what pets were meant to do, and said instead, "I'm investigating. I've got a job."

"What did you take from the house?"

Ah man. I hadn't taken anything, but there was no way he was going to believe me. *I* wouldn't believe me; I'd even patted my pockets as I left the house to make sure the USBs were still there, and he'd obviously seen that with his stupid super fae sight or whatever. I could have kicked myself for that.

"I didn't take anything," I said, sighing. "What was there to take? There were some photos and a few knick-knacks. Maybe some goblins, but I think they're next door and I wouldn't take one of those with me anyway."

"If I have to go through your pockets, I will," said Zero icily. "I won't have you interfering in my investigation."

"You've got no right to go poking your nose into my business," I protested. "You didn't want me in the house investigating, and now I'm out of the house! I don't answer to you!"

"This is a Behindkind matter."

"It's not, it's a human matter. Someone's trying to steal a little girl away from her parents."

"You're interfering with a changeling contract."

I managed to hide my surprise at the sudden influx of information that the single word *changeling* had prompted by tumbling into speech. "Yeah? Well, I remember you interfering with quite a few changelings yourself, not long ago."

My anger was growing, but it wasn't just because of how unreasonable Zero was: it was because I knew that if Zero really did search my pockets, he'd find both USBs. Why had I brought them out tonight? Why hadn't I taken the time to leave them back at the house before I came out?

"That's completely beside the point," said Zero. "What did you take from the house?"

"I didn't take *anything*!" I said exasperatedly. I didn't even know what there was I *could* have taken from the house that would do any good to either Sarah or my investigation.

Zero took a step down into the road, his jaw setting, and I skipped back an equal step back onto the footpath, fishing the USB Detective Tuatu had given me out of my pocket.

I held it up. "Oh, you mean this?"

Maybe I really had gone mad. But just like the situation with his father, it was the only way I could think to make sure he found the thing that I could most afford to lose. I mean, I was gunna try not to lose this USB either, but he didn't need to know that.

It stopped him in his tracks.

"How come you and your dad both want this?" I asked him. "Has it got something to do with my parents or your mum? Is that why North was hiding it? To give to you?"

I already knew the answer to the last two questions, but he didn't know that. I was beginning to think that Athelas had taught me a lot better than Zero knew. Maybe better than I'd realised, too.

Zero held out one hand commandingly. "Give it to me, Pet," he said.

"I'm not your pet, and you can't have it," I said. I mean, it wasn't like I could stop him, but beggar me if I wasn't going to fight all the way.

And when I say *fight*, I mean run away.

I shifted my weight back just slightly to turn and run, but as I did so, there was movement at my right shoulder, and the familiar scent of cologne.

Ah heck. Jin Yeong. Now I couldn't even try to run away.

Zero must have thought the same thing. He said, "Bring me the USB, Jin Yeong."

"Do your own dirty work!" I shot at him, hunching my shoulder against the warmth beside me that was Jin Yeong. It wasn't possible to watch both of them, but I couldn't help flicking a look up at Jin Yeong anyway, angry and defensive. He shouldn't have followed me to Morgana's house if he was just going to show up when Zero was around and force me to give up stuff to him.

JinYeong's eyes met mine for a brief moment before his head twitched sideways. He grinned lazily at Zero, his eyes all liquid darkness, and said, "*Shilloh*."

"I *beg* your pardon?"

Maybe I'd forgotten exactly how icy Zero could be, or maybe it was just that I'd never seen him this absolutely cold.

"I do not wish," said JinYeong, with great clarity, "to do as I am told."

Zero's sword came out, nothing like the umbrella it usually was in the human world, and it seemed to me that it was bluer than I remembered it being. Bluer—colder?

"Oi," I said, in more of a whisper than anything, "what have you done to the sword? It's gone all blue."

"It was always blue," said Zero. "You're the one who made it yellow. Give me the USB, Pet. I won't ask you again."

I looked away from him and up at JinYeong. "You okay?" I asked shakily.

"I knew today would be fun," he said, his eyes dark and bloody. "Get ready to run. We will meet afterward."

"Yeah," I said. "We'll get some *good* coffee."

His eyes met mine, one brow momentarily rising. He nodded.

Zero crossed the road in a single leap, with a slashing sweep that JinYeong darted beneath and emerged from again with two blades.

I'd only ever seen him with weapons while we practised: I'd never seen him really fight with weapons, just his teeth. And he was *beautiful*. Quicker than Zero, though not more savage, he slashed and swirled and parried, always just a little too fast for the heavier Zero. But I saw the strokes that landed on JinYeong, and I knew with a jolt of sudden fear that Zero was stronger, even in my shock at the deadly beauty of them both.

I scrambled back to get out of the way of a scurry of strokes and parries that brought them too close for comfort and kicked up loose bitumen on my jeans, completely woken from my daze.

"You," said Jin Yeong over his shoulder. "Run away now. You are in my way."

It took his attention away for the briefest moment, and Zero struck mercilessly with the hilt of his sword.

I couldn't help the breath that hissed in through my teeth at the weight behind it. Jin Yeong stumbled back into my arms and I caught him, but we fell heavily despite that. I had barely a moment to slip both of the USBs into his pocket before Zero's huge white hand seized me by the neck and plucked me away from Jin Yeong's prone body.

He went methodically through my pockets, then dropped me back to the ground with a definite jolt, and I caught myself up on a sob of anger, or fear.

"Pet," he said, through his teeth. "Where. Is. The. USB?"

"Swallowed it," I said, looking up the length of that blue blade. "You're gunna have to cut me open to get it."

Man, I have *got* to start thinking more before I open my mouth.

Zero stared at me for a cold moment, the tip of his sword slightly dropping.

Maybe it was the sweat trickling over his brow and into the corner of his eye that made him flinch. Maybe that was all that saved me from being sliced open in the brief moment before Jin Yeong collided with Zero in a snarling, bloody tumble that sent them both rolling down the alley.

I scrambled to my feet and ran for it.

I DIDN'T STOP RUNNING UNTIL EVERY BREATH HURT AND THERE was wetness all down my cheeks and below my nose. Then I stopped between someone's wheelie bins and sniffed and panted and tried not to cry properly. When everything was dry again but more swollen than before, I got back up and kept walking, trying to ignore the tight heat that was gravel rash through a torn patch in my jeans. I had to make sure I was ready to meet Jin Yeong again when he got away. He was still out there fighting like a streak of breathtaking lightning, too quick for Zero to land a significant hit if I wasn't there to get in the way. And Zero—Zero hadn't really been about to gut me, had he?

I moved up my pace a bit, sniffing defiantly. Athelas had told me clearly, but I'd still wanted to believe, even now, that even if Zero had been so lacking in concern for humans in general, that he cared enough to keep at least me safe.

I had been very wrong. Anything, *everything* that I had interpreted as genuine concern for me had been nothing more than his determination to keep me safe so long as he was contractually bound to keep me safe.

Well, so what? I thought, ducking up the street before Palfreyman's Arcade to approach from behind. I didn't need Zero—I was perfectly fine without him. And as soon as Jin Yeong got away, I'd be perfectly fine and have my USBs again, too.

I came across the parking lot less casually than I'd meant to, drawing a few looks from the blokes who were smoking out at the back of the steakhouse, and made myself slow down. I flicked my hood up, too, slouching my shoulders a bit, and they looked away again, cigarettes glowing bright as they sucked in a breath.

I tucked myself just inside the arcade at the back, from where I'd be sure to see Jin Yeong passing on his way to our meeting spot. I was sure he would understand exactly which coffee shop we were to meet at. Now that I was out of sight, the fight wouldn't last too long, would it? Zero was only interested in getting what he needed from me, not fighting with Jin Yeong. I'd never seen him even close to really fighting Jin Yeong before, despite Jin Yeong's very pointed provocations in the past, so I didn't think it would be too much longer.

It felt like a long time, though, and when I checked my phone for the time, it was already ten. I bounced on my toes, cold and hot and nervous. What was taking Jin Yeong so long? Zero wouldn't really kill him. I mean, Jin Yeong wouldn't kill Zero, either—would he? Not really? I'd seen them prowling around each other with death in their eyes and danger in their movements, but I didn't think I'd ever thought they'd really try to kill each other. I'd always thought that one of them would be sane enough when it came right down to it, even if the other went mad.

Too long. It was half past ten now, and too long—Jin Yeong should have gone past by now.

I tried to make myself wait there longer, but every moment stretched out and scratched at me unbearably, like the coil of wild graffiti that wrapped spikily around the ankle closest to the wall. I shook off the graffiti and strode through the arcade toward the street.

I came out of the arcade and headed back up the street the way I'd come, my heart beating just a bit too quickly. I stepped down between two cars to cross the road and saw something across the road, in the shadows of the gutter.

It was dark and crumpled and looked like roadkill: *really* big roadkill. Before knowing my psychos, the most I would have done was stay on the other side of the street to avoid the smell. That thought made me realise there *was* no smell to this roadkill, just the idea that there *ought* to be a smell. At the same time, I saw the faintest flutter of Between to the blood-matted bundle of flesh and cloth, and as I nipped between sporadic traffic and got closer, the wafting scent of Jin Yeong tickled my nostrils.

Oh heck.

CHAPTER NINE

I dropped to my knees beside the body, normal sight clashing with Between-aided sight that told me that even if the damage wasn't as bad as it looked to a passer-by, it was bad enough.

"Jin Yeong," I said. "You better not be dead."

I turned him over onto his back, blood slick beneath my fingers, and his head tumbled to the side, eyes slit open and unseeing. I steadied it with one hand beneath his ear and cheek, and used the other hand to check for a pulse. I don't know how vampires even have a heartbeat, but I do know they've got one—I'd heard Jin Yeong's before.

At first I thought there was nothing, then I felt the flutter of a heartbeat far too faint and far too quick.

"You flaming better not die!" I said fiercely to him.

There was a brief flicker of awareness to his slit eyes, and I heard the whisper of a laugh that sounded like, "*An chugo.*"

"You better not," I told him. "What can I—what do you need?"

Jin Yeong whispered stickily, "*Pi.*"

"Well, you're in luck," I said, swiping my cheek across the

shoulder of my hoodie to get rid of the wetness there. "Got a fresh supply right here. Better drink up."

I leveraged his head up a bit, sick at heart to hear the rattle of his breath when he gasped at the pain, and felt warm blood sink stickily into my jeans as Jin Yeong's weight settled against my legs. Usually his teeth don't hurt too much when they go in, but this time each one hurt like a wasp sting, sharp and burning cold, sinking deeper and deeper. I clenched my fist but didn't pull away, because Jin Yeong's head rested against my stomach in a welter of his own blood, too hot and heavy. He'd taken a heck of a lot more pain to make sure I got away safe. It was the least I could do.

The pain settled after a while, but in its place came a kind of sick dizziness. Just as I registered the feeling, Jin Yeong released my wrist and made a sticky mumble in Korean that I recognised as *enough*.

"You sure?"

"*Mm*," he mumbled; then, still in Korean, "Wait a little."

I don't know if it was too much of an effort to make himself understood through Between, or if he was just so exhausted and hurt that he'd forgotten about using it as a translator. It was a good thing that I'd learned as much Korean as I had simply for the pleasure of understanding him when he didn't want to be understood.

Sometimes spitefulness brings its own rewards, eh?

"You kill Zero?" I asked him, but I already knew the answer. There was no way Jin Yeong was here, looking like this, if Zero had been significantly hurt.

A bloody tooth showed between Jin Yeong's lips. "*Ma—ani tatchioseo*," he said, in low, drawn-out satisfaction.

"Oh, you hurt him lots? You're sounding pretty pleased for a bloke who looks mostly dead," I pointed out, but he already looked a little bit better.

Well, maybe not better—maybe just a little bit less dead. More alive? Still bloody and ragged, Jin Yeong gathered himself together, and let me help him to his feet. I saw the reflection of us in the empty storefront across the footpath, battered and bloody, with clothes in tatters and inky black dripping from our fingers.

"You could've worn something nicer if we were gunna meet for coffee," I said.

Jin Yeong gave a bloody chuckle that didn't sound anything like as bad as it had earlier, but he still weighed heavily across my shoulders.

Beggar me. What was I supposed to do with a nearly-dead vampire?

My eyes fell on the empty shopfront again, all black décor and dark wallpaper, with stairs only just noticeable far back in the darkness. That might work, if I could get Between to be properly useful for me.

"C'mon," I said. "We're going shopping."

"Nonsense," muttered Jin Yeong, with a faint touch of Between to the word.

I would have understood it anyway, but it was nice to know he was remembering it again—that he was capable of using it again.

I shuffled us forward toward the gothic door, looking for the familiar edge of Between that would give me the ability to push right through the door without opening it, and saw a fine filigree of lace around the edges of the door. Only it wasn't exactly lace— and it wasn't exactly *there*, either.

"Pretty!" I said, reaching out to touch it. It had a kind of shiny jet gleam to it, and I could feel it there, but when I tried to push through the door, everything was just a bit too solid and soggy to let us through.

"Um," I said. "Jin Yeong? Can you—?"

"Can't," he murmured. "Too hard...to hide us."

Right. I knew there had to be a reason that the people passing by on their way to the pub weren't staring at us. Jin Yeong was doing something to make us unseen, and it was already taking up all his energy.

"So you're lace," I said aloud. "But that's not useful. I can't push through lace."

"Not lace," Jin Yeong said tiredly, in my ear.

There was a dampness to my skin on the side that he pressed against, which was worrying. It meant the blood had soaked in, and I'd been hoping that he would have started healing by now, not bleeding worse. I probably shouldn't have gotten him on his feet so quickly.

"Not lace," he said again.

"It *looks* like lace," I told him. "Oh! Right! Paper doilies!"

Paper's a lot thinner and easier to get through than lace is. And it wasn't like we were really walking through paper—it was just a way to see the world so that I could get into the Between place where walls weren't boundaries.

This time when I dragged Jin Yeong forward, we stepped Between, and through the door.

"C'mon," I said. "Just a bit further, up the stairs and away from the front window."

We just made it to the top of the stairs before he collapsed, dragging me to the floorboards with him. There didn't seem to be much point in moving him from where he fell, so I took off my bloody hoodie and made a pillow of it, then rearranged him until he was half reclining, half leaning against me.

"Better stay down," I said. "Tell me when you need more blood."

"Don't need more," he muttered.

He was nearly white, though, and when I waved my wrist under his nose half an hour later, he bit into it briefly and carefully. This time, it didn't hurt, though it still made me dizzy for a few moments.

"Gotta start carrying chocolate around with me if we're gunna be fighting Zero these days," I said, swaying a bit where I sat.

There was a fizziness of energy to me, fighting the dizziness, and then I could sit upright again. "Oh, wait—vampire spit. I'm all good."

"Sit still," Jin Yeong said, short in his weariness. "Can still faint. Because you are human."

"Oi." I poked his cheek, and his eyes opened a gleaming slit.

"I will bite you."

"You already did," I said, and poked his cheek again.

This time his eyes didn't open, but a very slight point of tooth showed. "What?"

"Thanks."

I PROBABLY FELL ASLEEP, BECAUSE I DIDN'T HEAR MY PHONE going off, and I didn't remember the slow crawl of the dawn, or even the morning sunshine. By the time I woke up, feeling bright and immediately alert, it was already eight thirty by my phone and Jin Yeong was still sleeping with a slight but steady up and down of his chest.

I thought it was a good sign, but I don't know much about vampires.

He woke up when I tried to shift a bit of feeling back into the leg his head was resting on, and sighed, "*Ah, appa!*"

"Sorry," I said. "Didn't mean to hurt you."

That made him laugh beneath his breath, though I wasn't sure why.

I asked him, "What'd you do that for, anyway?"

Jin Yeong's eyes slit open, dark and reflective. "Do not be mistaken, Pet," he said. "I only wished to annoy *hyeong*."

"Liar," I said.

His brows went up. "Listen, you," he began.

"I know you can be nice sometimes," I explained, without giving him the chance to keep talking. I knew that a good ninety percent of what he'd done when I left the house originally must have been because he wanted to annoy Zero, but last night was the first time he'd really done something utterly unselfish. If he'd just wanted to annoy Zero last night, he already had ways that didn't involve near-death. As far as I could see it, Jin Yeong had acted on a genuinely good impulse. As if we were really friends, or at least equals. Maybe he'd remembered his sister, I don't know. Whatever it had been, it hadn't just been because he wanted to annoy Zero. "So don't pretend you're just a monster who likes to twitch other monsters' tails."

"I helped you because I wished to annoy *hyeong* and because I was once human," Jin Yeong said stuffily. "That is all. We are a little bit alike, you and me. Maybe we are companions these days."

"Yeah?" I said. "'Cos that's not the impression I got. I got the impression that you didn't much care for humans, whether or not you used to be one."

Jin Yeong appeared to ruminate on that for a while before he said, "You are different."

"That's a cop-out," I told him. "I'm not different. You just know me better than you know the rest of the humans these days."

"*Anindae.*"

"Garbage. You just want to keep thinking that way because it's easier to feed on humans if you don't have to think of them as a person like me."

"I am already a monster," he mumbled. "So I will be a *very good* monster."

"Maybe we are alike," I said. "We've both got a bad attitude."

"It is necessary to be a monster," Jin Yeong said, and he was grinning at the ceiling, his eyes reflecting as dark as the paint. "Because I am a monster."

"You been taking lessons from Athelas or something?"

Jin Yeong mumbled again.

"You're still alive, right?" I said, poking his cheek again. "What did you say?"

He said it in Korean and without any edge of Between this time, sulkily. I thought he might have said *You only try to understand the old man.*

"If you'd speak English, I wouldn't have to try to understand you," I retorted. "Oi. If you've started arguing, you must be feeling better. Maybe you should try sitting up."

"I don't feel well. I will stay here."

"Sook," I said, but I patted his head anyway, because even if he wasn't still bleeding, the evidence of his fight still spoke loudly in the condition of his clothes. "When you're feeling a bit better, I'll get you some clothes."

"Ah," he said, as if that had reminded him. "Where did you put them? Those little things?"

"You really wanna know?"

His eyes opened a slit again and glittered dangerously at my grin. "You had them and then you did not. Where are they?"

"Put 'em in your pocket," I told him, and now I was laughing. Companions or friends, whatever he wanted to call it, there was certainly something different between us this morning. "Better hope you moved fast enough not to lose any pockets."

Jin Yeong grinned a dark grin at the ceiling once again and said with a satisfied, rolling 'r', "I was *verrry* fast."

"Flamin' heck!" I said, impressed. "How'd you do that? There's not even an 'r' in that when you say it in Korean. How's stuff like that come through Between?"

"I am talented."

"Oh, right, that *must* be it," I said, but I didn't roll my eyes. I dug into his front pocket, surprising a stifled sound out of him, and found the two USBs. "Oh *beauty*! Here they are!"

"What are they?" he asked.

"Never you mind," I told him. "Just don't go telling Zero there's two, okay?"

"Shall I not?" asked Jin Yeong, looking up at me. "With what will you pay me?"

"I told you. This isn't a Behindkind deal. No paying. No deals. You either do it or you don't."

"Just once again," he said. "No more."

"Okay. Oi, if you're gunna be okay, I'll go out and get you some clothes. You can't walk around Hobart like that."

"I will have coffee, too," Jin Yeong said, sitting up easily.

I raised my brows at him, wondering how long it had been since he'd been able to do that, but left it alone. I nearly asked him for his card, but left that alone, too. At least I'd be able to afford decent clothes for him with the money I'd brought from my stash, even if they weren't exactly as expensive as he was accustomed to.

When I got back with my bag of clothes and a face-washer or two, still looking around fearfully for a sight of Zero, Jin Yeong was up and stretching, all ragged and black with dried blood, but whole.

"C'mon," I said. "Just get across the road here without stopping the traffic, and we'll be in the arcade. There's a toilet block there where you can wash and change."

I had to tug him along when he was inclined to snarl at one of the cars for nearly hitting him, but apart from that, it was a simple matter to get him across the road and into the toilet block. No sign of Zero, which I'd secretly been afraid of, though I was pretty sure I saw a familiarly raggedy figure lurking somewhere further up the road. The old mad bloke was still keeping tabs on me, then.

I'd bought a new hoodie but my jeans were black and didn't show the blood, so while Jin Yeong was still in the toilets cleaning and changing into his new clothes, I had a few minutes to call Morgana.

"Oi," I said. "Is there room for one more weirdo over there?"

"Your Korean friend?"

"Yeah."

"There are still rooms on the second floor," she said. I could hear the grin in her voice. "He can have the one beside yours, if you like. You gotta bring him up to meet me now, though, right?"

"I suppose," I said, sighing. "But if you're gassed out by his cologne, I'm not taking responsibility."

"I'll get the kids to open all the windows," Morgana said. The glee in her voice was much more obvious now. "Did you get what you went out for?"

"Yeah," I said. "Well, sorta. Maybe. See ya when we get back."

"Bring me coffee!" was the last thing I heard as I hung up. By then, JinYeong had finally emerged from the toilets and was sauntering across the road toward me.

He'd obviously tried to wet his hair and set it in his usual way, but he'd had to wash out too much blood and along with it the remains of his hair wax, and it wouldn't sit right. He was still trying to fix it as he stepped up onto the footpath, and I knew he could see me grinning.

JinYeong in a state of disarray, wearing a jumper and jeans instead of his usual sharp-edged suits, was far less annoying than JinYeong perfectly pressed and poised.

"What is *this*?" he demanded, plucking at the yellow jumper.

"It's a jumper."

"It is soft and ridiculous."

"You've got jumpers at home."

"They are *cashmere*."

"You're just cranky because you don't look dangerous, aren't you?"

JinYeong's eyes narrowed, molten caramel instead of black. "You bought me jeans. I do not wear jeans."

"You don't, and you'll probably get arrested," I pointed out. "What? You look cute. C'mon. Let's get coffee."

His eyebrows went up, but he followed me to the shop and stayed outside while I went in, leaning against the wall with his best smug *moue*. Maybe he was getting used to the jumper. Maybe he just wanted to lure in someone for a quick snack to top up his reserves.

The guy who was always there was still there: sitting at a booth with his computer out, his wheelchair snugly tucked underneath the table. I couldn't help looking at him as I came through the door—couldn't help smiling back at him when he smiled at me.

That didn't stop me noticing the little whispers of Between around his laptop, though. Whoever he was, this bloke knew something about Between and Behind. He was probably Behindkind, if it came to that, but I wasn't used to Behindkind smiling at me like that.

I smiled at him again on the way out—couldn't help that, either, or the warmth in my cheeks—then caught Jin Yeong's purse-lipped, impatient look at the window and hurried out. Technically, he was still healing, and the sooner we got back to Morgana's place, the better.

When I got out, Jin Yeong tipped his chin at the café door. "*Nuguya?*"

He must have been annoyed, because he didn't bother with Between translation.

"Who is who?" I asked, but I knew who he was talking about. Jin Yeong must have seen the bit of Between in use as well as I had.

"*Ku namja.*"

"I dunno who he is—a regular or something, I reckon. He's usually in there when I go in."

That must have satisfied him, because Jin Yeong took his coffee and sipped.

"All right," I said, to keep his mind otherwise occupied. He'd more than proved himself, after all. "There's a room for you back at Morgana's house, if you want. She said you could have it."

I actually thought I'd seen Jin Yeong at his smuggest by now.

Turns out I was wrong. This was Jin Yeong at his smuggest—nose up, lashes lowered, mouth plump and pleased.

"Zero wouldn't let you go back, anyway," I said, to remind him that there was no need to be quite so pleased with himself. I couldn't help grinning anyway, though. There was a weird little happy feeling somewhere deep in my chest: I hadn't expected anyone to stand up for me to Zero. Not even Jin Yeong. Especially Jin Yeong.

He shrugged. "I will live in the house of your friend. I will drink coffee every day."

"Knew that was the real reason," I said, still grinning. "C'mon, let's go home. We gotta find somewhere safe to put these USBs until we figure out how to use 'em."

Hyacinth was waiting for us outside when we got back, her little notebook at the ready. She smiled when she saw me, but looked askance at Jin Yeong, who didn't seem to appreciate it. He silently snarled at her and went ahead of me into the house.

"Sorry," I said to her. "He's in a mood because he got beaten up last night. He also doesn't like jeans or yellow, apparently."

The troll girl didn't look particularly soothed. "He's here a lot, isn't he?"

"Yeah. He's like me—got nowhere else to go. He's a friend."

"Really?" She didn't sound convinced, either. "Are you sure it's all right?"

"He's saved my life already this week," I said. "Pretty sure."

"All right," she said. "Just—you'll be careful, won't you?"

"Around a bloodsucking psycho? Yep."

That made her grin. "Any news for my lady?"

"Don't know yet," I said. "Anyway, how are you going to get the answer to her?"

"I have...a way," Hyacinth said.

She looked guilty, and that both annoyed and relieved me. It meant that somehow, somewhere, North was safe. It also meant that I wasn't being told where she was and wasn't to be given any more information for the time being.

"Listen," I said. "If North wants me to be sorting this out for her, she needs to give me a bit more info."

"I'll write it down," the troll girl said.

At first, I thought she was doing the equivalent of saying *I'll be sure to let my manager know, ma'am*, but her pen was at the ready, just like it was when she waited for my answers. The message would get to North one way or another.

"I need to know why she has two years' worth of photos of the Palmers. And I need to know why Sarah Palmer is important to Upper Management."

"Very well," said Hyacinth. "I will take the message."

"Is North okay?"

Hyacinth's apple cheeks grew a little plumper and rosier. "Yes, thank you. But she likes to do dangerous things and this time it looks like it will be a little more difficult. I have to go now. I'll come back again tomorrow."

I went in, slightly relieved and more than a little bit frustrated. I was beginning to feel like I was doing a lot of running around for not much of a result, and Sarah Palmer couldn't afford wasted time.

"*Wae?*" said Jin Yeong, from the couch. While I'd been out talking to Hyacinth, he had settled himself on the couch, barefoot and comfortable. Surprisingly, he hadn't tried to tidy his hair with any of the things in the bathroom that belonged to the lycanthropes—maybe they smelled too much of wolf, or maybe they just weren't expensive enough—and although the lycanthropes gave him a wide berth, they weren't glaring at him anymore. Daniel might already have told them the bad news.

"Nothing," I said, shoving his feet over to sit at the other end of the couch. "I'm just frustrated and I haven't got anyone to annoy until I feel better. You haven't even got a tie I can wreck."

"You can't find a way to help the human?"

"Yeah."

"We will not practise today."

I stared at him. "Of course not. You're still recovering."

"We will talk, instead."

"Oh," I said. He was offering to help me talk it out? "Hang on, I'll go get the coffee."

Jin Yeong must have been feeling pretty knocked about still, because he sipped coffee and let me talk through my annoyance with my lack of knowledge without being more than usually snarky. He didn't eat much of the lunch I put out for him, either.

Heck, maybe he was full from my blood. I was still pretty hopped up on vampire spit, so I felt bright and wide awake, and when he fell asleep leaning against me, I was feeling happy enough to just leave him be. I could count on one hand the amount of times I'd actually seen Jin Yeong sleep, so if he was sleeping now, he probably needed it.

The lycanthropes eventually settled down to watch tv instead of skulking about and keeping an eye on us, and when Daniel came down to sit on the couch, I felt safe enough to leave them all in the room together and went up to see Morgana.

We didn't talk much, just played video games and spilled cake crumbs all over the bedspread, then Morgana tried to show me how to do a smoky-eye makeup look and dissolved into giggles at my complete inability to know which brush I was supposed to use, let alone which colours.

"Rude," I said, making a dangerous dash with eyeliner that made me look like a surprised panda. "Heck. This is *hard*. Never thought I'd say I'm glad I do hand-to-hand training instead of makeup training. Who can even *do* this?"

"Not you, anyway," said Morgana, smudging her own eyeliner with tears of laughter. "Pet, I know you haven't done this before, but I didn't think it was possible to be as bad as you are."

"I'm expressing existential dissonance," I told her. "Soon I'll be a slightly larger clone of you."

"Oh, is *that* what you were trying to do?" she asked, looking at the result with a fascinated eye. "You're gunna have to practise, Pet."

"Heck no," I said, horrified. "What am I gunna do, half an hour of makeup tutoring and then down to sweat it off in a practise session?"

She shrugged. "You won't get better if you don't practise."

"Yeah, but I'm not likely to die if I don't practise my eyeliner skills," I said, and made my escape before she could try to convince me otherwise.

Down in the kitchen, I chopped up a good few kilos of vegetables for pumpkin soup, pondering the pros and cons of finding somewhere that *wasn't* Morgana's house to hide the glass USB until I could figure out how to access whatever was on it.

The house grew dark about me, and that felt familiar and normal until I lifted my head and saw the sunshine that was still outside the kitchen window but somehow not penetrating the house.

"What the heck?" I muttered, but then I saw the cracked little tile across the room.

Ah. The house was darker because this was the time in the afternoon when the shadow from Mount Wellington usually fell across my old house and made everything darker and colder. And *that* house, for whatever reason, was still trying to paste itself over *this* house.

"Heck," I said to myself, looking around worriedly. It seemed as though every line of Morgana's house had an overlapping line from my old house—far more than I'd seen over the last few days. "Maybe I'm gunna have to have a word with Athelas."

I left my pot of soup simmering on the stove and carefully exited the kitchen, worried about accidentally walking through a wall. It wasn't like it would hurt me, but I was concerned that it might do something else, like maybe pull *that* house a bit closer *here*.

There was a slow crawl of Between around the whole place, tickling at the edges of my sight until I felt dizzy, but when I checked on Jin Yeong he was still asleep, and the lycanthropes were playing a violent and noisy game of what was *almost* soccer out in the back yard.

Jin Yeong muttered in his sleep and made a faint noise of pain as he shifted, and I left looking at the house to gaze at him instead. Was that blood on the couch arm, beneath his neck?

"Flamin' heck!" I said, and went back to the kitchen to dampen a clean hand towel.

The first thing I saw when I came back out—or maybe it was the first thing my eyes naturally lighted on, like it would have been if I was actually home—was the huge figure of Zero, sitting where I usually sat, with a book open in front of him on the coffee table and a frown between his brows.

Jin Yeong was right—he had done a lot of damage. I could still see the slash that made a veiny blue line all the way from Zero's cheek to the neck of his t-shirt, and if all of Athelas' healing had only been able to get it to that point, Zero must have been a bit of a mess himself when he got home. There was blood on the floor, too. No one had bothered to clean it up, of course: it remained in the carpet, blue and sticky and far too plenteous.

"This is your fault," I said accusingly.

One of Zero's brows twitched up by the slightest margin, and I wondered for one cold moment if he'd actually heard me.

Nah. He was just reading his book. That was all. There was no way he could hear me when I was here in Morgana's house, and he was there in my house.

"It is," I said, flopping the wet towel at him in lieu of shaking my finger. "All your fault. If you wanted to stick your nose into the stuff I was looking at, you should have *asked*. I mean, I might not have told you, but at least it was better than—"

I stopped, because there was an ache in my throat, and I was pretty sure it was about to come out in my voice. Even if it was to an unhearing Zero, the impulse to hide all human emotion to make sure I was heard was strong.

"Sometimes I really hate you, you know," I said.

Zero's head dropped, and I heard him laugh. It wasn't an amused laugh; it was a tired, fed up sort of a laugh. "This house has too many ghosts," he said, as if to himself. He raised his head, and said into the room, "Stop talking to me."

What the heck? He actually *could* hear me?

"You're not my owner anymore," I said, but I said it quietly, and I was pretty sure he didn't hear it. His gaze was just slightly to the side of me, so I knew he couldn't see me, and that was a relief.

I took a step toward the sofa, toward Zero, and it seemed like I could feel the warmth, the slight disturbance in space and matter that usually came with the presence of someone's physical body.

No. That wasn't possible. If it was, it meant that my house really was trying to come to me. And if my house was trying to come to me, it was also trying to come *here*—to Morgana. That wasn't something that could happen; not if I wanted to keep this insane life away from her as long as possible.

Zero's eyes scanned the room, unhurriedly and meditatively, from one side to the other. I reached out breathlessly, and for a crazy moment I felt the material of Zero's shirt and the hint of warm skin beneath. Then a furious swirl of cologne snatched me away, scolding in rapid, unintelligible Korean, and the house shook itself into its proper appearance again, Zero vanishing with every other line of my old house.

"Oi!" I said indignantly at the stormy whirl of language. "Can you stop flamin' moving for a second? You're gunna bleed on your new jumper."

Jin Yeong stood still at once, which would have made me grin if

I'd been in the mood to grin, and tipped his head to the side to allow me to clean up the blood.

"Pretty sure you're supposed to be sitting still while you recover," I said, when I was done.

JinYeong cautiously felt the weepy wound, and said, "It is nothing."

His eyes dropped back to my face, and one of his brows went up. A slow, amused curl of the lips banished the remnants of irritation in his face. He said. "You. What have you done to your face?"

"What? Oh, that. Morgana was trying to show me how to put on eyeliner and stuff. I forgot I needed to wash it off."

He made a small *tsk*. "It is very bad."

"Yeah, yeah, I already know that."

"I can do it better than that."

"Hey, I don't care what you wear."

"That is not what I meant!"

"You can wear eyeliner if you want," I said, grinning. "You don't have to make excuses to me."

He glared at me. "I am naturally beautiful. I do not need it."

"All right, but you're naturally bleeding as well, so you should probably sit down again."

"No. You keep calling the house to you, and it is not safe."

"It's gone now," I said persuasively, and JinYeong looked around, slightly disgruntled.

"See?" I said. "So sit down, and I'll get us some coffee. And for pete's sake stop bleeding!"

CHAPTER TEN

Hyacinth came back the next morning, much to my relief. After dealing with my three psychos for so long, I'd come to think there was no limit to what Behindkind would do to avoid giving knowledge to humans if they didn't think it had any bearing on the situation. And of course, the likelihood of the knowledge having any bearing on the situation was always in the Behindkind's judgement, not mine.

So when I heard the knock on the door and went out to see that the troll girl had come back, it sparked a warm feeling in my chest. It would probably be too much to say that North trusted me enough to answer questions that were important in my own estimation, but at least Hyacinth was back again. She hadn't run away and not come back.

"Morning," I said.

"I have answers for you," said Hyacinth, beaming.

I let my relieved breath out very carefully so she wouldn't see how much I'd been expecting to have to fight for the information. She looked as though she was happy to be here, so maybe she hadn't been expecting to be able to bring back answers, either.

"Miss North says she doesn't know exactly why Sarah Palmer

is important, but she knows it has something to do with the fact that the girl escaped Behind to return to the human world without assistance. And she strongly suspects it has to do with the succession."

I thought about that for a while, frowning, while an idea tickled at the back of my mind. My psychos had been surprised every time I did something they thought a human shouldn't be able to do, but as far as I could see, I was far from the only one doing stuff like that. And I hadn't made it back from Behind without help, either.

Hyacinth asked hopefully, "Does it—does it mean anything to you?"

"Sorta," I said. "Almost. I need to think about it a bit more. What about the photos?"

"There was already someone there when Sarah got back, Miss North said. You know what they do—the ones who take over lives?"

"She came back and there was a changeling there pretending to be her?" So Zero had been right. No wonder the Palmers had pulled down the photos—they hadn't wanted to see the interloper with their daughter's face in their photos. "It was a couple of years that she was gone, wasn't it?"

"Yes. Miss North says the family gave her the photos because they didn't want them."

"Who would?" I said, shuddering. "Photos of someone else wearing your kid's face? Heck no."

"That's all Miss North told me about," Hyacinth said. "Do you have an answer for me?"

"I see." I wasn't sure I did see entirely, and I still didn't know why North was connected to the Palmers, but I saw enough for now. I was going to have to centre my next steps on Upper Management almost exclusively. It was a pity I couldn't talk to Zero or Athelas—they knew about Behindkind succession, when they chose to be forthcoming about it. "You can tell her I think I'm very close now. Come back again tomorrow."

"What does the little troll girl want?" said Jin Yeong in my ear, as I closed the door.

"She's my liaison with North," I told him, automatically hunching my shoulder against the tickle. "Are you still bleeding?"

"I wish to shower, but there is no soap that does not smell of dog," Jin Yeong said. "You did not purchase my cologne."

"I'm not gunna purchase it, either," I said frankly. "Having that pong in the other house was bad enough. Come up and meet Morgana: I told her you would. I'll get you some soap or shower gel or something later on. Hold still for a second."

Jin Yeong stood still as I circled him, nonplussed, and didn't pull away when I moved the neck of his jumper to check for the gash that had still been bleeding last night. It was gone, and I couldn't see any other blood.

"Okay, you're fine," I said. "You can come up. But no trying to charm her, and no trying to vamp her, either."

"I do not have to try," said Jin Yeong, sticking his nose in the air. "It is the natural reaction to me."

"Yeah? Then how come my natural reaction is to smack you one in the face?"

"There is something wrong with you," he said. "You are broken, I think."

"Don't think so," I said, with a brief, conscious thought of another pair of warm brown eyes and a smile I'd only seen a few times in a coffee shop. "You're just not as irresistible as you think you are."

"I am exactly as irresistible as I think I am," he said flatly, following me up the stairs. "You are certainly broken."

"Yeah? At least I'm not the one who's cracked."

"*Ya!*"

He was still scowling when we got to the room, which made Daniel stand up, his eyes wary.

"What's *he* doing here?"

"He's living here, too," Morgana said. "I said he could."

"No, I mean what's he doing in here?"

"Perhaps I should ask what you are doing?" suggested Jin Yeong, grinning. "You look so *com-fort-a-ble*."

"Morgana wanted to meet him," I said, shooting Daniel a warning look and jabbing Jin Yeong with my elbow.

"He's just as beautiful from close up!" Morgana said enthusiastically. To Jin Yeong, she said, "You're beautiful."

Jin Yeong, his mouth smug and pleased, raised his brows at me. "You are *broken*," he said, so that only I could understand him.

"You keep telling yourself that." To Morgana, I said, "Don't encourage him. He already thinks he's the world's gift to women."

"Let me know if you want a makeover," she said to Jin Yeong. "I've got some eyeliner that would look fantastic on you: I bet the camera would love you, too."

"Everything loves me," said Jin Yeong.

If he was a bird, he would have been preening. I rolled my eyes, and said to Morgana, "You don't have to tell him he's beautiful—trust me, he *knows*."

"Yeah, but sometimes it's nice to hear it, anyway," she said. "Are you out investigating or whatever today?"

"Yeah," I said, sobering. I didn't know exactly what or how I would be investigating, but I knew I had to at least find somewhere safe to store my USBs until I was certain Zero wouldn't commence an all-out attack on Morgana's place. I had an idea that I might, like the Palmers, one day need some leverage as a human. I couldn't use the glass USB as leverage if Zero had already taken it by force.

I mean, I wasn't sure I was going to use it as leverage, but if I was, Zero was the only one it had any hold over. He'd already proved how much he would do to get his hands on it. I glanced across at Jin Yeong and found that he was watching me, one brow up questioningly. I smoothed out the frown I could feel forming between my brows and returned his look with two raised brows of my own. He pursed his lips and looked away.

"All right," said Morgana. She added a little wistfully, "I know you don't have to tell me anything about your job, and maybe you *can't* tell me everything, but do you think you're getting somewhere?"

"Yeah, we're getting somewhere," I said, exchanging a look with Daniel. "But I don't know where it is we're getting. I had some more info this morning, and I keep thinking I *almost* know how it fits together, but it's not sitting right yet."

"Maybe you should try talking it out," said Daniel, with a pretty pointed look.

I grinned at him. "Sorry. I was gunna have a word with you but Jin Yeong was a bit under the weather. We'll have a chat when I get back home later, yeah? I have something I need to take care of first."

"All right," he said. "But if you're gunna make a habit of taking care of the v—Jin Yeong instead of talking to me, my feelings are gunna be hurt."

Jin Yeong would have come out with me that morning, but I managed to persuade him otherwise, and perhaps he was still recuperating, because he didn't try to push it too much. Daniel was inclined to try and come along, too, but I didn't have any clear idea in my mind of what I wanted to do, other than hide the glass USB somewhere that Zero wouldn't think to look for it. Obviously, Morgana's house was out of bounds until I knew he wouldn't hunt me down and make an all-out attack with Athelas for company. But mostly I needed to think about my next step in North's job, and bar sitting down on my own kitchen bench with a cup of coffee, walking was the best thing for thinking.

I'd only gotten to the top of the street when I realised I'd come out without having even a cup of coffee this morning. I sighed, and mentally weighed the necessity of coffee against the ridiculousness of spending my hard-earned money on shop coffee *again* when there was some at home.

Then I thought *beggar it, I'm gunna*, and marched toward the closest chain store instead of going to my favourite shop with the amazing coffee and mysterious, smiling stranger. It was probably better if I didn't visit that shop more than once a week—I didn't know if I could survive being smiled at more than once a week. I was also more than slightly suspicious of the owner of that smile, with his steady coil of Between that seemed to seep into his laptop.

I ordered a latte by way of a change, and when I turned around to carry it to a table, the first thing I saw was Athelas, leaning back in a window booth with his legs elegantly crossed and a steaming pot of tea in front of him.

I slid into the booth across from him and glared at him. "What are you doing here?"

"May I point out, Pet," said Athelas gently, "that I was here first? If either of us should be put out at the other's presence, I really do think I have more right to be so. I came here merely for a cup of their very excellent tea."

"Yeah? Well, I think you knew I was gunna be here. I don't have the USB on me, so if you're trying to pinch it, you're too late. I gave it back to my client."

I mean, I didn't know where North was, but neither did they. They didn't know I didn't know, either. Hopefully Athelas didn't guess I was lying about having the USB on me, either.

Athelas' brows rose. "Dear me! Your client! How very business-like of you, Pet!"

"What do you want?"

"Shall I point out again that I was here first?"

"You can point it out until the cows come home," I told him. "Doesn't mean I'm gunna believe you came here just for the fun of it."

"I believe I mentioned it was the tea I came for. Our pet recently left us without so much as a by-your-leave, and my lord is really not very good at making tea."

"Neither am I."

"Ah, but you are a quick learner, Pet," he said tranquilly. "Very well, if you will have it, I wished to ask you to refrain from causing *quite* as much trouble as you have hitherto caused. You're causing some difficulties at home, which is perfectly understandable, but difficulties abroad are a much harder harm to mitigate."

"What a shame," I said, without trying to disguise the sarcasm in my voice.

Athelas looked at me over his teacup and said, "Bitter mockery does not suit you, Pet."

"I ought to kick you in the shins!" I said indignantly. "You and Zero both!"

"I really urge you not to become too fond of Behindkind," he said. "We are not in the habit of self-sacrifice."

"Is this the part where I tell you not to change the subject, and you tell me you weren't changing it?"

"Even so."

"Then let's skip this part, because I already want to kick you in the shins."

"I wonder if you know what it is you had?"

"Do you? Why would I have taken it if I didn't know what it was?"

"I assume, Pet," he said gently, "that you took it because you were doing what you usually do—sniffing at something with the tenacity of a terrier until you uncover something. I should hate to think it was merely to annoy my lord."

"That was just a bonus," I said.

Athelas raised his brows. "Indeed. I wonder if Jin Yeong felt the same way last night?"

A deep stab of regret and shame pierced me. He was right—I

shouldn't be joking about stuff like that when I wasn't the one who'd paid the price for it.

"All right," I said, clearing my throat. It wasn't like he was really going to help, but I might as well ask, because sometimes he *did*. "What's on it that's so important?"

"You shouldn't have allowed JinYeong to help you," he said, instead of answering the question. "Zero doesn't approve."

I opened my mouth to say that I couldn't care less what Zero approved of, but Athelas wasn't finished.

"If it comes to that, I find I don't approve, either," he said. "Really Pet, has so little of my instruction remained with you since you left?"

"Instruction? Is that what you call it?"

Athelas' eyes dropped back to his tea. "Hm. Perhaps not. However, I really do caution against putting yourself in debt to the vampire."

"There's no bargain," I said.

He blinked once, and looked up again. "I beg your pardon?"

"No bargain," I told him again. "JinYeong's doing it without pay. I'm not in debt to him because he did it freely. So you can't go objecting to it."

"On the contrary," he said, straightening. "I object to it even more in that case, and I'm absolutely certain that my lord will be excessively unhappy about it."

"Oh," I said. "Well, you can feel however you like, but I'm not at home anymore and JinYeong's not coming back either. You two try and hurt him again and you'll have to deal with both of us."

"Then I take it the vampire is still clinging to life?"

There was something in his vanilla voice that made me look sharply across at him. "You came out to make sure he was all right, didn't you?"

"I repudiate the idea utterly."

"He's fine. I gave him some blood a couple of times and he's started asking for his cologne again, so he must be doing okay."

"I thought you said that you didn't owe him anything," said Athelas, very, very gently.

"I don't. I gave him the blood because he needed it, and because I could. I didn't have to do it."

"Do you really think so? I fancy you've merely traded one kind of balance sheet for another, Pet."

"Yeah?" I didn't believe it, but it seemed to be the only way Behindkind were capable of thinking. "Well, at least it's a human balance sheet."

Athelas looked down at his tea once again, this time meditatively. Then taking me completely by surprise, he asked, "If I asked you to come back, would you come back?"

"Can't," I said. "What's the point? What's changed?"

"You have unbalanced our existence."

"I didn't do anything," I protested. "I just left."

"Even the house is trying to bring you back," he said, and now he was looking at me steadily. He was trying to tell me something —trying to tell me something in his usual, tortuous, brain-worm-tricky way.

On the spur of the moment, I said to him, "There's no brain worm. You can just say stuff, you know."

Athelas' teacup clattered a little in the saucer as he set it down. "Ah," he sighed. "So you did meet my lord's father."

"Reckon so. Big bloke, no wrinkles? Puts a little worm in your brain to eat out the truth?"

"Pet, it really is the height of foolishness not to accept our protection if you've attracted the notice of one of the most powerful fae Behind."

"Have a biscuit," I said, sliding one across the table. They were just the free ones from the jar at the counter, and I'd taken two.

Athelas smiled faintly, but he accepted the biscuit. "Are you changing the subject, Pet?"

"Sorta," I said. "Actually, I haven't got much time to talk this morning."

"Ah, your client."

"Sorta," I said again.

"If it were me," said Athelas thoughtfully, "I would be wondering exactly why it is that this little human is so important to Upper Management. Not to mention your flighty friend North."

"I've been trying to figure that out," I told him. "North either doesn't know or isn't telling. There's gotta be something about her that worries them or interests them enough to keep tabs on her instead of killing her."

"Indeed," Athelas said.

I opened my mouth to add, "I mean, it's not like people just wander in and out of Behind, is it? You lot are always telling me that", but the words caught in the back of my throat in a startled intake of breath.

A bright, sparkling thought crystalized in my mind. Who else did I know who had escaped from Behind and come back to the human world, who had also been targeted by changelings?

The old bloke. The old bloke that Zero and Athelas suspected could be the harbinger. The old bloke that Upper Management and the Family both thought was dead.

What if Upper Management thought that Sarah Palmer was the next harbinger? I'd been told that whoever the harbinger favoured as heirling was most likely to become the next ruler of the Behind world. What if Upper Management and the Family had been fighting over the current harbinger until they had (as they thought) killed him? And now Upper Management thought they had the drop on the Family by finding the new harbinger.

I pulled in a very slow and steady breath through my nose, blinking away the brightness of my realisation and hoping that it hadn't been as obvious as I thought it must have been to Athelas.

I had it. I knew how I could leverage Upper Management into releasing Sarah Palmer and her parents from their contract.

It was going to be dangerous—for the Palmers and North as well as me—but it was doable.

Maybe Athelas saw a bit of that reflecting in my eyes, because he said, "We can protect you if you come back, Pet. No matter what you're up to, no matter what you're planning, if you come to Zero and ask for help, you'll get it. Despite all your efforts, didn't we protect you before?"

"Only from getting killed," I said. "And don't get me wrong, I'm thankful you did. I'd rather not die. But I'm not the only one in danger."

Athelas gazed at me over his teacup, and it seemed to me that he watched me in wonder, as if I was some species he couldn't quite fathom. "Do you expect us to help every imperilled human?"

"No," I said, sliding toward the edge of the booth. "Just the ones you find along the way. Just the ones who are in trouble because of Behindkind."

"And what of the danger while you're living alone? What of my lord's father?"

"I'm not alone," I said. "And even if I was, how am I supposed to come back? I told you: nothing's changed."

"You can't expect us to change all at once, Pet," he said. "I would have said you can't expect it at all, but it would seem I have been wrong in that. How can you expect a change when you're not there to bring it about?"

I felt a tug of desire to help, and that made me look at him suspiciously. Right; so tricky Athelas was back, was he? The glimpse of soft Athelas had been far too brief.

"I'm not medicine," I told him. "You can't just take a pet pill and get better. If you're not capable of changing by yourselves, you're not capable at all. Anything else will just be a lie."

I'd already been made gut-wrenchingly aware that the changes I thought I'd seen in Zero—the softening, the kindness, the care—hadn't been real. Despite Athelas' assurances that I would get help if I asked, I knew that any such help would come with a balance at the other end of it. Not to mention that any influence I had on them for the better could only be restricted while they still thought of me as an *it* instead of a person.

Athelas said on a sigh, "Then stay close to Jin Yeong—and do try not to get too attached, Pet! His teeth are sharp on friend and foe alike."

"Zero's teeth are pretty flamin' sharp, if it comes to that," I retorted. I would certainly trust Jin Yeong over Zero.

"What of your scraggly, bearded friend?" Athelas asked, without responding to that.

"Haven't seen him," I said. It wasn't quite true: I hadn't seen him for sure, but I was pretty certain I'd had a glimpse of him last night at least. Definitely not as much as I was used to seeing him, though. "Maybe he lost me when I moved."

"Perhaps," said Athelas, in a mild sort of way that suggested to me that he didn't agree with me. "Perhaps you have merely not seen him."

"Maybe," I said. I stood up and put my leftover biscuit in the well of the latte's plastic lid. "But I usually see him."

"It's unlikely that you would have seen him if he didn't want you to see him," said Athelas, sipping his tea. "Harbingers are notoriously hard to see when they don't wish to be seen."

"Maybe he's decided to hang around Zero instead, then," I suggested. "Wouldn't that be a good thing? You said the favourite of the harbinger is usually the one who winds up on the throne."

"I have the distinct impression that my lord isn't as eager for that outcome as yourself," Athelas said, smiling faintly. "I believe he hopes the harbinger has chosen elsewhere."

"Oh. Well, even if the harbinger chooses him, he doesn't have to be the next king if he doesn't want to be, does he?"

Athelas smiled at his own reflection in the tea. "Certainly, he can refuse—and has so refused—to acquiesce in training for the role, but there are methods and *methods* of persuasion, Pet!"

"Yeah? Well, if you've taught me anything, it's that there are methods and *methods* of getting other people to do what you want them to do, so I s'pose you've got your own thing going on."

"I believe we've discussed your suggestions that I'm working under anything other than my lord's orders," said Athelas gently.

At one time, his tone would have frozen me. Since then, though, I've been killed by him about six times, and I was pretty sure I wasn't the only one who came out of that with scars.

So I said, "Don't worry, I won't tell Zero I think you're up to mischief all the time. Reckon he already knows, anyway."

Then I kissed him on the cheek, feeling the movement of that cheek in a smile beneath my lips, and trotted away with my coffee. He'd come to tell me something, and I was grateful for that. I was also not planning on going back to the house: not unless Zero came to tell me the same thing, that is.

And I knew that wasn't going to happen.

I waited until Zero's huge, leather-and-denim figure strode down the street before I sneaked in through the window on the second story of my old house again. The house sort of folded around me as I slipped in, and this time I knew it wasn't just nostalgia flooding my senses: it was the house itself, welcoming me back as though it was alive.

"Pretty sure this isn't normal," I said to it, since none of the psychos were there to say the same thing.

I would have borrowed from North's repertoire by filling a glass of water and dropping the USB in it, but I was afraid that might be too much water exposure, so I dug it into a bowl of marbles in my room instead, and put the red USB in the tiny chest of drawers that sat on the same shelf.

That done, I pinched Jin Yeong's bottle of cologne with the

feeling that I was going to regret it, and left by the window again, feeling the tug of the house at my heart and limbs as it tried to get me to stay.

"Definitely isn't normal!" I panted. I worked my second leg free, nearly falling, and said into the empty living room, "Don't worry, I'll come back. I'm gunna get you back off Zero as soon as I can."

It seemed to surrender reluctantly, and I was able to climb to the ground safely. From there, I headed toward Detective Tuatu's place, still vaguely unsettled and wondering what the outcome of the house's evident fondness for me would be. Appearing faintly to me while I was in another house was one thing—trying to keep me there indefinitely when I visited was another.

I was still worrying about that when I reached Detective Tuatu's house. There was a kind of soft greenery to the feeling of the front door, but it opened for me without complaint, and I felt a draught of fresh air sweep down the hall toward me. I smiled without meaning to, the scent of forest and bright skies clear and refreshing around me. I didn't stop to think what it meant until I was in the kitchen and saw North sitting on Detective Tuatu's kitchen table with her tiny, bare feet perched on the back of one of his seats.

"Flaming heck!" I said explosively.

Detective Tuatu jumped compulsively and dropped the toast he'd just taken out of the toaster. "Pet! How did you get in here!"

"The dryad let me in! How come you pinched my client and didn't tell me?"

"He didn't steal me," said North, sending a tiny breeze swirling through the kitchen to scoop up the toast and bring it to her. She must have been another five-second-rule person, because she dusted it off and bit into it. Through her mouthful, she added, "I stole him."

"Thank you!" said Detective Tuatu. "Pet, I have been kidnapped and terrorised."

"You should be grateful to me," North said to him, sunnily. "Someone has been laying a nice little trail of crime and deception all the way to your front door. They've been doing the same to me, so when the Family made a grab to stop me handing over something to Lord Sero, I decided to come to you. I'm surprised you weren't already in jail."

"Someone tried that," he said grimly. It sounded like they'd been discussing it for a while. "They threw a dead body into a house while I was in it."

"Gotta talk to you about that later, too," I remarked.

"Humans don't cope very well when Behindkind try to frame them," said North, as if excusing herself. "And he has a nice face, so I thought we could work together, but he's done nothing except complain."

"Excuse me for not appreciating being kidnapped," said Detective Tuatu beneath his breath. "Do you have enough toast now?"

She smiled at him. "Yes. Thank you."

"Oh," I said, watching as Detective Tuatu managed to go very faintly red through the warm brown of his usual complexion. "Well, I've got the feeling things are going to get worse for a while, so..."

He closed his eyes. "What did you do?"

North, her eyes bright and fierce, said, "You found a way!"

"Yep. But if I do it, there's gunna be a heck of a lot more danger for Sarah and her parents for a while. You still got Zero and Athelas on board?"

"Yes. Tell me your plan."

"Tell *us* your plan," the detective corrected her. "If I've been kidnapped and terrorised, I'm going to make sure it was for a good reason."

"You're such a nice little thing," said North, beaming at him. "I'll keep you."

"I'm a human," said Detective Tuatu slowly. "You. Can't. Keep. Me."

"I know," she said, laughing in delight. "But you're so adorable when you get annoyed about things that I can't help it."

I cleared my throat. "If you blokes are finished flirting with each other, I need to clarify some things."

"We're not—we're not flirting!" said Detective Tuatu, flushing.

"I was," North said, without embarrassment. "Go on, Pet. What did you need to ask?"

"The changeling that was there when Sarah got back from Between—it was you, right?"

Her smile vanished utterly.

"Sorry," I said. "But I need to know for sure."

"Before I was the North Wind," she said, slowly, reluctantly, "Upper Management had me do a spell as a changeling with the Palmers. It was supposed to stick, but Sarah came back after a year, and they knew straight away that she was theirs. They wouldn't have anything to do with me until Upper Management trapped them into a contract to ensure Sarah's safety."

"You were the one who won the ribbon," I said. It was the only way the photos and the ribbon made sense. The only way the Palmers knowing what they seemed to know made sense. "And you kept it to remember your time as a human."

"I didn't keep it to be reminded of my time as a human," North said, her voice husky. "I kept it to remember what it was like to be loved. I never had that before. I won't let them take it away from her as well. Do you really have an answer for me?"

"Yes," I said. "But it's mostly leverage so it's going to be dangerous for a while."

"If there's danger, I'll see to it."

"Did you know Sarah was special?"

"I wasn't told. I assumed that if she wasn't an heirling it was her parents who were special."

"Nope," I said. "Upper Management think she's the harbinger."

North laughed incredulously. "That's nonsense! At the most, she's an heirling."

"That's what the Troika say, too," I said. "They've already got a good idea who the harbinger is. But Upper Management thinks otherwise, and they've been trying to make sure they've got a good hold on her."

"You're saying we should threaten to take that knowledge to the Family," North said, her pointed jaw setting firmly. "That's—"

"Yeah, dangerous. But we only need them to break the contract. They'll do it and regroup. It gives us a bit more time. And I'm willing to bet they already think I'm in with the Family. Pretty sure one of them saw me with Zero's dad, so..."

North's eyes grew bright and fierce again. "Can you get out again without dying? I can protect Sarah and her family, but I can't make sure you get out of there safely again once you're in."

"I'll take the Jin Yeong with me," I said. Well, so long as he was recovered well enough. "We'll be fine. How much time do you need to get the Palmers safe before I can go in?"

"Give us until tomorrow morning," she said. "They'll need...a little convincing. Sarah understands but her parents are still wary of anything coming from Behind."

"Call it ten?"

"Ten," she confirmed. "When you go in, find Richard—he's the one who technically holds the contract."

"What's Richard look like?"

"You won't need to see him: you'll smell him. He's a harpy. He's the one who brokered the contract." She hesitated, then added, "Your part will be more dangerous in that moment. The vampire might not be enough, although he'll be able to scent the harpy for you. You should think about asking for more help."

"I'll think about it," I said, but I don't think I convinced her. I wasn't convinced either.

She nodded, and sank into her own thoughts, eyes far away and her hair wafting around her in the breeze that scurried around the kitchen. It was a good time for me to leave: I had my own preparations to make, and some cologne to deliver that might help with those preparations.

"Oi," I said, on my way out. "Found that USB you left for Zero. I can—I can give it back to you if you want."

"No," she said, after a moment's pause. "I left it for Lord Sero, and you are...connected with him. I fulfilled my part of our bargain by leaving it for him. I will trust you to convey it to him when it seems good to you."

I don't speak fluent Behindkind, but I know permission when I hear it. North was giving me permission to keep the USB for as long as was necessary—and to take advantage of whatever leverage it might give me when I inevitably had need to give it up.

The detective walked me out, almost as if he was looking for an opportunity to get out of the house while North was caught up in her thoughts and plans.

He didn't try, though; he just asked, "Why did you bring up the changeling stuff? She looked like she really didn't want to talk about it."

I'd brought it up because it was important. Because if North told me what I already knew must be true, I knew she could be trusted utterly to look after Sarah and her parents. It meant she had had everything a human could have, had loved it, and had given it up.

"I needed to know for sure what kind of person she is," I said. "Because I knew that if it was true, it would mean she's an actually good person. Someone told me a bit of what it's like to grow up as Behindkind, especially fae, and I needed to know that North is one of the good ones. She is, but goodness knows *how*."

"You're telling me to trust her?"

I grinned at him. He'd been pretty comfortable with her when I walked in, and as far as connections go, both of them were likely being framed by the same people. "As if you didn't already know that!"

He went that very dark shade of red again, and opened his mouth to protest, but I didn't give him the chance.

"Oi," I said. "What's with the stuff on that USB you gave me?"

"Can't say," he said. "And believe me, Pet, it gives me absolutely no joy to say that to you despite the fact that your lot never tells me anything."

"Okay, but I don't understand why Athelas had you looking into these things. These are things he could have found himself."

"Yes," Detective Tuatu said. "He could have. *Anyone* could have."

"Then why bother to put them on a USB? If anyone's looking for 'em they're easily accessible—they just need a bit of digging to find, and someone who knows the right places."

"Yes," he said again.

"Right," I said grumpily. "You can't say any more."

"I've already said enough," he said, and he sounded a bit testy himself.

"Looks like everyone's taking lessons off Athelas now," I said. I felt pretty sour. "Did he say he wanted anything else from you?"

"No."

"Did he say anything about the debt being cleared?"

Detective Tuatu froze. "Do you mean he's going to come back and ask me for *more?*" His voice sounded appalled, and I didn't blame him.

"You need to be a heck of a lot clearer about what you agree to and what you get back, next time," I advised him. "Make sure he knows the debt is cleared, and get him to *say* that. There's some stuff the dryad can't help you with. And if someone's still trying to frame you for stuff, you probably don't want to be messing around with things for Athelas."

"I don't want to be messing around with stuff for him at all!" Tuatu said feelingly, as I stepped out the door.

CHAPTER ELEVEN

"Pet, you *said* you were going to tell us what your plan is once we were up here," protested Daniel. "I've already lent you my phone, so you ought to have started talking by now!"

"All right, all right!" I protested. "I just wanted my coffee. Shove over, Jin Yeong; how are you taking up so much space when you're so flamin' skinny?"

"It's the size of his personality," said Morgana, and Jin Yeong gave the smallest of approving nods.

"This girl understands me," he said to me in Korean.

"You're encouraging him again," I complained.

Daniel, impatiently, asked, "So what is the plan?"

"I'm going to break into Upper Management's new place."

Jin Yeong said, "*Koll! Jaemitkaetda!*"

"Sure you're okay?" I looked him up and down, and he grinned at me.

"I am beautiful," he said. "And healthy."

"What'd he say?" asked Morgana, her eyes wide.

"He says he's in and it sounds like fun," I told her. "Also that he's beautiful and healthy."

Daniel protested, "Pet, we can't just break into their new place! That's how people end up dead!"

"We're not doing it, *I'm* doing it. You're gunna be helping to watch out for the Palmers: you and the boys downstairs. Detective Tuatu will help with that bit, and so will North. Tomorrow morning at ten."

"If you're going there, I'm going too."

"I will go with her," Jin Yeong said, with great clarity. "You look after your dogs."

I punched him in the arm and he said a quiet *ow* in Korean but didn't seem abashed. Morgana's eyes narrowed a bit.

"I'm not breaking in to take something out," I explained. "I'm breaking in to tell 'em something."

"Yeah, because that's *much* safer," muttered Daniel.

"I reckon it'll be safe enough while we're in there," I said. "It'll be when we get out that it gets dicey. They'll try to kill me before I can get to Zero's dad, that's all. We'll have to go to ground pretty quickly then."

"Pet—!"

"What? Don't tell me you're gunna complain about Zero's dad, now? Strike, ya just can't please some people! You don't like me messing with Upper Management, and you don't like me messing with the Family!"

"That's because they'll *all* kill us!" Daniel said indignantly.

"Is he exaggerating, or is it really that dangerous?" asked Morgana. The frown was more obvious now, and I wished we'd discussed this business anywhere else other than in front of her. We'd gotten too comfortable discussing stuff around her that we shouldn't have been talking about, even if we were careful not to get into the really Behind things.

"It's pretty dangerous," I said. "But there's enough of us to make a difference. Don't worry about it."

"How long have we got to prepare?" asked Daniel.

"Tonight. Everything goes down at ten tomorrow morning. I

reckon North's already with the Palmers, trying to persuade them that they're gunna need the help, and I'm certain she's conscripted help from Zero and Athelas, too."

"It was promised," Jin Yeong agreed unexpectedly, warming me with the realisation that this time, he was reporting things *to* me instead of *about* me. "There was an exchange."

I asked him, "Is that what the USB was exchanged for?"

"Yes."

I couldn't help grinning. By fudging the line of my connection with Zero, North had outmanoeuvred Zero, and given me the chance to look at whatever was on the USB before he could. Or perhaps she had just wanted to give me my own leverage for a change.

North might value the human way of doing things, but she was obviously fully prepared to get things done in the fae way if it suited her. Maybe one day I'd be like that. Maybe I was already becoming like that.

I wasn't sure whether to be chilled about that or pleased by it.

"You can make real plans around dinner tonight," I said. "Fill the boys in, see if they're willing to help out."

"They'll help," said Daniel. "I'll call the others if it looks like we'll need 'em."

"I thought you said you weren't the mafia," Morgana said suspiciously.

"I'm not the mafia!" Daniel said indignantly. "I just have a…I just have a lot of friends. And they're willing to help when I tell them—ask them!—to help."

"It still sounds like the mafia to me," Morgana said, but she was grinning.

"Quick," I said to Jin Yeong. "Let's get out before she thinks we're part of it, too."

I dragged him out with me while Daniel was still protesting that we weren't a *part* of it, we were the *whole* of it. I would have started back down the stairs to put something on for dinner later, but Jin Yeong shut the door behind him and pulled me back by the hood of my hoodie.

"You," he said. "I think you have something for me."

Rats. I'd been meaning to put the cologne in his room when he wasn't looking, but now he was making it look like I'd gotten him a present. He must have smelled it in my pocket.

"Pinched it from your room," I said. "I was already at the house, so I figured I might as well. Oi. It's rude to be all *you* this and *you* that."

Jin Yeong said with a touch of indignation, "You are not Pet. So what then should I call you?"

I shut my mouth, taken aback. Truth to tell, I'd been *Pet* for long enough—and completely without a name for longer than that again—that I hadn't thought anything about Morgana and Daniel calling me Pet. Or what I would answer anyone who asked me my real name. I was still instinctively unwilling to give up my real name to Jin Yeong, so I just pulled the cologne out of my pocket and tossed it to him.

"Here," I said. "Stink the place up. You can fight it out with the lycanthropes."

DANIEL CAME BACK DOWN AGAIN A BIT LATER, AND THE lycanthropes gathered around him as he came, making me wonder again exactly how much of the communication amongst them was verbal.

"All right, Pet," he said. "What really happened, and what's going down tomorrow?"

I gave them the quick run-down that I'd already given to Jin Yeong, minus the details of what Jin Yeong and I would actually be up to. I had a feeling that if I told Daniel how shaky that particular part of my plan actually was, he would insist on coming with us. The Palmers were going to need all the help they could get, and he would be far more useful there. As for me and

Jin Yeong, so long as we got in safely, getting out safely was more likely. We just had to find Richard the harpy, threaten him a bit, and get out while he still didn't know what had hit him.

"You lot keep Sarah safe; that's all we need you to do," I said. "Me and Jin Yeong are the match, but the gunpowder's all with the Palmers. Once we light her up, it's gunna blow pretty fast. We'll need to keep the Palmers safe for as long as it takes North and Zero to sort out something for them."

"What are we supposed to tell the little sister?" asked Cameron, tipping his head up toward Morgana's room. "It could take us days. She'll notice."

"You're not supposed to be telling her anything," Daniel said, and there was a threat to his voice. "You're not supposed to be bothering her at all."

"She talks to us through the mirrors when we're playing outside!" protested Cameron. "We can't just ignore her!"

"Don't get too comfortable with it," Daniel told him, after a pause. "We're not supposed to be interacting with humans—"

"We interact with humans all the time," interjected one of the others.

"Yeah, and *you* interact with her all the time, so—"

"*Will* you lot shut up!" snapped Daniel. "We're meant to be making plans for tomorrow!"

I left them to their argument and eventual planning and went upstairs, moving through the confusing lines of this house and that with one hand against the wall to make sure I didn't fall down the stairs in the confusion of it all. When I opened the door, I found that the room looked about a fourth of the size as it usually did, and that was confusing, too, until I caught on to the fact that I was seeing my old room superimposed on the actual room here.

"Weird," I muttered. Downstairs, everything seemed to match up with where it would have matched were the houses to occupy the same space. Upstairs in Morgana's house, that should have meant I was walking into my parents' room and part of the upstairs living room, but it was definitely my old room instead.

That was probably why when I saw the huge shadow over in the corner, I thought it was just the tallboy that was always there. Then it moved, and I tumbled back out through the door in my hurry to get away. I collided with something soft and woolly in the doorway that muttered in Korean as it caught me, and panted, "Heck! How'd he get into my room?"

"Who is in your room?"

"Dunno," I said, but for a horrible moment, I'd thought I was having my nightmare again. That didn't make sense, because I hadn't had it since JinYeong came to stay in Morgana's house. I added, "Thought it was the nightmare again."

"I will see," said JinYeong, pushing past me.

"It's fine," I told him, pulling vainly at the sleeve of his jumper and stretching the knit. I'd just recognised the familiar, broad shoulder line by now: it was Zero, leaning his hips against what looked like my windowsill but was the wall parallel with my bed here at Morgana's house.

"Ah," muttered JinYeong, catching sight of him at the same time as me. "Why is *hyeong* here again?"

"Beggared if I know," I said, beneath my breath. It was already off-putting to find him in my bedroom here—that he was in my bedroom back at home was even worse. Did he know I'd hidden the USBs in there? "What's he doing in my room, that's what I want to know!"

JinYeong silently put one long finger over his lips, and I shut my mouth.

As we watched, Zero pushed away from the wall and paced slowly around the room, his eyes roaming over the whole place as he walked. Beggar me. He knew *something*. Suspected something. At the very least, it looked as though he knew I'd not only been in the house, but in my old room.

He kept strolling until he got to the shelves, and my heart

dropped. How did he know where I'd been? Because he definitely knew.

Zero scanned the shelves until his eyes lighted on the tiny chest of drawers. I would have sworn I saw the faintest lift of his usually serious lips, and he reached for the miniscule drawers. He didn't bother with the unmanageably small drawer knobs, just tipped the whole thing forward until the heaviest drawer slid out by itself, disclosing the red USB.

My heart sank a little bit more as he removed the drawer and shook the USB into his palm. It wasn't like it would be the end of the world for him to take that one, but I'd wanted to keep it. At least it might stop him from finding the other one, and I still had all the hard copies of the images on it. It might be disruptive if he discovered that Athelas was the one who'd been interested in this stuff, though, since he was more likely than me to be able to guess why Athelas *would* be interested in it.

I watched helplessly as he held it to the light, turning it between his fingers as he gazed frowningly at it. Like he was trying to make up his mind about something.

Jin Yeong's fingers closed around my arm with deceptive gentleness, and I looked up to meet brown eyes that were dark with warning. I gave the smallest of nods back: I wouldn't have tried to do anything after the last time, when Zero had given every sign of coming through with the house. I didn't want him to know we were here—for my sake and the sake of the still-hidden glass USB as much as for Jin Yeong's sake.

A phone rang, distantly, and Zero said, "Yes?" while I was still frantically feeling for my own phone to stop the noise. "North. We have some things to discuss."

That was a relief. For a second, I'd thought it was my phone, and that everything was about to smash again like it had when Jin Yeong grabbed me as I touched Zero's shoulder that time.

I let out a breath nice and slowly, and I had the impression that Jin Yeong was doing the same next to me.

Zero, still gazing at the USB, said, "There is some question of our exchange."

A pause, where I was very sure North was telling him exactly what she'd told me, but probably with a lot more mendacity.

Zero's eyes grew lighter blue, amusement breaking through against his will. He said, "Very well. We will be there," and hung up.

He looked at the USB for a few seconds longer, and then, to my utter surprise, put it back in the drawer, and the drawer back in the tiny chest of drawers. I looked across at JinYeong in surprise, and he stared back, his mouth dropping open the slightest bit.

While we were both still caught up in the surprise of it, Zero left the room.

I said, "Heck. What was that?"

JinYeong closed his mouth, eyes narrowing, and gazed at the section of wall that had swallowed Zero. "I wonder," he muttered. "Is he being very stupid, or very clever? Ah, I *wonder*."

"Don't care!" I said, with feeling. I pulled away from his grip on my arm and crossed the room toward the familiar set of shelves, reaching for the bowl of marbles before it could occur to me that it might not be possible for me to do what I was doing.

That was probably a good thing, because it meant I grabbed the USB before I knew it wasn't possible to grab it. JinYeong said something startled in Korean behind me and nudged up to look over my shoulder as I took back the red USB, too.

I grinned at him, which made him roll his eyes as if I was showing off, and maybe I was. It was just so *nice* to do stuff they said I wasn't supposed to be able to do. You know. Because I'm just a feeble little human.

The grin faded pretty quickly, though. I mean, fine; I'd gotten the USBs back safely, and that was good, but where was I supposed to hide them *now*?

"This is the day that just keeps giving," I said sourly to

Jin Yeong, and shoved the USBs back in my pocket. Looked like I was going to have to go out again.

"You went out again last night," said Jin Yeong broodingly the next morning at breakfast.

"Yep," I said. I'd gone to visit an old friend. Well. Not exactly a friend. More of a tree. A friendly tree? But he wasn't a tree exactly. He was a green man made of moss on the side of one of the buildings that lined the stairwell side of the carpark in Argyle street. It had once given me some advice on how to look after a dryad, and I figured it might be able to hold onto something as small as a USB in one of its crumbly bricks.

It had agreed to do so after a gentle susurration of slowly growing vines that tickled my hair and planted something small and viney there. I had trotted off home with my extra green hair, comforted in the knowledge that it would brush out on its own in a couple of days, and it seemed to me that someone was following me.

Luckily for me, it hadn't been the sandman or any of Upper Management's people: it was the old mad bloke, wearing a new t-shirt and a battered hat. Well, not new—different. I didn't think he had access to much stuff that was actually new.

I'd stopped in at a coffee shop afterward to buy a coffee and a couple of muffins to leave for him: he was looking a bit skinnier than usual.

I didn't tell that to Jin Yeong, of course. To Jin Yeong, I just said, "You ready to go?"

"*Caja*," he said, straightening his tie.

I'd noticed he was in a suit again, but it hadn't occurred to me until now to wonder where he'd gotten it from. "Oi, where'd you get that lot from? Have you been pinching clothes from the shops around here?"

"I needed a suit," he said coldly. "All I had were *jeans* and a wool jumper."

"Well, you could have worn that," I pointed out. "If you hate it that much, you could just get it all mucky while we're out and about instead of messing up that pretty little suit."

"I will not be taken seriously if I go to war in those clothes."

"Well, it's not like I take you seriously in that getup," I said, flicking his tie. "Why d'you wear a tie, anyway? Someone could strangle you with that."

"No," said Jin Yeong, very precisely straightening the tie. "They could not. They do not have the ability."

One of the lycanthropes said something rude about that from the living room where they were all milling about, restless with the urge to brawl, but Jin Yeong only grinned and stayed where he was. As if he knew that restless feeling before a fight and was refusing to be drawn into a confrontation. It was possible that he was refusing to be drawn into a fight because he wanted them to live a bit longer in their extreme twitchiness, but I preferred to think it was because he had just a smidgen of fellow feeling.

The lycanthropes left before we did, when Daniel came downstairs from having breakfast with Morgana, even the oldest of them playing leapfrog and whooping and galloping down the path like they were the local rugby team going out to murder the opposition on the perfect day for a game.

Jin Yeong and I waited until ten on the dot before we left the house.

"Hope you can sniff out a harpy," I said to him. "Otherwise we're in for some trouble." I already knew he could, but I was sick with nerves, and I was about as inclined as the lycanthropes to be incendiary and snarky when I was just waiting for the other shoe to drop.

"I can sniff out anything," Jin Yeong said, with a certainty that should have been comforting but annoyed me anyway.

"Except me," I said. And yeah, I know I shouldn't have, but

sometimes I just can't stop my mouth saying stuff. "You didn't know I was in the house for at least a week at the start."

"That is different."

"That's what you always say," I argued. "Whenever I ask you about stuff, it's always *that's different*. What's different?"

"You," he said. "You are different."

"We already talked about this."

"Yes," said Jin Yeong. "But you are *wrong*. It is irritating."

"So's your face," I said, before I could stop myself. "But you don't hear me complaining about it."

Jin Yeong stopped in a quick swirl and turn of the heel that put him directly in front of me. He ducked his head until his narrowed eyes were level with mine, and said, "You complain about it *all the time*."

"Yeah, okay, that's fair," I said. "Oi. If we don't die today, let's get some good coffee afterward. I need coffee."

"You already had coffee," Jin Yeong said, but he made a neat turn that put him back by my side, and kept walking. "Very well. But if you can't sleep tonight, I won't sit with you to frighten away the nightmares."

I KNOW I'VE SAID IT BEFORE, BUT I'M PRETTY SURE THE MOST useful thing about Behindkind is that they're so *flamin'* sure they're superior, that they don't check for things that any self-respecting human criminal would check for as a matter of habit.

For instance, when Jin Yeong and I strolled into the office where the Behindkind Richard sat behind a desk, pretending to be a middle-aged businessman, he didn't even think to check if I was recording on the phone I had sticking out of the front pocket of my jeans.

What a galah.

We hadn't stopped walking since we entered the shoe store, me and Jin Yeong. Straight down the stairs, following the scent of harpy that Jin Yeong had in his nose, without having to do more than show our little card from the clothes shop to the human at the entrance at the bottom of the stairs. There were more humans in the halls when the walk-up mirrors lining the end of the store's basement let us walk right through them and into what looked like an Alice-in-Wonderland version of a hospital.

Upper Management might not think much of humans, but as an organisation, it seemed to have a definite *penchant* for using them as staff.

Kinda dumb, because they didn't look at us twice, either. No one looked sideways at us until Jin Yeong turned precisely at an office door, opened it, and ushered me in ahead of him.

"Richard," I said, beaming, to the big, untidy bloke behind the desk. Today was just getting better and better—he was the same Behindkind I'd seen in the hall the day the Family grabbed me out of North's apartment. "G'day. We're here to talk about an acquisitions deal."

"You're a human," he said, starting from his chair. A strong scent of dirty feathers and bird droppings wafted over. His eyes flickered to Jin Yeong warily, then back at me, wide with recognition. "You're *that* human! The one the Family had."

"That's me!" I said cheerfully. "Glad you remember me. This is gunna make things a *lot* easier."

Again. Behindkind really need to rethink their attitude toward humans. The poor wally didn't even try to call for his security straight away. Just a human and a vampire—nothing to worry about.

Instead, he let his human appearance drop and said with more of a screeching edge to his voice, "It was a very big mistake to come here, human. Do you want to die?"

"Yeah, you probably think it's a mistake," I said. "But there are about three different questions you should have asked before that one."

The harpy laughed, shaking his feathers, and another gust of bird-poop-and-old-feather scent hit us. "I suppose you think your vampire master will save you."

Jin Yeong, with a dangerous smile, his eyes dark and glittering, shut the door behind him and leaned against it.

"Is that supposed to frighten me?"

"You're really not good at the questions," I said. "I mean, if it were me, I would have asked who I was. Then maybe what I wanted. And I would *definitely* have asked why a pet you'd seen last with the Family was barging into your office."

He tried to laugh again, but it sounded a bit breathless this time. "I don't have to ask any of that," he said. "You're just a human. You'll be dead before you get out of here."

"You reckon? Okay. Ask me what I'm here for, then. Just for fun."

"*Ya*," said Jin Yeong from behind me, in a lazy voice. "Stop having fun."

He didn't layer it with Between, so I was left to explain to the increasingly puzzled Richard, "He thinks I'm enjoying myself too much. Right. Down to business, then."

"I don't do business with humans."

"Well, that's a lie. I saw at least ten humans out there."

"They're staff. Some humans are bright enough to appreciate the use in allying themselves with Behindkind. Business and staff are different."

"Yeah, and you've got a contract with a human family."

"I don't know what you're talking about."

"If you're going to be making contracts with humans to make sure you've got your mitts on the next harbinger," I said, grinning at him without humour, "you really gotta make sure you don't let other people know about it. Especially when it comes to people with Family connections."

"You—you—how did you know about that!"

"Living with Behindkind is useful," I said to him. "You get to learn which questions are good questions to ask. But you—you're still asking the wrong questions. What you should really be asking me now is what I want."

It's weird to see a bird swallow. Or maybe it was weird because he wasn't exactly a bird, and he was just enough human to swallow convulsively and just enough bird for it to look wrong.

"What do you want?" he asked, in a voice like chalk.

"I want you to break your contract with the Palmer family," I said.

Richard looked toward Jin Yeong in what was pretty close to helplessness. "Are you going to let a human get away with this?"

Jin Yeong shrugged. "I am here for amusement. She does not belong to me."

"What—what makes you think I'm going to break a contract at your say so?" he blustered. "There's nothing you can do to me. There's nothing you can do to us."

"You were there, too," I said. "That night that Lord Sero's father turned up—you saw me with the Family. If you want me to tell them that you lot have an eye on the next harbinger and where to find her, keep your contract. Reckon it won't do you much good, but that's your business. I can make a call in less than five seconds."

"You would be dead once you'd done so," he said.

Jin Yeong gave a small, scornful sniff of laughter. "You would be dead also," he said.

The Behindkind's feathers spread up and around his face. It could have been a ruff to intimidate us, but it gave me the impression that he had been badly frightened.

"Yeah, maybe," I said to him. "But by then, I reckon you'd have lost your big secret to the Family. And I'm pretty sure that if you're the one to let that happen, you'll end up flamin' uncomfortable even if Jin Yeong doesn't kill you."

"Even if I do make the call," he said. "You still have to get out of here alive."

"Yeah," I said. "That's why I'll be on the phone with the

Family while we walk out of here. Think about it: even if you don't have a contract, you're still the only people who know what she is and where she is. And maybe they'll be persuaded to make a new deal."

His side-feathers twitched and turned slightly sideways. A sign of thoughtfulness? That he was listening? Or just that he was likely to attack? I didn't know. One huge, feathered wing slowly reached toward the desk in front of him, and the hand hidden in the feathers there hefted open what looked like a small filing cabinet drawer in the desk.

Very slowly now, Richard put a piece of paper on the top of the desk, then lifted his hand above it, palm and fingers flat.

"Hang on," I said. "I need to see it first."

He snapped his beak, and snatched the paper off the desk, shoving it back into the desk drawer and replacing it with another. This time, he handed it to me straight away, and I didn't know if his hand shook with anger or fear of what was coming.

JinYeong took a look over my shoulder, but I didn't need his nod to know I was looking at the Palmers' contract. It was exactly the same as the copy North had given me.

I handed it back to the harpy and said, "Dissolve it. Permanently. If I don't get a text in the next couple of minutes, I'll be making the call to Lord Sero's father regardless. Got it?"

He didn't answer me. He was probably too angry. He spread his hand over this paper, and I didn't know what he did, but there was a hot flash of something and the contract burst into flames.

A few seconds later, the extra phone I'd borrowed from Daniel rang. I picked it up, and Athelas' voice asked tranquilly, "Are you well, Pet?"

"Yeah," I said. "Piece of cake. You blokes?"

"The contract is completely dissolved. Perhaps one day you'll tell me how you did it?"

"Yeah, perhaps." I looked across at JinYeong and jerked my

head toward the door. He opened it, and I said to the harpy, "Sorry Richard. We gotta go."

"Are you coming here?"

"Not just yet," I told him. "Maybe in a bit."

"Do you need assistance?"

"Dunno just yet. Are you allowed to offer help?"

"I have not been told that I may not," said Athelas.

"Stay there," I said. "Things are about to get fun."

He hung up, but I kept the phone to my ear: I could still see Richard in the reflective surface of the white walls, a feathery menace who could call for help any second if he thought he could kill us before we told what we knew. We were in the hallway now, Jin Yeong and I, but there was still a good hundred metres of cold hallway to walk before we got to the exit, dotted with humans and Behindkind alike. I felt as though it stretched itself out as I watched, longer and longer, and the Behindkind were definitely starting to look at us. Had some sort of silent alarm gone out? I would have bet pretty good money on it.

Involuntarily, my steps grew longer and faster.

"Slowly," murmured Jin Yeong. "Smile at them. Make them afraid."

He did as he'd told me to do, directing a sharp-edged smile around at the hall as we sauntered back out. I grinned, too, fierce and dangerous, and when we finally emerged at the top of the stairwell into the shoe store, it felt like it wasn't possible to stop grinning.

"*Hajima, museowo!*" Jin Yeong complained.

"Don't think I can stop," I said, massaging my cheeks. "And you *told* me to be frightening!"

"*Wae?* You are frightened?"

"Flamin' terrified," I told him, a shudder running over me as we finally stepped into glorious, human sunshine. I dug out my phone with cold fingers, and had to stab at the red button three times before I managed to stop it recording.

"You looked as though you were having fun."

"Figured we were gunna die," I explained, pushing the phone back into its usual pocket. "Reckoned I might as well worry him while we were about it."

JinYeong said offendedly, "I would not have allowed you to die."

"Oh. Thanks," I said. "Reckon he's got someone following us?"

"Of course."

"All right. We better not go back to the house or the Palmers, then."

"You said we would have coffee."

"All right, let's go to Isle Coffee. They've got a couch up on the top floor."

The walk back up out of the centre of Hobart did something to shake the weirdness out of my legs and set my heart beating normally again. I followed JinYeong as he made some darting little detours that passed through normal streets and sudden bursts of Between that brought us out in odd places, willing to let him do the hard work of trying to lose the followers that were almost definitely behind us somewhere.

When we got to Isle Coffee, and JinYeong had ruthlessly ordered a couple off the sofa so that we could sit on it instead, I tossed my own phone at him and said, "Oi. Can you fix it?"

His brows went up, but he looked over the phone. A very small smile came and went on his lips, and he said, "*Hyeong* has been busy."

"Yeah," I said. So it really hadn't been JinYeong. That was... nice, I supposed? "Can you fix it?"

"It doesn't need fixing, just removing," he said. "It is a spell."

I don't know what he did, but by the time the waitress came with our coffee, a small patch of the couch's stitching was trying to wriggle free from the leather, and there was the distinct feeling of thinness to reality.

"I do not use magic often," explained Jin Yeong, when we were alone again, though I didn't ask. "So I am slow. Here. It is done."

"Thanks," I said, and gave him the free little bikkie that had come with my coffee to add to his. That made him smug and pleased for some reason, and while he was contemplating the perfectly matching biscuits, I sent the video file I'd recorded to Detective Tuatu.

It's for North, I texted. *Don't show it to Zero or the others.*

It took a while to go through, so I sat back with my coffee and my feet up on the coffee table, wondering if things were really going as smoothly as it seemed they were. I mean, it'd be nice for a change. Just kinda...unusual.

I'd just started to relax when my phone rang.

"Heck," I said, jumping, and looked down at the display. It was Tuatu. He must have got the message that it was safe to call and text now. I picked up the call and said, "What's up? Other than my flamin' heart rate?"

"Sarah ran away," said Tuatu breathlessly in my ear.

CHAPTER TWELVE

"She went to the toilet twenty minutes ago, just before the contract went up. She didn't come back, but we thought she'd just gone to her room. I think she's trying to keep her parents safe. North and I are out looking, but if they find her first...!"

"I'll get JinYeong on it," I said. "See what he can sniff out. Where are Zero and Athelas?"

"Out looking, too. If you see her, North says to say *macaron* and she'll know you're safe."

"We're on it. Call if you find her; we'll do the same." I hung up, and said to JinYeong, who was looking at me enquiringly, "The kid's run off. We've gotta try to find her before Upper Management does, or they won't need a contract to keep a hold of her."

We left our half-finished coffee and took to the streets again, and this time JinYeong grabbed me by the arm to pull me Between at the first sign of a fluttering *moreness* at the edges of reality. I caught a brief glimpse of the old factory as we passed it: here Between I could see the smoke still puffing from the old, brickwork industrial chimney like the human world hadn't seen from them in probably a hundred years, and I wondered fleetingly exactly what Behindkind were making in there.

There was no time to try and fathom what was going on, no time to do anything but dodge the lumbering beasts that were part of the work as they spilled out onto the main road to the honking of cars. I didn't have time to try and see what the people in the cars saw them as, either.

I just ran with Jin Yeong.

We stopped when we got to the Mexican place on the corner of Lefroy and Elizabeth, and Jin Yeong scented the air in satisfaction.

"Ah! I have it!"

As he said it, I saw a small figure far ahead of us on the street, dodging between pedestrians and leashed dogs. Blonde hair, school hoodie, black shoes. Could be a schoolkid wagging it from school, but I didn't think so.

"Hang on!" I yelped. "I think—I think I saw her!"

"The smell is *this* way," Jin Yeong said.

"Yeah, but—"

"*This* way."

"Fine—you go that way; I'll go this way."

"It is dangerous," objected Jin Yeong.

"Yeah, but it's dangerous for her, too," I said. "We might find her quicker if we split up, anyway. Just...try to stay within yelling distance, all right?"

"I will," he said. "If you need me, *call*."

He darted down Lefroy, leaving me to follow Elizabeth Street upward again at a quick trot. I saw a flicker of loose blonde hair as I jogged past the opshop, and turned on my heel, gasping a bit. The door jingled as I went in, which was a shame, because Sarah was jumpy and saw me straight away.

Her face went pale at the sight of me, but she said, "Just try and take me. I can fight, too, you know."

"Heck," I said, impressed. "Relax, will you, kid? North said to tell you *macaron* so you'd know I'm with her."

She relaxed, but only a little bit. "I'm not going back with you, either. They'll kill my parents this time."

"You've got it wrong," I said. "They'll only kill your parents if you're *not* there. You were the only thing keeping them a little bit safe."

"What?"

"The stuff you can do—you know you're not normal, right?"

"Look who's talking!" she shot back.

Heck. What did she know? I couldn't help grinning, though. "Yeah, I know. But that kind of not normal is useful to the people who want you, and they just broke their contract with you. So if they get you now, they can force your parents to do whatever they want, because you're their bargaining chip."

"Man, I hate these guys," Sarah said. "Everything's about leverage."

"Tell me about it," I said.

The doorbell jingled, and I looked instinctively over my shoulder. Three men? Nope, three men and a woman, dressed like pretend security. They looked familiar, but it was their guns that really told me they were probably with Upper Management. Had they been following me, or Sarah?

"Heck," I said again, turning to face the threat. "You said you can fight? How are you with guns?"

"Know what I hate more than Behindkind?"

"Humans working with Behindkind," I agreed, nodding. Under my breath, I added, "Make a break for the staff exit as soon as we get a distraction."

"Stay right there," said one of the men, across the shop. He moved warily, and so did the others, which made me wonder exactly which one of us they were afraid of.

"Their guns won't work," said Sarah, edging toward a wall that displayed alternate flowers and handbags. "They're just water pistols."

"What?"

"They look like water-pistols, right?" she said, and her eyes were pleading.

I looked over at the closest bloke and saw his gun flicker between green plastic and black metal, and said, "Heck yes. You gunna shoot us with water-pistols?"

A single drip of water dropped to the ground, and one of the men said, "Call the boss, *now*. She's doing it again."

None of them picked up a phone, but I heard a rustle of movement, and maybe the slight click of a button releasing.

"Be careful," Sarah said softly. "They'll have spells, as well. Little magic stuff that they can point at people."

I didn't notice when the flower display began to move slightly, but the sandman must have been pretty close already, because the flowers split apart a moment later to allow it to step through into the shop.

Sarah screamed, short and sharp, but it already had her with its nebulous, sticky hands.

"Heck," I said, feeling ill, and the sandman looked at me consideringly.

I'd swear I saw the thought process pass across its face. Richard had definitely been talking to it. It needed Sarah to take back to Upper Management, but it couldn't let me go free to run off to the Family and tell what I knew, either.

So I ran for it.

I snatched up one of the walking sticks from the bin by the staff exit as I sprinted through the curtain, and felt the weight of it falter as it went from wood to steel and back again as I crashed through the back door and into the alley.

The poor kid probably thought I was abandoning her, but it was the only way I could think of to get them all out of range of unwary humans, and toward my hidden vampire. I mean, he wasn't exactly hidden, but he wasn't close enough to be useful, either.

I flew down the alley and turned left onto Lefroy where I'd

last seen Jin Yeong, skidding across gravel that spilled out from the unsealed carpark beside the footpath. I scented cologne, and saw Jin Yeong across the park, crouched by the side of a graffitied wall. Gravel scattered beneath my feet as I ran for him, too noisy to be able to hear how close behind me the pursuit was.

Jin Yeong stood at once, catching me by the elbows with a snarl at the dust on his pointy shoes, and narrowly avoiding a good bruise or two across the shins from the walking stick I'd pinched.

"Quick!" I said. "Givus a kiss!"

Jin Yeong looked up from his shoes, completely still but without any of the usual catlike, tail-twitching elegance that came with such stillness. He said blankly, "*Mwoh?*"

"I need some more vampire spit! Bite me or something!"

"I am not," he said, very precisely, releasing my elbows, "a vending machine."

"You flamin' better be, or we're gunna be over-run by the sandman and some of its friends. Anyway, you're the one who's always biting me or kissing me, so I should be able to—"

"Do it," said Jin Yeong, teeth showing dangerously in a smile. "It does not bother me."

"Come down here, then!" I said testily, yanking him down by his tie.

He made a startled, choked sort of a noise, but I kissed him anyway—just long enough to make sure I tasted the bitterness, or life, or pure electricity that was vampire spit. Then I let go of the tie and stepped back, the walking stick sweeping out in my left hand. Back in the shop it had been a walking stick, but here behind the carpark, amidst wild-growing graffiti, it gleamed with another form beneath the easily seen wooden exterior.

I rolled my wrist to flick it into its other form, a slender, flexible blade, automatically swiping the back of my other hand over my mouth to get rid of the feeling of Jin Yeong's lips touching mine.

"*What* are you doing?" he demanded, one hand automatically rearranging his untidy tie.

"Wiping off your kiss," I said.

His translating bit of Between dropped in outrage. "*Ya! Na aniya*, noh—!"

"No time to argue," I said urgently. A shock of sticky fear prickled over my ribs as the Sandman squished its way into sight around the edge of the building, far too close for comfort. "You better find something to fight with. Try not to die this time."

"My body is a weapon," JinYeong said, with cold certainty, easily understandable again.

"Yeah, and so is your flamin' perfume," I said. "But I've seen what the Sandman does to people who bite it, and it's not pretty."

"Watch me, then," he said, eyes narrow and liquid.

He went straight for the Sandman, who threw Sarah toward one of the humans and grew vast and sticky and fluttery. I didn't see him fight but I heard it: my eyes were on Sarah, who kicked and punched and fought the human who tried to hold her. I came for them with my walking stick sword, my eyes only on Sarah, and maybe my training had done some good, because my guard came up in just the right way.

If I'd thought about it, I probably would have hesitated and been shot. I didn't: I just swung, and slashed, and I must have thrust at some point, too, because I remember warmth and resistance, and blood on my hands and hoodie.

And I was *quick*. With the edge of vampire spit, I was too fast to shoot, too quick to avoid. Sarah broke away when her captor came to help, running and then skidding through the gravel to slip through the gap between me and the wall. She stayed behind me, out of reach of my sword, and as safe as she could be from bullets, and I had a moment to be utterly thankful for that before there was a flutter of dark blue suit and a flying tie, and JinYeong was between us and danger.

Over near the wall, wild graffiti crawled over a white and red mess that had once been the Sandman, but Jin Yeong still snarled. Three humans were left, and unlike the ones we'd come across in Upper Management's first quarters, these ones didn't run away.

"These ones are human," Jin Yeong said, without taking his eyes off them.

"I know," I said.

"I have to be at least this much of a monster," he said. "Or shall I stop?"

"No," I said huskily. I had blood all over me: he wasn't the only monster here. "They have guns and they're helping. I understand. Kill 'em if you have to. I'd help, but—"

"The child is looking."

"I know. I'll cover her eyes. Do what you have to do."

"I don't need my eyes covered," Sarah said, but her voice shook, and she didn't try to pull my hand away from her eyes.

She covered her ears, too, when the screaming and gunshots started. I didn't have that luxury—didn't think I was allowed it, if it came to that. Not when I was a part of the cause of their death. I watched the humans fall, every one, and tried to remember that it wasn't just Behindkind who could be evil.

I tried to remember that these humans were part of an underworld, otherworldly company that traded in slavery, death, and human lives. I tried to remember that they did it for money and special privileges.

And maybe I cried a bit.

One of them was still moving feebly when Jin Yeong said crisply, "*Caja*," and swept away toward the street.

"The blood—!" I protested, but he didn't stop.

"He's doing something to hide it," Sarah said, in a snubby little voice.

I'd already seen the film of Between on everything, but I still felt horribly noticeable with the cooling blood on my hoodie and the stickiness of it on my hands. It wasn't like we could stay back there Between, after all. Sooner or later, Upper Management would come looking for its henchmen.

Across the road and down the street a bit, Jin Yeong did something weird that sealed off the walkway between the patisserie and the burger house, and we sat down on the benches there while he straightened himself out and I called the detective to let everyone know where to find us. Then Sarah and I just sort of stared at the painted flowers and painted dog, and tried to ignore Jin Yeong muttering about the bloodstains on his tie.

I wanted to ask Sarah a few questions, and I think she wanted to ask me some, but there wouldn't be much time before everyone got there, so I just cleared my throat and said, "Don't run away again. You're the only one who can keep your parents safe. No one's gunna hurt your parents if you're with them: you're too valuable to...well, everyone, apparently."

"I don't want to be important to Them," she said.

"I know," I said. "But it won't be forever. Just until they find out who the real harbinger is. Then you won't be important, but you'll still be protected—North will take care of it."

"That's all right, then," said Sarah, her jaw firming up. There was a shine to her eyes that made me understand the picture of North that I'd found hidden away on her dresser. "If Aunty North says she'll do it, it'll happen."

Nearly everyone arrived at once: North with the Palmers and Detective Tuatu, and Daniel with a black eye and some clothes for me. Daniel gave me a very obvious once-over for injuries, and I returned the favour before I swapped the clothes for his phone.

"What happened?" he asked.

"Killed someone," I said shortly. "Don't reckon I got hurt."

"Good," he said, and walked me to the public toilet block so I could change.

There was a hubbub of noise from the walkway when we got back, and Daniel's brows went up a bit as we pushed through Jin Yeong's curtain of Between.

"Where is the pet?" demanded Zero's voice. "Jin Yeong, get *out* of my way!"

"I'm over here," I said. "And if you're gunna have a go at me for saving people's lives, you can flaming well stop right there. I'm not your pet and I can do what I want."

He looked me up and down, frowning, then said icily, "Stop causing trouble," and walked away again.

"What the heck?" I complained, looking at Athelas, who was sitting where I had been earlier, one leg crossed over the other. "What'd *I* do? I saved peoples' lives *and* I didn't die!"

Zero must have heard, but he just kept walking.

"Oi!" I called after him, dropping my bag of bloody clothes. "That's flamin' rude!"

"Ah," sighed Jin Yeong. "So irritating! I will have more coffee."

"Hang on, what?" I demanded, but he was already walking away.

"What bit him?" asked Daniel.

"Dunno," I said. "But I think he's annoyed because his coffee went cold while we were out saving Sarah."

Athelas looked amused. "Do you really think so? Then by all means go and buy him some more."

"Haven't got any money on me," I said, and this time it wasn't to avoid paying for Jin Yeong's coffee.

"Allow me," said Athelas, surprising me a great deal. He passed me a twenty, which was also surprising, and explained, "I have a vested interest in Jin Yeong's emotional state at the present."

"Yeah?" I said suspiciously, but I took the money.

"Athelas," said Zero from the street, his voice deep and carrying.

"You better go before you get in trouble," I said to Athelas. "I'll buy Jin Yeong a coffee and see if he gets any more reasonable."

After all, I *did* kinda owe him, and I very much wanted something warm to drink.

"Oh, I should doubt that very much," said Athelas pleasantly. "Do enjoy your afternoon, Pet!"

"Well, that was flamin' sus," I said, as he left. "Wonder what he's up to."

"How does he manage to make stuff like that sound like a threat?" wondered Daniel.

"That's what I keep wondering," I said. "North already take the Palmers with her while I was changing?"

"Yeah. The detective, too. I think they're planning something."

"Okay. I'll see you back at the house, then. Some of the boys out there, too?"

"Yeah."

"Make sure you're not followed on your way back, all right?"

"You too," said Daniel. "They'll be out for your blood if they see you, and they have people everywhere."

"Yeah," I said, remembering all the normal-looking human staff I'd seen at Upper Management. "I'm starting to get that feeling."

I caught up with Jin Yeong in the street, and if he'd looked like he was sucking on a lemon before, now he looked as smug as usual.

"I'll get ya another coffee," I said. "But then we've gotta go home the long way around. If they catch up with us again..."

"I can get us home safely," he said. "But I must have coffee."

"You're pretty flamin' fond of coffee these days," I said, but I wasn't too inclined to really complain. I still felt pretty high and heady from vampire spit, and I was pretty sure that Zero had only come to the alley with the others to make sure that I wasn't hurt.

Maybe not pretty sure. Maybe I just still hoped there was a human part of him that really cared what happened to me, and not just because it said in a contract that he had to make sure I didn't die.

Still, it was enough to keep me high and heady until we got to the little two-storey Isle Coffee café again, where the last barista was trying to close the shop for the afternoon.

"Too late," I said. "C'mon, I'll make you some coffee at home."

"We wish to have *coffee*," said Jin Yeong to the barista, ignoring me. "You may make it and leave."

I left the whole twenty on the counter while Jin Yeong ordered and went upstairs. I was cold and tired, and it seemed as though I could still feel blood on my hands even though I'd washed it off. I wanted to sit down.

Jin Yeong came up a few moments later and threw himself carelessly on the couch beside me. "I am a very good teacher," he said.

"Is that meant to be you telling me I did a good job?"

"You didn't tell me that I did well," he pointed out.

"Fair enough," I said, and a bit of the cold feeling left me. "Thanks for looking after us."

"You did well, too," he said, as the barista climbed the stairs, like he was granting a concession.

"Thanks," I said, and somehow I was grinning again.

The barista set a tray on the coffee table in front of us, then made a beeline for the stairs again. It wasn't just a couple of cups of coffee, like I'd expected: there was also a box of chocolates. You know, the expensive ones that come in a huge box and are individually wrapped, that cost more than a decent meal at a burger place. There was a big seal on the front that looked expensive, too.

"Oi!" I said in surprise. "What'd you order this lot for? I haven't got the money for it!"

"*Na aniya*," he said, but he looked very pleased with himself as he sat back against the couch. "People like to give me things."

"Of course they do," I muttered.

Jin Yeong grinned at me. I tried to roll my eyes, but somehow ended up grinning again instead, and peered over the balcony to check that the waitress had made it back safely down the stairs in the fog she was definitely in.

What I saw wasn't what I had expected. "Hang on," I said. "She's run for it."

Jin Yeong's eyes narrowed. "*Mwoh?*"

"I mean, literally," I told him, still gazing after the woman in surprise. Mobile phone to her ear, she was literally running from the café. "What's the go? Did you bite her?"

He rose swiftly to his feet, grabbed me by the arm, and dragged me down the narrow wooden staircase. I tripped over the stairs and caught myself against the walls, tumbling down the last few after Jin Yeong.

"What the heck? Ow!"

Jin Yeong grimly pulled me along, ignoring my complaints, and shoved at the front door. It didn't budge, and I had just a moment to be surprised at that before there was a staticky kind of stillness that made me wonder if I'd suddenly gone deaf.

In a flurry of movement, Jin Yeong pressed me down into a crouch, covering my head with his arms and wedging me between his chest and his knees. Something very big and powerful exploded an instant later, and Jin Yeong's cologne, edged with dust, filled my nostrils. I felt the impact of small, stinging things; and bigger ones that must have hit Jin Yeong instead of me, because they didn't hurt. I don't know how long it lasted, but when the pressure let off and I could cautiously straighten, my forearms were leaning against Jin Yeong's knees and I could see the tattered edges of his blue suit coat fluttering in my peripheral, with blazing edges to the holes. I looked up into Jin Yeong's face and he looked down at me, then with outrage at the fiery holes in his suit jacket. When he looked back at me the outrage was still there. He wagged one finger right in my dusty, confused face, and said in English, "Bad *Petteu!* You are *bad Pet.*"

"What?" I said. I wasn't sure which was more confusing; Jin Yeong protecting me from a few cuts and scrapes at the expense of his clothes, or Jin Yeong speaking English.

He rose abruptly, tipping me backward into the debris, and stripped off his tattered coat. He surveyed it with pursed lips, and I heard the annoyed "*Aight!*" that was becoming familiar. As if *I* was the one who'd set off the explosion and ruined it!

"What?" I protested. "It wasn't my fault!"

Jin Yeong gazed down at me with impotent dislike, as if he was trying to find the words to speak but couldn't think of any bad enough. At last, he said "Bad *Petteu!*" once more and stalked away through the ruins of the shattered glass door, his back rigid with outrage.

I scrambled to my feet and hurried after him. There was a gaping hole in the back of his shirt, too, with a decent smearing of blood. I told him that, in Korean, but all he said was, *"Hangook mal hajima."*

"How else am I supposed to talk to you?" I argued. "You don't usually speak English."

"Do not understand things I wish not to be understood!"

"Reckon you'll have to stop talking altogether if that's what you want," I told him. "'Cos whether you talk in Korean or English, I'm gunna understand you."

"So annoying!" he muttered in Korean. "The old man is right again! I won't. I refuse!"

I gazed up at him suspiciously. "You been drinking something other than coffee?"

"*Hyeong* is already angry that you're out of the house," he said. "And the old man would cut me open if you didn't come home. Otherwise, you would be full of holes. No more free help!"

"I *was* going to tell Athelas that you're talking about him behind his back," I said placatingly. "But since you stopped me from having my eyebrows blown off, I'll make you some kimchi instead."

Sulkily, he said, "I want *kimchi jjigae*."

"Fine, I'll make you *kimchi jjigae*."

"I still want coffee," muttered JinYeong, unappeased. "Buy me coffee. We will go to that coffee shop with the good coffee."

"Don't have any money," I told him. And I *had* already used the money Athelas gave me, but I could have gotten some more if I'd wanted to.

Truth was, there was no way I was going to be sitting down with a bloke as good looking as JinYeong in that other coffee shop. For a start, every waitress within cooee would be hanging around the table. Secondly, I didn't like the idea of the bloke who smiled at me seeing me sitting down with JinYeong, like we were on a date or something.

I also didn't know where else Upper Management had people, and now that they seemed to know my face so well, I could probably count on a repeat of the exploding chocolate box if I wasn't careful.

"We've got coffee at home," I said. "And you look like you were just blown through a bush sideways, so…"

"Ah!" he said impatiently.

"Anyway, I'd rather not hang out in the streets so Upper Management can have another pot shot at us," I reminded him. "If you know a good way home that doesn't involve us being followed, now is the time to use it."

"You," said JinYeong coldly, "are a *bother* to me!"

"Well, you're a pain in the neck, too, but what are we gunna do?"

"*Jibae caja!*"

"That's what I *just said*," I told him, but JinYeong was already on the move again, Between blurring the concrete beneath his feet. I caught up with him so I wouldn't be left behind with no way of knowing which way to go, and grinned across at him. "Thanks," I said.

Maybe I was just shaken and slightly discombobulated, but I still felt warm.

JinYeong seemed to sulk all the way home, and when we got there he vanished upstairs into his room to sulk there, too. I made a face at his retreating back, feeling a bit snubbed, but once I'd gone to let Morgana know things had gone well, I retreated into my own room, too.

I let myself down on the bed slowly, feeling as though I'd aged a few years in the last few hours, and gazed at the ceiling that wasn't quite right. It seemed like every time I got back to Morgana's place these days, my old house was quicker to connect with it. It looked like I wasn't going to be able to stay here much longer without bringing trouble down on Morgana and her parents.

I fell asleep while I was still worrying about that, and when I woke up it was twilight. I was in my old house, and Zero was sitting on the edge of the bed at my feet.

"Flaming heck!" I said, sitting up hastily. I knew I was still at Morgana's place because I could smell the age and the damp of it, but if I hadn't been able to do so, I would have thought I was really back at the old place.

Zero looked around as though he'd heard, but his eyes passed right over the space I occupied. "You're not really there, are you Pet?" It wasn't a question; it was more of a plea.

"Nah, it's your imagination," I said. "Maybe the house. I mean, you could be going mad, but I doubt it."

He gave a short huff of laughter. "I am almost certainly going mad."

"Yeah, but at least there's no one there to see you," I said. I mean, it wasn't like he really thought I was there, after all.

"You have to come back," he said. "It's not safe out there for you anymore. Not now that my father has seen you."

"We don't have a contract anymore. You don't have to look after me."

"I don't want you to die," said Zero, and even though he couldn't see me, even though he didn't think I was really there, he still didn't seem to be able to look at the place where I should have been. Instead, he gazed out through the window. "I can't do that again. I can't see it happen again."

"I don't particularly want to die, either," I said. There was a relieved warmth in my chest that came from the knowledge that he really did care enough to look after me even without a contract. But there was a cutting edge of sorrow to that knowledge.

"Then *why* won't you let me look after you without arguing all the time?"

"Because you think you know best all the time," I told him sadly. "And you don't care if someone else gets hurt while you're looking after me."

"That's on my conscience, not yours."

"Rubbish."

"You don't know—you're not capable of understanding—"

"We're getting to the bit where I want to bash you one really quickly," I said. I said it quietly, but he stopped. Into that quietness, I said, "You didn't even say you were sorry."

That brought his head around sharply, but his eyes still searched and found nothing. "Would that have changed anything?"

"Yeah."

"How? *Why?*"

"Lemme know when you figure it out," I said, scrambling off the bed.

"Pet? Where are you going?"

"Somewhere not here," I said.

"You can't go," he said, sounding more perplexed than before. "This is *my* dream."

"Says you," I said, and left the room.

I sat on one of the couches downstairs to brood for a while

but fell asleep again instead. By the time I woke it was morning and two lycanthropes in wolf form were curled up beside me.

"Rude," I said, but it didn't feel right to wake them up, so when I got a text from Detective Tuatu that said, *We need to meet up*, I sent back an answer that said, *Can't right now. Got two wolves asleep on me. How about two hours at your place?*

See you then, he texted back.

I was a bit quicker than two hours. The lycanthropes woke up after about half an hour, and since Jin Yeong was refusing to put in an appearance downstairs, there was nothing to do but pop my head into Morgana's room and let her and Daniel know where I was going. I frowned at Jin Yeong's door on the way out, but that didn't do any good, so I shrugged and headed out.

The first thing Detective Tuatu said to me when he opened the front door was, "Did you blow up a coffee shop yesterday afternoon?"

"Not personally, no," I said. "Upper Management took a pot-shot at me and Jin Yeong. How's Sarah and the Palmers?"

"Safe," he said, leading the way down the hall. "And likely to be much safer soon."

"Good," I said, and then, startled, "What the heck?"

Athelas was sitting at Detective Tuatu's kitchen table with a cup of tea, one leg politely crossed over the other.

"Good morning, Pet," he said pleasantly.

"Good grief! The dryad let you in?"

"Yes, I was marginally surprised myself," he said.

"What are you here for?" I demanded, helping myself to one of the detective's coffee cups and starting up the jug.

"I'm here to offer some advice to the detective."

"Oh. Why?"

"That's what I wanted to know, too," said Detective Tuatu

grimly. He must have taken to heart the last conversation I had with him about Athelas.

"I believe you'll find it useful, however."

"Thanks," said the detective. He didn't look much happier about it. "I hope you don't expect payment for it, because if so, you can keep your advice."

I found a packet of biscuits at the back of the cupboard under the bench and brought them out gleefully as Athelas said, "It adds nothing to the ledger."

Yeah, that's a big *comfort*, I thought, sniffing as I opened the biscuits. By the looks of Detective Tuatu, he didn't find it comforting, either.

"When a person—are you listening to me, Pet?"

"Yeah, yeah, I'm listening," I said, taking a couple of biscuits in one hand and my coffee in the other.

"I really don't think you are."

"Well, if you'd stop pontificating instead of—"

"I hesitate to say so, Pet—"

"Yeah? Doesn't look like it."

"—but you have become even more headstrong and impertinent since you were with us."

"You lot threw me out, so you can't blame me if I've gone to the bad," I told him.

"Neither correct regard for your own conclusions nor cheekiness is inherently bad," Athelas said, surprising me. "In my experience, however, it tends to be painful more often than I would like."

I couldn't picture Athelas being cheeky, even when he was young. Bitterly sarcastic, yes. Devastatingly, incisively honest, yes. Cheeky, no. Come to that, I couldn't picture Athelas being young.

"You were talking to the detective, anyway," I complained. "Why should I have to listen?"

"I've not noticed that the recipient of any given conversation determines your interest in it."

I grinned. "Yeah, that's fair. Oi. Zero know you're here?"

"He does. He was the one who sent me."

"Yeah?" I looked at him suspiciously. I didn't know why, but I had the distinct feeling that he wasn't telling the truth. No—that he was telling the truth, but *very carefully* telling the truth to mislead us as much as possible. The question was, what was it he was very carefully saying—or *not* saying, as the case may be?

"What exactly are you trying to advise me about?" asked Detective Tuatu, his impatience simmering over. "We've been sitting here for the last twenty minutes, and all you've said is that you have a message for North. What is it?"

"The message is regarding the recording you gave her."

"What about it? North said she's giving it to the parents."

"When a person has something that another party desires to have, it is generally considered necessary to negotiate."

Tuatu frowned a bit. "She's a nice lady. She just wants to give it to the parents and she doesn't need anything from them."

"While that is no doubt very laudable," said Athelas, "Behind, there is the expectation of contract even between friends."

"You lot really gotta work on your definition of friends," I said. "If North doesn't want to throw a contract at someone to make an exchange for something she doesn't need, why can't she just give it to them?"

"Because gifts are dangerous Behind," said Athelas. "Sometimes for the receiver, sometimes for the giver. Even a nominal exchange put to contract is safer than willy-nilly generosity!"

"You mean Behindkind wanna pin each other down just in case something goes sideways," I translated.

"Something of the kind," he said. "I would encourage you to inform your friend, detective, that it is best to solidify her gifts on paper."

"She's not my friend," said Detective Tuatu. "She's a force of nature, and I'm pretty sure if I try to tell her anything, it'll be the last thing I do."

"Perhaps Pet will do so, then," Athelas said lazily.

"Yeah, p'raps," I said. North wasn't likely to try to hurt me on purpose, but she was potentially even more powerful than the psychos, and it's always easier to cry about the squashed bug after you squash it than it is to mind your feet.

"I see that I can do no good here," said Athelas, rising in a leisurely way. "I'll tell my lord that my attempts to convince you of the necessity of contractual certainty were useless. Do make sure you remind your friend that since her young protégé's parents were not the ones who called an end to the contract, it's their right to dictate the terms of any following contract that might be formed. Pet. Detective."

I blinked a bit. Athelas had given me a very good idea, and that was a bit concerning. Any idea I got from him was probably an idea he meant to give me, and if that was the case, there was a fifty-fifty chance that the idea was actually a Very Bad Idea.

Well, I mean: good for Athelas, but likely bad for me.

I stared at his back as he disappeared down the hall, trying to figure it out. Was he trying to tell me something, or had I actually figured it out by myself?

"Don't ask me," said Tuatu gloomily, somehow managing to correctly interpret the way I was gazing after Athelas. "I don't know what's going on anymore."

"Good heavens," said Athelas' voice from the doorway, while we were commiserating with each other.

Still, he didn't seem really shocked, so I wasn't surprised when Zero and Jin Yeong came down the hall, with Daniel close behind.

"If you're here to offer more advice—" began Detective Tuatu.

"I'm here to speak with the Pet," said Zero.

CHAPTER THIRTEEN

I was pretty sure Detective Tuatu had had enough for the day, so I chivvied everyone outside and made them talk on the front steps instead.

There were probably a few dozen things I'd imagined Zero would say if he came looking for me. At least a dozen I wanted him to say. He didn't say any of them. Instead, he said, "Come back to the house. We'll make a bargain: that USB for ownership of your house and our protection."

"Yeah? What about the house?" I demanded. I was trying not to read too much into the fact that nobody had mentioned chattel ownership, or even going back to being a pet. Yet. "It keeps trying to come across to me. That upsets the balance a bit, and I'm pretty sure that means I should be getting more in the exchange."

"We can discuss it when you're home."

"You're not taking her home until she's happy to go," Daniel said.

"We do not need to go back," said Jin Yeong at the same time. "We have coffee elsewhere."

He didn't look as fully dressed as usual: he was missing a tie and one of his buttons wasn't done up. Had he left the house in a hurry?

"It's no longer safe for the pet to be out alone," Zero said, pinning them both with an icy blue look. "And I have need of the information she possesses."

"I can look after her," said Jin Yeong, shrugging. "She will look after me. We do not need you."

"I fail to see how the pet can possibly protect you," Athelas said. "Jin Yeong, do you think you could refrain from needling my lord long enough to begin negotiations?"

Ignoring Jin Yeong completely, Zero said to me, "Come back, Pet. I apologise. We can—we can talk about conditions at home."

"I'm not going back with you," I said. "Not without talking about it, anyway. If you don't wanna talk, me and Jin Yeong and Daniel will go home now and you can have a conversation between you and Athelas. At least that way no one's gunna be disagreeing with you."

"What do you want to talk about?"

"I want to make some ground rules," I said. "Because right now I don't trust you."

"You—" Zero stopped, his shoulders very stiff, and said at last, "I have always kept you safe."

"You kept me safe because we had a contract," I said. It was easier than saying the whole truth to his face, and I didn't yet know if I wanted Zero to know how much access I still had to the house. "And you lied to me to keep me safe, because we had a contract. So don't pretend you were keeping me safe for anything else. I want to be able to trust you to tell the truth before I trust you about anything else."

Zero's feet shifted just slightly. "Pet—"

"I mean, Jin Yeong kept me safe, too, and he didn't lie to me about it. Even Athelas told the truth. You're the only one who lied to me."

Zero, as if frustrated beyond what he could endure, said, "I'm not the only one who lied!"

Jin Yeong's mouth dropped open, and he said in utter shock, "*Hyeong!*"

"If you're talking about Athelas, it's not like he *actually* lies, he tells the truth in a sneaky way, so—"

"Jin Yeong—" began Zero, still rather hastily, and Jin Yeong, his gaze dark and bloody, said something sharp that I didn't understand. Zero held those eyes coolly, and said to me, "Jin Yeong was with you on my orders the entire time. I told him to follow you, to keep you safe. I didn't do that because we still had a contract, I did it—"

Jin Yeong gave an incredulous little laugh, and said softly, "Ah, I should really kill you this time! *Hyeong*, you're cheating!"

I stared at him, and there was a pointy, warm ball of rage somewhere above my heart. "You flamin' *liar*!"

"*Ya!*" said Jin Yeong.

"Don't you *ya* me! You trotted along behind me like you were watching out for me off your own bat! You didn't tell me Zero sent you!"

"*Yopae isseosseo!*"

"It doesn't matter whether you were behind me or beside me!"

"To Jin Yeong, I believe it does," said Athelas. "But I don't see why we should allow that to affect us in any way, after all."

Jin Yeong snarled at him, silent and warning, and one of Athelas' brows went up.

"You pretended to be my friend," I said, scowling at Jin Yeong.

Jin Yeong muttered something about not being friends, his shoulder turned to me as if *he* was the one with the right to be sulking instead of me.

"Would you have allowed him to stay around the place if you thought I'd sent him?" Zero asked briefly.

"No," I said, turning the glare reflexively on Zero. I'd guessed at the first that Jin Yeong had been reporting the odd thing or two back to Zero, but after the fight, things had changed—Jin Yeong had changed. Maybe I'd changed. And for just a little while, I had trusted him completely.

"Very well."

"No, it's *not* very well. That's *my* choice."

"This is what she was talking about when she said she couldn't trust you," said Daniel in disbelief. "Seriously, do you three even *listen?*"

Jin Yeong snarled at him, but Athelas only sighed. He looked like he was ready to give up on the whole thing. Zero said tightly, "This has nothing to do with you, wolf. You're fortunate that your trial has been indefinitely postponed."

"Don't threaten my friends," I said indignantly.

Zero's voice sounded as helpless as I'd ever heard it. "I didn't—I didn't threaten..."

"Yeah you did," I said.

"Perhaps we could offer an apology to the wolf, my lord?" gently suggested Athelas.

"Very well." Zero drew in a deep breath through his nose. "I apologise. Pet, at the moment we need you, and you need us. We should at least talk about making a new contract."

"Are you sorry?" I asked him, because that was important.

I saw that same flicker in one eye—the same thing I'd seen as he hesitated just a fraction of a second too long to gut me—and even though he said, "No," sharply, I was content. As much as Jin Yeong had been deceptive about his friendship, Zero was deceptive about withholding it.

For now. I was content for now.

I said, "Okay. I'll make a deal. I'll come home tonight and we'll talk about it properly tomorrow."

Because even if I was content for now, I was going to make my bargain count this time.

"Are you sure, Pet?" asked Daniel uneasily.

"Yeah," I said. It was too dangerous for Morgana if I stayed much longer at her house. Besides that, I'd done what I could while I was on my own, but I couldn't deny that things were easier to do and find out when I was with my psychos. And there was no way I would be able to access all that was on the USB without Zero's password.

Then there was the matter of my house, and my parents' murders.

There was too much to find out. Too much to solve. Too many humans who, like the Palmers, were terrorised by Behindkind with no way out. Too many turning to Behindkind for their cut of the power.

If I went back, I could do something about all of those things. If I went back, maybe things would be different this time. Because Zero hadn't gutted me, and Athelas had come to me when he didn't need to. Because Athelas and even sometimes Zero, had begun to call me *she* instead of *it*.

And because this time, I would have some leverage for making my bargain.

"I've gotta get my stuff," I said to Zero. "Meet you back at the house."

"I'll come with you."

"No," I said. "I'll meet you at home."

He hesitated, and looked as though he were about to say something, but bit his lips over it. "Very well. Don't be long."

Daniel and I turned back up Elizabeth street, and a familiar flutter of cologne began to follow us as if by sheer force of habit.

"I don't *want* you!" I said. "Go away!"

"*Nado shilleoh!*" snapped Jin Yeong, turning on his heel, and then Daniel and I were alone.

MORGANA'S FACE DROPPED AS SOON AS SHE SAW ME. "YOU'RE going, aren't you?" she said, before I had even shut the door behind me.

"Yeah," I said, because there didn't seem to be much use in drawing it out. "Me and the other blokes back at my house are trying to reach an agreement."

"Is it safe? Daniel doesn't like them much."

"I'm still not sure I like them much," I said honestly. "But there's still work for me to do there. And I think...I think maybe they can change. It's just gunna take a lot longer than I thought it would."

"I suppose that means everything went well tonight."

"Yeah. Daniel wants to tell you about it and I have to grab my stuff tonight anyway."

"Are you going to—will you be back?"

It must seem weird to her—rude even. Me picking up and leaving as quickly as I could. But it had never been safe for her to have me here, and I didn't want to think what would happen if my house got much closer to overlaying her house. She had every right to be angry, though I wasn't sure if she was angry or just sad.

"I'll come past and say hi to Daniel every now and then," I said. "You won't know I'm here. You don't have to talk to me—don't have to look at me if you don't want to."

"No!" said Morgana, her face brightening. "I want to talk! You have no idea how lonely it is here when you're out!"

"There's a whole bunch of people downstairs," I said.

"Yeah," she said. "All blokes, did you notice? I love them all, but sometimes I just want to talk to another female, you know?"

I thought about that doubtfully. "Dunno," I said, at last. "I'm not really used to talking to anyone, so I s'pose I'll get there."

I still remembered how hard it had been to stop myself from listening obsessively to everything that went on in the house when I was still hiding from my psychos—that warm, lingering, aching desire to hear other people speak and see the movement of life around the place. Maybe there was a version of that which came after a person was used to the basic companionship of people again, one that focused on a particular kind of companionship.

"I'll feed the kids before I go," I said. It wasn't what I wanted to say, but it was all I could say. I had to get my stuff and go before the houses tried to merge any more: I'd already seen the blurring of the stairs around me as I walked up to see Morgana.

"I'll see you next time?" she asked, briefly perky.

"Yeah," I said, even though I knew it wasn't likely that I'd be back any time soon. "Thanks. For everything."

It didn't leave me feeling wonderful, so I was already in a pretty foul mood by the time I got back to my old house. The familiarity of knowing that all three of my psychos were in the house, and exactly where they were, twitched at my lips and tried to make me smile, and the tension that had been building in my shoulders seemed to melt away. That is, until I saw what was in the Jin Yeong-tinted patch of the living room as I walked up the hall.

It was Jin Yeong, of course. But it was Jin Yeong in jeans and a yellow jumper, padding across the carpet barefoot from the direction of the kitchen.

"Don't wear that!" I said to him, aware of my own unreasonable annoyance but unable to stop myself. He hadn't done worse than Zero, but for a while, I had trusted him even more than I'd trusted Zero, and now I was *angry*.

Jin Yeong only shrugged elegantly at me and sat down on our couch. "I wish to drink coffee," he said pointedly.

"Yeah? Well, so do I, and I'm not your pet, so get it yourself."

He shrugged again and went back into the kitchen. Athelas, who was sitting in his own chair with a cup of tea, looked amused.

"Let me guess," I said, my voice sour to my own ears, "Zero told him to get in by any means, and they planned that fight together."

The thought made me angrier. I couldn't believe I'd felt sorry for the perfumed little git. I couldn't believe I'd given him so much of my blood. Couldn't believe I'd bought clothes for him instead of making him walk home in a bloody mess.

"There was such an order," said Athelas, "but my lord made no such plan. Jin Yeong is...unpredictable. We certainly didn't expect him to disobey orders to the extent he did."

The extent didn't really matter: outwardly or not, Jin Yeong had been following orders the whole time he was with me in Morgana's house. Lying to me. Pretending that somehow we could be friends.

"By the way, I trust that you're suitably grateful, Pet," said Athelas, so smoothly and naturally that I knew there had to be more to it than was readily apparent.

"What for?" I demanded bluntly. "If you want me to say thank-you, you'd better tell me why."

"Do you really think we leave that window open willy-nilly?"

"Heck!" I said, catching my breath at last. "Which one of you did it, though?"

"Ask each of us," he said, and his smile was now more than a faint one. "We'll each tell you it wasn't us."

"Thanks a lot," I said sourly. In other words, one of them had left it like that for me, knowing that it was likely I would at least come back for my money, but none of them would admit to it because that would be *human* and *soft*. "I ought to kick all of you in the shins!" I yelled at the ceiling, even though Zero was the only one not downstairs.

Either my yelling spurred him into action, or he'd been waiting for me to get home. A few minutes after I yelled, Zero came down the stairs with a piece of paper that had enough Between to it to have hidden a whole sheaf of papers, and put it down in front of me on the coffee table.

"Sign it."

"Nope," I said, folding my arms. "We're gunna renegotiate properly. You're the one who declared the first contract over, so I have the right to set the terms on a second one."

Zero's eyes flitted over Athelas and then rested on me. "How did you know that, Pet?"

"Been studying. Anyway, I've got some terms to add before I go signing anything."

"What terms?"

"Lots of stuff," I said. "I'll obey you unless you tell me to do the wrong thing. Then I'll stop. You have to do any jobs I bring to you, but I'll only bring you jobs if it's humans who're in danger from something to do with Behindkind."

"I see," said Zero; a heavy, but not necessarily forbidding couple of words. "Go on."

"I help out on those jobs—and you share info with me like you would with Athelas and Jin Yeong. If it's your own stuff, you make the decision about whether to share or not."

"Go on." His voice was very nearly a rumble, but still not as forbidding as I had expected.

"*And,*" I added, tipping my chin at Jin Yeong as he came back into the living-room, "I'm not gunna be *his* pet."

Jin Yeong's brows went up, but to my surprise, he seemed amused instead of annoyed.

No, not amused. He was smugly, purringly *pleased.*

Heck. What had I done that I didn't know about?

"*Kurae, johah,*" he said exultantly. And then, very clearly, he told me, "I don't want you as a pet."

"Rude!" I said. "I've been a good pet. You're just biased."

"*Anindae,*" said Jin Yeong. "You: from now on I will be very annoying, because you have annoyed me."

"*I* didn't blow holes in your coat! I didn't go around pretending to be your friend!"

Athelas gave vent to a low, soft laugh, as if he could no longer contain it, but when I turned to him, he asked only, "And what of me, Pet?"

"Haven't decided yet," I said, glaring at Jin Yeong before I turned my attention fully on Athelas. "I'll let you know."

I still wasn't sure he hadn't given me the knowledge of how to renegotiate on purpose, though I didn't know why he'd given it to me if he *had*.

There was a sigh from Zero: huge and slightly frustrated and somehow amused, too. "Bring me the contract," he said. "I'll sign it."

"That's brave," I said. I'd expected him to want to read it over very carefully first. "Haven't written it yet. Gotta get some help."

"I'll be very glad to assist, Pet," Athelas said.

"Not from you!" I said firmly. "You'd probably write yourself in as chief beneficiary."

"It would be highly unusual in a contract, I believe."

"Yeah, but you're highly unusual, too," I pointed out. "I've got someone else who can help."

I was pretty sure North would help, when she had a bit of breathing space. She hadn't paid me yet, so maybe that's what I'd ask for when the question came up.

"Bring it to me when you've finalised it," Zero said. "Until then, I'll consider you my pet again. Decisions will be mutually agreed upon, and we'll assist humans at your request if the attacker is Behindkind."

I caught myself up just before I said, "Deal!" and agreed verbally to something that I wanted to be very sure was in black and white, and above all, *detail*, before I did.

Instead, I said, "That'll do for now."

Maybe it was a dream I had that night when I fell asleep on the couch. I mean, I doubt it, but it *could* have been. Annoyingly, I'd fallen asleep with my back against Jin Yeong, which meant I was going to smell like his cologne for another couple of hours when I went up to my own bed. He seemed to be asleep, or as close as he usually gets to it, so that couldn't be what had woken me.

I wasn't even sure, with the fuzziness of the dark room around me, that I *was* awake.

Then someone knocked at the linen closet door, and a huge shadow moved silently across the room.

Zero opened the door while I was gummily blinking my eyes and wondering why the world smelled so overwhelmingly of Jin Yeong and coffee, and I saw a fractured version of the golden fae I'd met a few times before.

I gave up trying to blink and just gazed blankly through my slit eyes.

"I'll take the job," Zero said.

I saw victory flash across the golden fae's face as my eyes inevitably shut again. "I will be sure to—"

"But I have my own terms, and I'll write the charter myself. Any attempt to work around the conditions this time, and I'll not bother to bring it to a Behindkind court: I'll carry out the sentence myself. You can tell my father that."

I COULD HAVE VISITED MORGANA ANY TIME OVER THE following week. She messaged me every day, but I didn't dare answer because I knew if I did, I'd go around to see her. Then I would have to talk about why I was back with my psychos, because she was concerned and would *ask*, and I didn't know how I could answer because I wasn't exactly sure how I felt about it myself. There was a perilous sense of freedom to it: there was no contract yet, and for the first time I felt as though I was nearly on the same level as everyone in the house. Or maybe just that it was close to being acknowledged. It was probably wishful thinking. I'd just got used to being treated like an equal by Morgana and Daniel—and even, to some extent, by Jin Yeong's lying little carcass. Now that I could understand him most of the time, he was mostly grumpy and annoyed rather than superior. Sort of like an old human man stuck in a ridiculously pretty body.

A lying, manipulative old man stuck in a ridiculously pretty body.

Or maybe just a lying manipulative teenager who never grew up.

I was definitely going to start calling him *ahjussi*. It wouldn't change much, but it would make me feel a lot better. And at least now that we both knew where we stood, there *was* a kind of evenness to our relationship: I disliked him and he disliked me, but at least he wasn't coldly supercilious like Athelas or ruthlessly condescending like Zero.

Nope. Jin Yeong was just a liar.

I wasn't sure about how it was all going to work from now on, but I *was* sure about one thing: I was glad to be back. There was a slightly different edge to everything, but it still felt like home. And there was a hopeful sort of feeling to that edge of difference, if you didn't count the fact that Jin Yeong had gone back to smouldering at Zero again.

It was enough for now.

But I still missed the human interaction with Morgana, and to a certain extent, the slightly-less-human interaction with Daniel that felt like family anyway. When I woke up to another message from Morgana one morning about a week after I'd left her house, it put me out of synch with the Between-laced world around me.

"I'm going shopping!" I yelled to the house in general, making myself coffee. It would be good to get out for a walk—away from all the Betweenness of this world. The patch of Zero-tinted space upstairs shifted a bit, and Jin Yeong's shadow flitted past in the kitchen, where the percolator was doing its good work. "I'll make breakfast when I get back."

I started off in the right direction; heading for the grocery store. Despite that, I soon found myself drifting in the direction of Morgana's building when I left the house. It took me longer than the halfway point before I realised it was because I'd wanted to talk to her.

That realisation made me stop dead in my tracks. It was bad enough that I was visiting her at all—if anyone had been following me, I would be leading them right to her. I couldn't keep going to see her just because I felt the urge to talk to her. It wasn't fair to her—it wasn't *safe* for her, not if people like the Sandman were going to start following me as a normal thing now.

A feeling of unease settled in my stomach. Oh yeah. I should probably swing by anyway—check that she was all right. I didn't need to go in and see her; I would just pass by and make sure there was nothing weird about the building. Nothing Between lingering around the corners of it or anything.

Yep. That's what I would do. No need to speak to Morgana at all. Maybe just pop up the stairs to make sure there was nothing weird hanging around her room. Make sure Daniel had been keeping up with feeding the kids.

I was still debating on whether or not to go inside when I turned down the street that Morgana's building was on. My first feeling was relief, because I could see the building, and there wasn't anything *Between* about it. My second wasn't so comforting.

There *was* something different about the building.

Fear pierced me in a single, cold shock. Someone had already found Morgana. What had they done? I ran the last ten metres until I stood, panting, at the front gate.

In the coldness of my fear, it took me far too long to see the huge shadow by the corner of the building. I didn't see it until, dashing forward to find out what had happened to the house, a huge hand grabbed me by the collar and effortlessly reefed me backwards.

"Strike a light!" I panted. "Why can't you call when you want me instead of popping out of nowhere?"

"Didn't I tell you to pay attention when you're out by yourself?" said Zero coldly, one white brow twitched up in disapproval.

"Yeah, you say that," I began, on the attack because I was still too startled and too relieved to think better of it, "but you're the one who made the building hard to see, aren't you?"

"It's hard to see; not impossible. And those who are used to seeing it shouldn't have any difficulty."

"What are you doing here?"

"I don't think that's the question that's important right now," Zero said dryly. "Stop flailing, Pet."

"If you don't want me to flail you shouldn't scare the spit outta me!" I said indignantly.

"I'm referring to your verbal flailing."

"Oh. Well, if you hadn't scared the spit outta me—"

"Why are you here, Pet?"

"That's what I keep asking myself. Out of all the places in the world, why am I here with three non-human psychos? Just down to flamin' bad life choices, I reckon."

"Pet," said Zero, ducking his head down to my level and pinioning me with a blue look. "I am willing to talk all morning and into the night, if that's what it takes."

"Can't," I said. "Gotta get home and cook breakfast, and it's JinYeong's turn to pick dinner tonight, so—"

"JinYeong can wait," said Zero; and usually, I would have approved of this attitude.

"Yeah," I protested, "but—"

"Keep going," he said, tilting his head at the entrance. "You're visiting someone, I believe."

I cleared my throat. Was that all he knew? Was that what he thought? That I was visiting someone as a friend? Not that I was going back to the place where I'd spent the last couple of weeks?

I said slowly, "Yeeah. Okay."

But as I stepped through the entrance, a huge shadow followed me.

I turned around and put my hands on my hips. "What?"

"I'm coming with you."

"What?"

"I'm coming with you."

I sighed. "When did that little rat tell you?"

"He told me where you were staying the first night when he came back."

"Wait until I see him!" I muttered. "I'll soak his ties in so much holy water that he sneezes himself out of his socks!"

I stopped, dithering in my indecision. It was bad enough that Morgana had seen JinYeong and Daniel; I wasn't going to bring more Behindkind into her life, even if that Behindkind was Zero. I didn't want to put her in that kind of danger.

Zero waited for me, his eyes lightest blue, and it occurred to me that he was smiling. Actually smiling, and not just with his eyes. *Fine* time for him to show that he could display emotions. I said crossly, "Forget about it! I'm going home!"

Zero, still smiling, followed me out the door. I knew he was still smiling because I could see his face reflected in the mirror. I wondered if Morgana had seen a reflection of us coming and going, too, and felt a pang of regret. I really wouldn't be able to see her much from now on. It wasn't until I realised as much, that I could acknowledge the fact that I'd been planning, somehow, on still going to see her.

The heaviness of regret in me grew. I stomped ahead of Zero, who didn't try to catch up or call me back but opened Between ahead of me and followed me as I stumped into it without looking around.

It was a short distance through Between, but I wasn't paying attention to it as much as I should have been, and when the smudgy edges of somewhere damp grew solid and turned into carpet and a familiar staircase, I was surprised to find myself back in the house.

Zero shouldered past me, and he was no longer smiling. For once, I didn't care. I was just cranky enough to not worry that he now looked annoyed.

Athelas looked up as we came into the room, and if I'd

wondered whether or not he already knew about Morgana, his amused glance left me in no doubt. Jin Yeong was smirking, too, so I stuck out my tongue at him.

"I understand that you've made a new friend, Pet!" said Athelas, and his voice was mildly congratulatory. "Well done!"

"She's not Behindkind," I said. "Just a human. She's not important."

"Ah, but if she's your friend, naturally she's important," said Athelas, and there were layers of meaning to his voice that I had already spoken to myself.

"Yeah," I said flatly. "I'm not gunna keep visiting her, so you don't have to worry."

"I've already put protections around her building," Zero said abruptly. "There's no need to avoid it. I didn't go to the trouble for nothing."

I blinked at him and felt a lightening of my heaviness. I didn't mean to smile at him, but I did, and I saw his smile come out again for the briefest moment before he turned away to his book-case. Choosing a book or avoiding emotion, who knew? I decided to leave my thanks at a smile instead of confusing him by saying it aloud.

Behind me, Athelas said, "However, if what Jin Yeong told us is right, it might behove him to pay her a visit and give her protection of a more...permanent kind. Give her the ability to take care of herself, so to speak."

I turned sharply.

"*Kurae,*" said Jin Yeong, looking pleased with himself. It had probably been his idea. "*Hae bolkka?*"

"Don't you lay a tooth on her!" I said furiously. "She's human and she's going to stay human!"

Jin Yeong, offended, said, "*Wae?*"

"Really, Pet," said Athelas placidly, "you might consider that your little human is quite unwell and might like to be turned."

"She's not *my little human!* She's a human girl, and she doesn't need Behindkind shoving their noses in her life!"

I took in a deep breath; trying to calm down, trying to remember that Athelas had once had a little worm chewing away in his brain. That the people he took care of usually only had one fate.

Remembering that even if he had a twisted way of expressing it, he was trying to suggest something helpful; maybe even something he thought was kind.

My anger dissipated into the heaviness of regret again. No good would come of me continuing to visit Morgana, not now that I was back with my psychos. She had Daniel now, and she would always have the kids. It would be far better if I didn't go back to see her.

"You lot leave her alone," I said to them, more calmly. "She doesn't need you hanging around. I'll stay away, too."

I would go back once to see her, make sure she was okay—to let her know I wouldn't see much of her anymore. And then her life would stay as it was, unlike the Palmers' lives.

I put a pot of chilli mince on to simmer, because that felt a little bit normal and life was a bit too much up and down these days. When I came back out from the kitchen again, feeling familiar and weird and sad all at the same time, it was as though nothing had ever happened. Zero sat by himself, sharpening knives, a crease between his brows, Athelas sat elegantly in his favourite chair alternately smiling at the ceiling and gazing quietly around the room, and Jin Yeong, eyes dark and stormy, glared at the world around him as he sucked on a blood bag.

I went and sat down on Zero's desk, crossing my legs beneath me. Usually there were books out on it, but today he was just sharpening knives, slow and steady and mindless.

I said, "Thanks."

Zero looked up briefly. "For what?"

"Whatever thing you put on Morgana's house. And for listening to my terms, I s'pose."

"Sarah Palmer and her family are still in danger," he said. "Don't expect me to do anything more for them."

"I don't," I said. "North will take care of it. I'd be surprised if she didn't already have terms in mind. She'll get the Palmers through it."

"You trust too easily," said Zero. "She's the North Wind."

"Incarnation of," I told him. "I know. But I know she's not going to hurt them."

"You don't know that."

"Yeah, I do," I said. If there was one thing I was sure about when it came to North, it was that she'd do everything up to the point of death and probably beyond, to look after human children in general and Sarah Palmer in particular. "She knows what it's like. She knows what it's like to have human warmth and love, and lose it all. She can't do anything like that to anyone else."

"I had all of that," Zero said, his voice quiet. Across the room, JinYeong looked up, his eyes dark and narrow, and Zero's voice sank a little further. "I had it all and lost it. And I could still allow it to happen to someone else. So don't trust too much."

"I saw you," I said, my voice low to match his. "I saw you find the USB, and I saw you put it back. Don't pretend you couldn't have had everything you wanted much earlier."

There was a silence long enough to make me look up at Zero; and having done so, to find that he was staring at me, his ice-blue eyes for once dazed instead of icy.

"How did you see that? You couldn't have seen it!"

"Too late to tell me that now," I said. "I told you this house is mine. Kick me out, and it just tries to come to me."

Zero, with the very faintest hint of darkness to his pale cheeks, said stiffly, "I was waiting for—I was waiting for a better—"

"A better time?" I suggested, when he stopped. "You mean

when no one knew you were taking it, no one knew you had it, and you could have had the info you actually wanted?"

This time he managed to say it. "I thought it would be safe to leave it there until I knew how you'd gotten it into the house to leave it there. I would have taken it without a second thought if I knew I wouldn't get the chance to look at it."

I didn't believe him, but I couldn't prove it. It seemed as though Athelas had given me a way to negotiate, but Zero had allowed me to have the leverage to do so.

"Anyway," I said. "Pretty sure your problem isn't a lack of empathy: it's too much. You shut it off after a while when it hurts too much to keep. And North had two good parents for a while— you only ever had one."

"Don't make excuses for me, Pet."

"I'm not," I said. "I still remember that you let a bloke die, and too much empathy isn't an excuse for that. But I reckon you can be better than that, so I'm just gunna keep hoping that you start thinking like that too."

"Don't expect the best of us, Pet," said Athelas, making me jump.

I don't know when he'd got out of his chair, but he was standing beside me with a cup and saucer in one hand, and a coffee mug in the other. He passed the coffee to me, which startled me even more.

"Spent all me money," I said, sliding off the desk.

"No charge, Pet," he said, smiling tranquilly at me. "But rest assured that this momentary lapse is not something in which you ought to think of me more highly."

"I don't," I said, and hugged him before he could step away with his cup of tea.

I heard him say, "Good heavens," and with the warm scratchiness of his wool waistcoat beneath my cheek, I was almost certain that I felt one of his arms curl around me slightly, his hand resting lightly on my back for a bare moment.

"Don't corrupt my steward," said Zero, tugging me away from Athelas by my hood.

I staggered backwards, sloshing coffee, then turned around and hugged him around the waist for good measure, too.

"Don't—don't hug me, either!" he said.

"Too late!" I said, hugging him tighter when Athelas gently removed my coffee mug and took it with him to put on the coffee table. "You blokes are really bad at hugs, you know."

"No one is bad at hugs," protested Zero, awkwardly patting my back with one huge hand. "Stop it."

"You're very bad at them. You're meant to hug me, not pat me; that's weird."

For the second time, Zero tugged on my hood, this time to pull me away from himself. "It's not weird. I know how to hug people."

"Says you," I muttered, following Athelas over to the coffee table to reclaim my coffee.

JinYeong, looking put upon, stood up from his usual seat and said as if conferring a very great favour, "Be quick. I wish to shower."

"Go shower, then," I said, sitting down and picking up my coffee with relish. "I'm not stopping you."

"*Ya!*" said JinYeong indignantly. "*Naman wae an junun koya?*"

"Because you lied to me," I told him. "No hug for you."

"I saved your life!"

"Saved yours, too," I pointed out. "You've probably still got my blood doing loop-de-loops in your veins or wherever it is it goes."

"*Petteu—*"

"Nope," I said. "No hugs for you."

"I do not want your hugs!"

"Good—"

"*Dwaesso!*"

"—'cos you're not getting one."